VINTAGE
SCI-FI STORIES

Book 1

Anthology by Maree Hubbard

Title: Robots
Sub Title: Vintage Sci-Fi Stories
Anthology by Maree Hubbard

Subject Category: Fiction/Science Fiction
ISBN: 978-0-6483854-1-7

Registered with the National Library of Australia - Trove.

EMPIRE
OF
EXUBERANCE

Website: www.empireofexuberance.com.au

Maree Hubbard - An entrepreneur and an advocate for the further studies of exploring the natural evolution of human consciousness and for humanity to achieve full potential.

Dedicated to lovers of Science Fiction, and Science Fiction Writers, past, present and future.

I would also like to dedicate this book and thank my husband Colin, daughters Chantelle and Bianca for the hours you endured Science Fiction movies and TV shows on my behalf.

Please note the stories have retained the spelling as per originally published, (U.S. or U.K.).

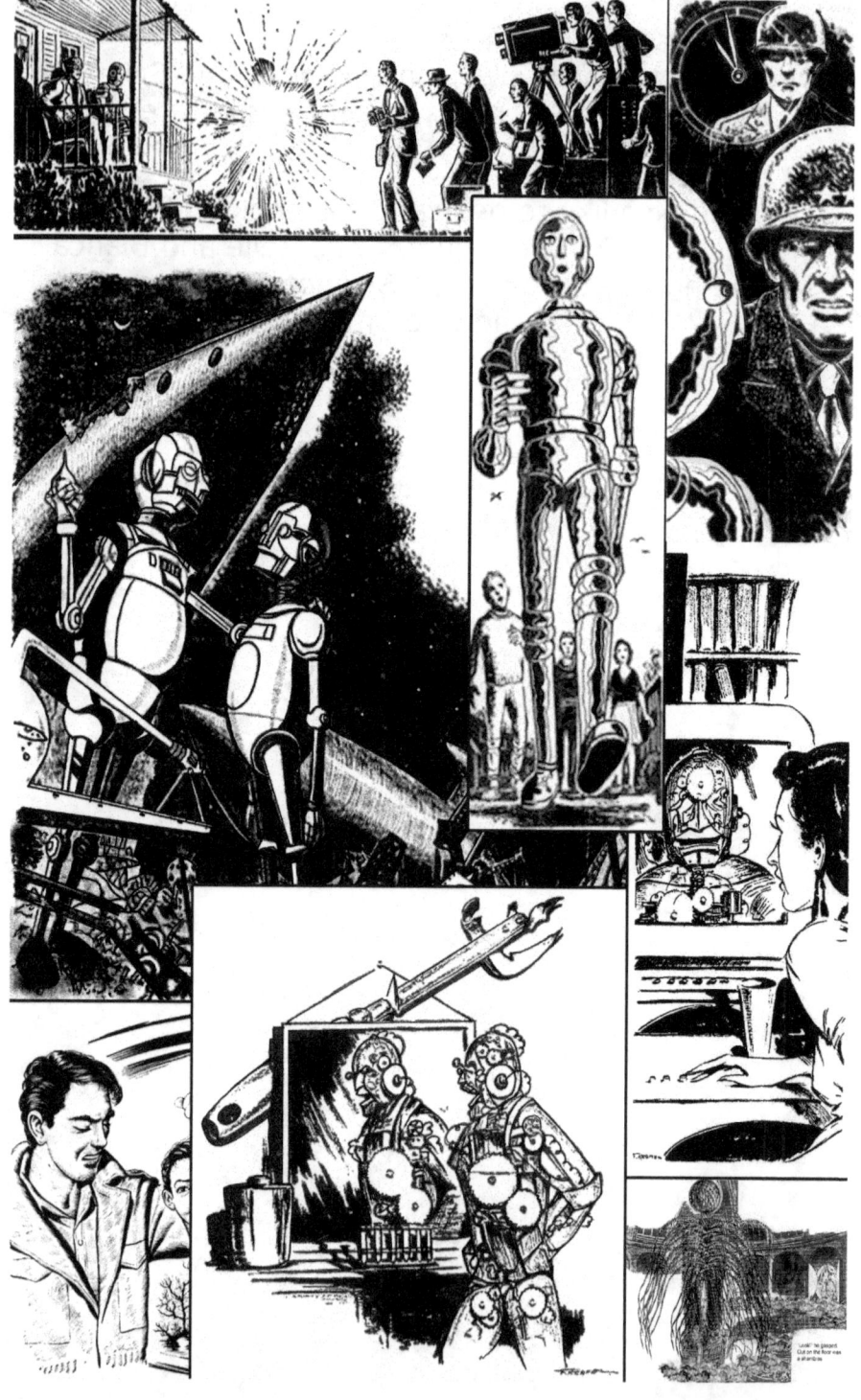

CONTENT

B-12's MOON GLOW

By Charles A. Stearns
Published 1954

Among the metal-persons of Phobos, robot B-12 held a special niche. He might not have been stronger, larger, and faster than some ... but he could be devious ... and more important, he was that junk-yard planetoid's only moonshiner.

I am B-12, a metal person. If you read the *Day* and the other progressive journals you will know that in some quarters of the galaxy there is considerable prejudice directed against us. It is ever so with minority races, and I do not complain. I merely make this statement so that you will understand about the alarm clock. An alarm clock is a simple mechanism used by the Builders to shock themselves into consciousness after the periodic comas to which they are subject. It is obsolescent, but still used in such out of the way places as Phobos.

My own contact with one of these devices came about in the following manner: I had come into Argon City under cover of darkness, which is the only sensible thing to do, in my profession, and I was stealing through the back alleyways as silently as my rusty joints would allow.

I was less than three blocks from Benny's Place, and still undetected, when I passed the window. It was a large, cheerful oblong of light, so quite naturally I stopped to investigate, being slightly phototropic, by virtue of the selenium grids in my rectifier cells. I went over and looked in, unobtrusively resting my grapples on the outer ledge. There was a Builder inside such as I had not seen since I came to Phobos half a century ago, and yet I recognized the subspecies at once, for they are common on Earth. It was a she. It was in the process of removing certain outer sheaths, and I noted that, while quite symmetrical, bilaterally, it was otherwise oddly formed, being disproportionately large and lumpy in the anterior ventral region. I had watched for some two or three minutes, entirely forgetting my own safety, when then she saw me. Its eyes widened and it snatched up the alarm clock which was, as I have hinted, near at hand.

"Get out of here, you nosey old tin can!" it screamed, and threw the clock, which caromed off my headpiece, damaging one earphone. I ran.

If you still do not see what I mean about racial prejudice, you will, when you hear what happened later. I continued on until I came to Benny's Place, entering through the back door. Benny met me there, and quickly shushed me into a side room. His fluorescent eyes were glowing with excitement. Benny's real name is BNE-96, and when on Earth he had been only a Servitor, not a General Purpose like myself. But perhaps I should explain.

We metal people are the children of the Builders of Earth, and later of Mars and Venus. We were not born of two parents, as they are. That is a function far too complex to explain here; in fact I do not even understand it myself. No, we were born of the hands and intellects of the greatest of their scientists, and for this reason it might be natural to suppose that we, and not they, would be considered a superior race. It is not so.

Many of us were fashioned in those days, a metal person for every kind of task that they could devise, and some, like myself, who could do almost anything. We were contented enough, for the greater part, but the scientists kept creating, always striving to better their former efforts.

And one day the situation which the Builders had always regarded as inevitable, but we, somehow, had supposed would never come, was upon us. The first generation of the metal people—more than fifty thousand of us—were obsolete. The things that we had been designed to do, the new ones, with their crystalline brains, fresh, untarnished, accomplished better.

We were banished to Phobos, dreary, lifeless moon of Mars. It had long been a sort of interplanetary junk-yard; now it became a graveyard. Upon the barren face of this little world there was no life except for the handful of hardy Martian and Terran prospectors who searched for minerals. Later on, a few rude mining communities sprang up under plastic airdromes, but never came too much. Argon City was such a place. I wonder if you can comprehend the loneliness, the hollow futility of our plight. Fifty thousand skilled workmen with nothing to do. Some of the less adaptable gave up, prostrating themselves upon the bare rocks until their joints froze from lack of use, and their works corroded. Others served the miners and prospectors, but their needs were all too few.

The overwhelming majority of us were still idle, and somehow we learned the secret of racial existence at last. We learned to serve each other. This was not an easy lesson to learn. In the first place there must be motivation involved in racial preservation. Yet we derived no pleasure out of the things that make the Builders wish to continue to live. We did not sleep; we did not eat, and we were not able to reproduce ourselves. (And, besides, this latter, as I have indicated, would have been pointless with us.)There was, however, one other pleasure of the Builders that intrigued us. It can best be described as a stimulation produced by drenching their insides with alcoholic compounds, and is a universal pastime among the males and many of the she's.

One of us—R-47, I think it was (rest him)—tried it one day. He pried open the top of his helmet and pouted an entire bottle of the fluid down his mechanism. Poor R-47. He caught fire and blazed up in a glorious blue flame that we could not extinguish in time. He was beyond repair, and we were forced to scrap him. But his was not a sacrifice in vain. He had established an idea in our ennui-bursting minds. An idea which led to the discovery of Moon Glow. My discovery, I should say, for I was the first.

Naturally, I cannot divulge my secret formula for Moon Glow. There are many kinds of Moon Glow these days, but there is still only one B-12 Moon Glow. Suffice it to say that it is a high octane preparation, only a drop of which—but you know the effects of Moon Glow, of course. How the merest thimbleful, when judiciously poured into one's power pack, gives new life and the most deliriously happy freedom of movement imaginable. One possesses soaring spirits and super-strength. Old, rusted joints move freely once more, one's transistors glow brightly, and the currents of the body race about with the minutest resistance. Moon Glow is like being born again.

The sale of it has been illegal for several years, for no reason that I can think of except that the Builders, who make the laws, cannot bear to see metal people have fun. Of course, a part of the blame rests on such individuals as X-101, who, when lubricated with Moon Glow, insists upon dancing around on large, cast-iron feet to the hazard of all toes in his vicinity. He is thin and long jointed, and he goes "creak, creak," in a weird, sing-song fashion as he dances. It is a shameful, ludicrous sight. Then there was DC-5, who tore down the 300 feet long equipment hangar of the Builders one night. He had over-indulged.

I do not feel responsible for these things. If I had not sold them the Moon Glow, someone else would have done so. Besides, I am only a wholesaler. Benny buys everything that I am able to produce in my little laboratory hidden out in the Dumps. Just now, by Benny's attitude, I knew that something was very wrong. "What is the matter?" I said. "Is it the revenue agents?"

"I do not know," said BNE-96 in that curious, flat voice of his that is incapable of inflection. "I do not know, but there are visitors of importance from Earth. It could mean anything, but I have a premonition of disaster. Jon tipped me off."

He meant Jon Rogeson, of course, who was the peace officer here in Argon City, and the only one of the Builders I had ever met who did not look down upon a metal person. When sober he was a clever person who always looked out for our interests here.

"What are they like?" I asked in some fear, for I had six vials of Moon Glow with me at the moment.

"I have not seen them, but there is one who is high in the government, and his wife. There are half a dozen others of the Builder race, and one of the new type metal persons."

I had met the she who must have been the wife. "They hate us," I said. "We can expect only evil from these persons."

"You may be right. If you have any merchandise with you, I will take it, but do not risk bringing more here until they have gone."

I produced the vials of Moon Glow, and he paid me in Phobos credits, which are good for a specified number of refuelings at the Central fueling station.

Benny put the vials away and he went into the bar. There was the usual jostling crowd of hard-bitten Earth miners, and of the metal people who come to lose their loneliness. I recognized many, though I spend very little time in these places, preferring solitary pursuits, such as the distillation of Moon Glow, and improving my mind by study and contemplation out in the barrens.

Jon Rogeson and I saw each other at the same time, and I did not like the expression in his eye as he crooked a finger at me. I went over to his table. He was pleasant looking, as Builders go, with blue eyes less dull than most, and a brown, unruly topknot of hair such as is universally affected by them.

"Sit down," he invited, revealing his white incisors in

greeting. I never sit, but this time I did so, to be polite. I was wary; ready for anything. I knew that there was something unpleasant in the air. I wondered if he had seen me passing the Moon Glow to Benny somehow. Perhaps he had barrier-penetrating vision, like the Z group of metal people... but I had never heard of a Builder like that. I knew that he had long suspected that I made Moon Glow.

"What do you want?" I asked cautiously.

"Come on now," he said, "loosen up! Limber those stainless steel hinges of yours and be friendly."

That made me feel good. Actually, I am somewhat pitted with rust, but he never seems to notice, for he is like that. I felt young, as if I had partaken of my own product.

"The fact is, B-12," he said, "I want you to do me a favor, old pal."

"And what is that?"

"Perhaps you have heard that there is some big brass from Earth visiting Phobos this week."

"I have heard nothing," I said. It is often helpful to appear ignorant when questioned by the Builders, for they believe us to be incapable of misrepresenting the truth. The fact is, though it is an acquired trait, and not built into us, we General Purposes can lie as well as anyone.

"Well, there is. A Federation Senator, no less. Simon F. Langley. It's my job to keep them entertained; that's where you come in."

I was mystified. I had never heard of this Langley, but I know what entertainment is. I had a mental image of myself singing or dancing before the Senator's party. But I cannot sing very well, for three of my voice reeds are broken and have never been replaced, and lateral motion, for me, is almost impossible these days. "I do not know what you mean," I said. "There is J-66. He was once an Entertainment—"

"No, no!" he interrupted, "you don't get it. What the Senator wants is a guide. They're making a survey of the Dumps, though I'll be damned if I can find out why. And you know the Dumps better than any metal person—or human—on Phobos."

So that was it. I felt a vague dread, a premonition of disaster. I had such feelings before, and usually with reason. This too, was an acquired sensibility, I am sure. For many years I have studied the Builders, and there is much to be learned of their mobile faces and their eyes. In Jon's eyes, however, I read no trickery—nothing. Yet, I say, I had the sensation of evil. It was just for a moment; no longer. I said I would think it over.

Senator Langley was distinguished. Jon said so. And yet he was cumbersomely round, and he rattled incessantly of things into which I could interpret no meaning. The she who was his wife was much younger, and sullen, and unpleasantly I sensed great rapport between her and Jon Rogeson from the very first.

There were several other humans in the group—I will not call them Builders, for I did not hold them to be, in any way, superior to my own people. They all wore spectacles, and they gravitated about the round body of the Senator like minor moons, and I could tell that they were some kind of servitors. I will not describe them further.

MS-33 I will describe. I felt an unconscionable hatred for him at once. I cannot say why, except that he hung about his master obsequiously, power pack smoothly purring, and he was slim limbed, nickel-plated, and wore, I thought, a smug expression on his viziplate. He represented the new order; the ones who had displaced us on Earth. He knew too much, and showed it at every opportunity.

We did not go far that first morning. The half-track was driven to the edge of the Dumps. Within the Dumps one walks—or does not go. Phobos is an airless world, and yet so small that rockets are impractical. The terrain is broken and littered with the refuse of half a dozen worlds, but the Dumps themselves— that is different.

Imagine, if you can, an endless vista of death, a sea of rusting corpses of space ships, and worn-out mining machinery, and of those of my race whose power packs burned out, or who simply gave up, retiring into this endless, corroding limbo of the barrens. A more somber sight was never seen.

But this fat ghoul, Langley, sickened me. This shame of the Builder race, this atavism—this beast—rubbed his fat, impractical hands together with an ungod-like glee. "Excellent," he said. "Far, far better, in fact, than I had hoped." He did not elucidate.

I looked at Jon Rogeson. He shook his head slowly.

"You there—robot!" said Langley, looking at me. "How far across this place?" the word was like a blow. I could not answer.

MS-33, glistening in the dying light of Mars, strode over to me, clanking heavily up on the black rocks. He seized me with his grapples and shook me until my wiring was in danger of shorting out. "Speak up when you are spoken to, archaic mechanism!" he grated.

I would have struck out at him, but what use except to warp my own aging limbs.

Jon Rogeson came to my rescue. "On Phobos," he explained to Langley, "we don't use that word 'robot.' These folk have been free a long time. They've quite a culture of their own nowadays, and they like to be called 'metal people.' As a return courtesy, they refer to us humans as 'builders.' Just a custom, Senator, but if you want to get along with them—"

"Can they vote?" said Langley, grinning at his own sour humor.

"Nonsense," said MS-33. "I am a robot, and proud of it. This rusty piece has no call to put on airs."

"Release him," Langley said. "Droll fellows, these discarded robots. Really nothing but mechanical dolls, you know, but I think the old scientists made a mistake, giving them such human appearance, and such obstinate traits."

Oh, it was true enough, from his point of view. We had been mechanical dolls at first, I suppose, but fifty years can change one. All I know is this: we are people; we think and feel, and are happy and sad, and quite often we are bored stiff with this dreary moon of Phobos.

It seared me. My selenium cells throbbed white hot within the shell of my frame, and I made up my mind that I would learn more about the mission of this Langley, and I would get even with MS-33 even if they had me dismantled for it.

Of the rest of that week I recall few pleasant moments. We went out every day, and the quick-eyed servants of Langley measured the areas with their instruments, and exchanged significant looks from behind their spectacles, smug in their thin air helmets. It was all very mysterious. And disturbing. But I could discover nothing about their mission. And when I questioned MS-33, he would look important and say nothing. Somehow it seemed vital that I find out what was going on before it was too late.

On the third day there was a strange occurrence. My friend, Jon Rogeson had been taking pictures of the Dumps. Langley and his wife had withdrawn to one side and were talking in low tomes to one another. Quite thoughtlessly Jon turned the lens on them and clicked the shutter.

Langley became rust-red throughout the vast expanse of his neck and face. "Here!" He said, "what are you doing?"

"Nothing," said Jon.

"You took a picture of me," snarled Langley. "Give me the plate at once."

Jon Rogeson got a bit red himself. He was not used to being ordered around. "I'll be damned if I will," he said.

Langley growled something I couldn't understand, and turned his back on us. The she who was called his wife looked startled and worried. Her eyes were beseeching as she looked at Jon. A message there, but I could not read it. Jon looked away.

Langley started walking back to the half-track alone. He turned once and there was evil in his gaze as he looked at Jon. "You will lose your job for this impertinence," he said with quiet savagery, and added, enigmatically, "not that there will be a job after this week anyway."

Builders may appear to act without reason, but there is always a motivation somewhere in their complex brains, if one can only find it, either in the seat of reason, or in the labyrinthine inhibitions from their childhood. I knew this, because I had studied them, and now there were certain notions that came into my brain which, even if I could not prove them, were no less interesting for that.

The time had come to act. I could scarcely wait for darkness to come. There were things in my brain that appalled me, but I was now certain that I had been right. Something was about to happen to Phobos, to all of us here—I knew not what, but I must prevent it somehow.

I kept in the shadows of the shabby buildings of Argon City, and I found the window without effort. The place where I had spied upon the wife of Langley to my sorrow the other night. There was no one there; there was darkness within, but that did not deter me.

Within the airdrome which covers Argon City the buildings are loosely constructed, even as they are on Earth. I had no trouble, therefore, opening the window. I swung a leg up and was presently within the darkened room. I found the door I sought and entered cautiously. In this adjacent compartment I made a thorough search but I did not find what I primarily sought—namely the elusive reason for Langley's visit to

Phobos. It was in a metallic overnight bag that I did find something else which made my power pack hum so loudly that I was afraid of being heard. The thing which explained the strangeness of the pompous Senator's attitude today—which explained, in short, many things, and caused my brain to race with new ideas. I put the thing in my chest container, and left as stealthily as I had come. There had been progress, but since I had not found what I hoped to find, I must now try my alternate plan.

Two hours later I found the one I sought, and made sure that I was seen by him. Then I left Argon City by the South lock, furtively, as a thief, always glancing over my shoulder, and when I made certain that I was being followed, I went swiftly, and it was not long before I was clambering over the first heaps of debris at the edge of the Dumps.

Once I thought I heard footsteps behind me, but when I looked back there was no one in sight. Just the tiny disk of Deimos peering over the sharp peak of the nearest ridge, the black velvet sky outlining the curvature of this airless moon. Presently I was in sight of home, the time-eaten hull of an ancient star freighter resting near the top of a heap of junked equipment from some old strip mining operation. It would never rise again, but its shell remained strong enough to shelter my distillery and scant furnishings from any chance meteorite that might fall. I greeted it with the usual warmth of feeling which one has for the safe and the familiar. I stumbled over tin fuel cans, wires and other tangled metal in my haste to get there. It was just as I had left it. The heating element under the network of coils and pressure chambers still glowed with white heat, and the Moon Glow was dripping with musical sound into the retort.

I felt good. No one ever bothered me here. This was my fortress, with all that I cared for inside. My tools, my work, my micro-library. And yet I had deliberately—something—a heavy foot—clanked upon the first step of the man-port through which I had entered. I turned quickly. The form shimmered in the pale Deimoslight that silhouetted it. MS-33. He had followed me here.

"What do you want?" I said. "What are you doing here?"

"A simple question," said MS-33. "Tonight you looked very suspicious when you left Argon City. I saw you and followed you here. You may as well know that I have never trusted you. All the old ones were unreliable. That is why you were replaced."

He came in, boldly, without being invited, and looked around. I detected a sneer in his voice as he said, "So this is where you hide."

"I do not hide. I live here, it is true."

"A robot does not live. A robot exists. We newer models do not require shelter like an animal. We are rust-proof and invulnerable." He strode over to my micro-library, several racks of carefully arranged spools, and fingered them irreverently. "What is this?"

"My library."

"So! Our memories are built into us. We have no need to refresh them."

"So is mine," I said. "But I would learn more than I know." I was stalling for time, waiting until he made the right opening.

"Nonsense," he said. "I know why you stay out here in the Dumps, masterless. I have heard of the forbidden drug that is sold in the mining camps such as Argon City. Is this the mechanism?" he pointed at the still.

Now was the time. I mustered all my cunning, but I could not speak. Not yet.

"Never mind," he said. "I can see that it is. I shall report you, of course. It will give me great pleasure to see you dismantled. Not that it really matters, of course—now."

There it was again. The same frightening allusion that Langley had made today. I must succeed!

I knew that MS-33, for all his brilliance, and newness, and vaunted superiority, was only a Secretarial. For the age of specialism was upon Earth, and General Purpose models were no longer made. That was why we were different here on Phobos. It was why we had survived. The old ones had given us something special which the new metal people did not have. Moreover, MS-33 had his weakness. He was larger, stronger, faster than me, but I doubted that he could be devious.

"You are right," I said, pretending resignation. "This is my distillery. It is where I make the fluid which is called Moon Glow by the metal people of Phobos. Doubtless you are interested in learning how it works."

"Not even remotely interested," he said. "I am interested only in taking you back and turning you over to the authorities."

"It works much like the conventional distilling plants of Earth," I said, "except that the basic ingredient, a silicon compound, is irradiated as it passes through zirconium tubes to the heating pile, where it is activated and broken down into the droplets of the elixir called Moon Glow. You see the golden drops falling there.

"It has the excellent flavor of fine petroleum, as I make it. Perhaps you'd care to taste it. Then you could understand that it is not really bad at all. Perhaps you could persuade yourself to be more lenient with me."

"Certainly not," said MS-33.

"Perhaps you are right," I said after a moment of reflection. I took a syringe, drew up several drops of the stuff and squirted it into my carapace, where it would do the most good. I felt much better.

"Yes," I continued, "certainly you are quite correct, now that I think of it. You newer models would never bear it. You weren't built to stand such things. Nor, for that matter, could you comprehend the exquisite joys that are derived from Moon Glow. Not only would you derive no pleasure from it, but it would corrode your parts, I imagine, until you could scarcely crawl back to your master for repairs." I helped myself to another liberal portion.

"That is the silliest thing I've ever heard," he said.

"What?"

MS-33 moved closer and said, "It's silly. We are constructed to withstand a hundred times greater stress, and twice as many chemical actions as you were. Nothing could hurt us. Besides, it looks harmless enough. I doubt that it is hardly anything at all."

"For me it is not," I admitted. "But you—"

"Give me the syringe, fool!"

"I dare not."

"Give it here!"

I allowed him to wrest it from my grasp. In any case I could not have prevented him. He shoved me backwards against the rusty bulkhead with a clang. He pushed the nozzle of the syringe down into the retort and withdrew it filled with Moon Glow. He opened an inspection plate in his ventral region and squirted himself generously. It was quite a dose. He waited for a moment. "I feel nothing," he said finally. "I do not believe it is anything more than common lubricating oil." He was silent for another moment. "There is an ease of movement," he said.

"No paralysis?" I asked.

"Paral—? you stupid, rusty old robot!" He helped himself to another syringe full of Moon Glow. The stuff brought twenty credits an ounce, but I did not begrudge it him.

He flexed his superbly articulated joints in three directions, and I could hear his power unit building up within him to a whining pitch. He took a shuffling sidestep, and then another, gazing down at his feet, with arms akimbo.

"The light gravity here is superb, superb, superb, superb, superb," he said, skipping a bit.

"Isn't it?" I said.

"Almost negligible," he said.

"True."

"You have been very kind to me," MS-33 said. "Extremely, extraordinarily, incomparably, incalculably kind." He used up all the adjectives in his memory pack. "I wonder if you would mind awfully much if—"

"Not at all," I said. "Help yourself. By the way, friend, would you mind telling me what your real mission of your party is here on Phobos. The Senator forgot to say."

"Secret," he said. "Horribly top secret. As a dutiful subject—I mean servant—of Earth, I could not, of course, divulge it to anyone. If I could—" his neon eyes glistened, "if I could, you would, of course, be the first to know. The very first." He threw one nickel-plated arm about my shoulder.

"I see," I said, "and just what is it that you are not allowed to tell me?"

"Why, that we are making a preliminary survey here on Phobos, of course, to determine whether or not it is worthwhile to send salvage for scrap. Earth is short of metals, and it depends upon what the old ma—the master says in his report."

"You mean they'll take all the derelict spaceships, such as this one, and all the abandoned equipment?"

"And the r-robots," MS-33 said, "They're metal too, you know."

"They're going to take the dismantled robots?" I said

MS-33 made a sweeping gesture. "They're going to take all the r-robots, dismantled or not. They're not good for anything anyway. The bill is up before the Federation Congress right now. And it will pass if my master, Langley says so." He patted my helmet, consolingly, his grapples clanking. "If you were worth a damn, you know—" he concluded sorrowfully.

"That's murder," I said. And I meant it. Man's inhumanity to metal people, I thought. Yes—to man, even if we were made of metal.

"How's that?" said MS-33 foggily.

"Have another drop of Moon Glow," I said. "I've got to get back to Argon City."

I made it back to Benny's place without incident. I had never moved so swiftly. I sent Benny out to find Jon Rogeson, and presently he brought him back. I told Rogeson what MS-33 had said, watching his reaction carefully. I could not forget that though he had been our friend, he was still one of the Builders, a human who thought as humans.

"You comprehend," I said grimly, "that one word of this will bring an uprising of fifty-thousand metal people which can be put down only at much expense and with great destruction. We are free people. The Builders exiled us here, and therefore lost their claim to us. We have as much right to life as anyone, and we do not wish to be melted up and made into printing presses and space ships and the like."

"The damn fools," Jon said softly. "Listen, B-12, you've got to believe me. I didn't know a thing about this, though I've suspected something was up. I'm on your side, but what are we going to do? Maybe they'll listen to reason. Vera—"

"That is the name of the she? No, they will not listen to reason. They hate us." I recalled with bitterness the episode of alarm clock. "There is a chance, however. I have not been idle this night. If you will go get Langley and meet me in the back room here at Benny's, we will talk."

"But he'll be asleep."

"Awaken him," I said. "Get him here. Your own job is at stake as well, remember." "I'll get him," Jon said grimly. "Wait here."

I went over to the bar where Benny was serving the miners. Benny had always been my friend. Jon was my friend, too, but he was a Builder. I wanted one of my own people to know what was going on, just in case something happened to me.

We were talking there, in low tones, when I saw MS-33. He came in through the front door, and there was purposefulness in his stride that had not been there when I left him back at the old hulk. The effects of the Moon Glow had worn off much quicker than I had expected. He had come for vengeance. He would tell about my distillery, and that would be the end of me. There was only one thing to do and I must do it fast.

"Quick," I ordered Benny. "Douse the lights." He complied. The place was plunged into darkness. I knew that it was darkness and yet, you comprehend, I still sensed everything in the place, for I had the special visual sensory system bequeathed only to the General Purposes of a bygone age. I could see, but hardly anyone else could. I worked swiftly, and I got what I was after in a very short time. I ducked out of the front door with it and threw it in a silvery arc as far as I could hurl it. It was an intricate little thing which could not, I am sure, have been duplicated on the entire moon of Phobos.

When I returned, someone had put the lights back on, but it didn't matter now. MS-33 was sitting at one of the tables, staring fixedly at me. He said nothing. Benny was motioning for me to come into the back room. I went to him.   Jon Rogeson and Langley were there. Langley looked irritated. He was mumbling strangled curses and rubbing his eyes. Rogeson laughed. "You may be interested in knowing, B-12, that I had to arrest him to get him here. This had better be good."

"It is all bad," I said, "very bad—but necessary." I turned to Langley. "It is said that your present survey is being made with the purpose of condemning all of Phobos, the dead and the living alike, to the blast furnaces and the metal shops of Earth. Is this true?"

"Why you impudent, miserable piece of tin! What if I am making a scrap survey? What are you going to do about it? You're nothing but a ro—"

"So it is true! But you will tell the salvage ships not to come. It is yours to decide, and you will decide that we are not worth bothering with here on Phobos. You will save us."

"I?" Blustered Langley.

"You will." I took the thing out of my breastplate container and showed it to him. He grew pale.

Jon said, "Well, I'll be damned!"

It was a picture of Langley and another. I gave it to Jon. "His wife," I said. "His real wife. I am sure of it, for you will note the inscription on the bottom."

"Then Vera—?"

"Is not his wife. You wonder that he was camera shy?"

"Housebreaker!" roared Langley. "It's a plot; a dirty, reactionary plot!"

"It is what is called blackmail," I said. I turned to Jon. "I am correct about this?"

"You are." Jon said.

"You are instructed to leave Phobos," I said to Langley, "and you will allow my friend here to keep his job as peace officer, for without it he would be lost. I have observed that in these things the Builders are hardly more adaptable than their children, the metal people. You will do all this, and in return, we will not send the picture that Jon took today to your wife, nor otherwise inform her of your transgression. For I am told that this is a transgression."

"It is indeed," agreed Jon gravely. "Right, Langley?"

"All right," Langley snarled. "You win. And the sooner I get out of this hole the better." He got up to go, squeezing his fat form through the door into the bar, past the gaping miners and the metal people, heedless of the metal people. We watched him go with some satisfaction.

"It is no business of mine," I said to Jon, "but I have seen you look with longing upon the she that was not Langley's wife. Since she does not belong to him, there is nothing to prevent you from having her. Should not that make you happy?"

"Are you kidding?" he snarled.

Which proves that I have still much to learn about his race.

Out front, Langley spied his metal servant, MS-33, just as he was going out the door. He turned to him. "What are you doing here?" he asked suspiciously.

MS-33 made no answer. He stared malevolently at the bar, ignoring Langley.

"Come on here, damn you!" Langley said. MS-33 said nothing. Langley went over to him and roared foul things into his earphones that would corrode one's soul, if one had one. I shall never forget that moment. The screaming, red-faced Langley, the laughing miners.

But he got no reply from MS-33. Not then or ever. And this was scarcely strange, for I had removed his fuse.

THE END

THE PROUD ROBOT

By Lewis Padgett (Henry Kuttner)
Published 1943

Originally the robot was intended to be a can opener. Things often happened that way with Gallegher, who played at science by ear. He was, as he often remarked, a casual genius. Sometimes he'd start with a twist of wire, a few batteries, and a button hook, and before he finished, he might contrive a new type of refrigerating unit. The affair of the time locker had begun that way, with Gallegher singing hoarsely under his breath and peering, quite drunk, into cans of paint.

At the moment he was nursing a hangover. A disjointed, lanky, vaguely boneless man with a lock of dark hair falling untidily over leis forehead, he lay on the couch in the lab and manipulated his mechanical liquor bar. A very dry Martini drizzled slowly from the spigot into his receptive mouth.

He was trying to remember something, but not trying too hard. It had to do with the robot, of course. Well, it didn't matter.

"Hey, Joe," Gallegher said.

The robot stood proudly before the mirror and examined its innards. Its hull was transparent, and wheels were going around at a great rate inside.

"When you call me that," Joe remarked, "whisper. And get that cat out of here."

"Your ears aren't that good."

"They are. I can hear the cat walking about, all right."

"What does it sound like?" Gallegher inquired, interested.

"Just like drums," said the robot, with a put-upon air. "And when you talk, it's like thunder." Joe's voice was a discordant squeak, so Gallegher meditated on saying something about glass-houses and casting the first stone. He brought his attention, with some effort, to the luminous door panel, where a shadow loomed—a familiar shadow, Gallegher thought.

"It's Brock," the annunciator said. "Harrison Brock. Let me in!"

"The door's unlocked." Gallegher didn't stir. He looked gravely at the well-dressed, middle-aged man who came in, and tried to remember. Brock was between forty and fifty; he had a smoothly massaged, clean-shaved face, and wore an expression of harassed intolerance. Probably Gallegher knew the man. He wasn't sure. Oh, well.

Brock looked around the big, untidy laboratory, blinked at the robot, searched for a chair, and failed to find it. Arms akimbo, he rocked back and forth and glared at the prostrate scientist.

"Well?" he said.

"Never start conversations that way," Gallegher mumbled, siphoning another Martini down his gullet. "I've had enough trouble today. Sit down and take it easy. There's a dynamo behind you. It isn't very dusty, is it?"

"Did you get it?" Brock snapped. "That's all I want to know. You've had a week. I've a check for ten thousand in my pocket. Do you want it, or don't you?"

"Sure," Gallegher said. He extended a large, groping hand. "Give."

"Caveat emptor. What am I buying?"

"Don't you know?" the scientist asked, honestly puzzled.

Brock began to bounce up and down in a harassed fashion. "My God," he said. "They told me you could help me if anybody could. Sure. And they also said it'd be like pulling teeth to get sense out of you. Are you a technician or a driveling idiot?"

Gallegher pondered. "Wait a minute. I'm beginning to remember. I talked to you last week, didn't I?"

"You talked—" Brock's round face turned pink. "Yes! You lay there swilling liquor and babbled poetry. You sang 'Frankie and Johnnie.' And you finally got around to accepting my commission."

"The fact is," Gallegher said, "I have been drunk. I often get drunk. Especially on my vacation. It releases my subconscious, and then I can work. I've made my best gadgets when I was tizzied," he went on happily. "Everything seems so clear then. Clear as a bell. I mean a bell, don't I? Anyway—" He lost the thread and looked puzzled. "Anyway, what are you talking about?"

"Are you going to keep quiet?" the robot demanded from its post before the mirror.

Brock jumped. Gallegher waved a casual hand. "Don't mind Joe. I just finished him last night, and I rather regret it."

"A robot?"

"A robot. But he's no good, you know. I made him when I was drunk, and I haven't the slightest idea how or why. All he'll do is stand there and admire himself. And sing. He sings like a banshee. You'll hear him presently."

With an effort Brock brought his attention back to the matter in hand. "Now look, Gallegher. I'm in a spot. You promised to help me. If you don't, I'm a ruined man."

"I've been ruined for years," the scientist remarked. "It never bothers me. I just go along working for a living and making things in my spare time. Making all sorts of things. You know, if I'd really studied, I'd have been another Einstein. So they tell me. As it is, my subconscious picked up a first-class scientific training somewhere. Probably that's why I never bothered. When I'm drunk or sufficiently absent-minded, I can work out the damnedest problems."

"You're drunk now," Brock accused.

"I approach the pleasanter stages. How would you feel if you woke up and found you'd made a robot for some unknown reason, and hadn't the slightest idea of the creature's attributes?"

"Well—"

"I don't feel that way at all," Gallegher murmured. "Probably you take life too seriously, Brock. Wine is a mocker; strong drink is raging. Pardon me. I rage." He drank another Martini.

Brock began to pace around the crowded laboratory, circling various enigmatic and untidy objects. "If you're a scientist, Heaven help science."

"I'm the Larry Adler of science," Gallegher said. "He was a musician—lived some hundreds of years ago, I think. I'm like him. Never took a lesson in my life. Can I help it if my subconscious likes practical jokes?"

"Do you know who I am?" Brock demanded.

"Candidly, no. Should I?"

There was bitterness in the other's voice. "You might have the courtesy to remember, even though it was a week ago. Harrison Brock. Me. I own Vox-View Pictures."

"No," the robot said suddenly, "it's no use. No use at all, Brock." "What the—"

Gallegher sighed wearily. "I forget the damned thing's alive. Mr. Brock, meet Joe. Joe, meet Mr. Brock—of Vox-View."

Joe turned, gears meshing within his transparent skull. "I am glad to meet you, Mr. Brock. Allow me to congratulate you on your good fortune in hearing my lovely voice."

"Uh," said the magnate inarticulately. "Hello."

"Vanity of vanities, all is vanity," Gallegher put in, sotto voce. "Joe's like that. A peacock. No use arguing with him, either."

The robot ignored this aside. "But it's no use, Mr. Brock," he went on squeakily. "I'm not interested in money. I realize it would bring happiness to many if I consented to appear in your pictures, but fame means nothing to me. Nothing. Consciousness of beauty is enough."

Brock began to chew his lips. "Look," he said savagely, "I didn't come here to offer you a picture job. See? Am I offering you a contract? Such colossal nerve— Pah! You're crazy."

"Your schemes are perfectly transparent," the robot remarked coldly. "I can see that you're overwhelmed by my beauty and the loveliness of my voice—its grand tonal qualities. You needn't pretend you don't want me, just so you can get me at a lower price. I said I wasn't interested."

"You're cr-r-razy!" Brock howled, badgered beyond endurance, and Joe calmly turned back to his mirror.

"Don't talk so loudly," the robot warned. "The discordance

is deafening. Besides, you're ugly and I don't like to look at you." Wheels and cogs buzzed inside the transplastic shell. Joe extended his eyes on stalks and regarded himself with every appearance of appreciation.

Gallegher was chuckling quietly on the couch. "Joe has a high irritation value," he said. "I've found that out already. I must have given him some remarkable senses, too. An hour ago he started to laugh his damn fool head off. No reason, apparently. I was fixing myself a bite to eat. Ten minutes after that I slipped on an apple core I'd thrown away and came down hard. Joe just looked at me. 'That was it,' he said. 'Logics of probability. Cause and effect. I knew you were going to drop that apple core and then step on it when you went to pick up the mail.' Like the White Queen, I suppose. It's a poor memory that doesn't work both ways."

Brock sat on the small dynamo—there were two, the larger one named Monstro, and the smaller one serving Gallegher as a bank—and took deep breaths. "Robots are nothing new."

"This one is. I hate its gears. It's beginning to give me an inferiority complex. Wish I knew why I'd made it," Gallegher sighed. "Oh, well. Have a drink?"

"No. I came here on business. Do you seriously mean you spent last week building a robot instead of solving the problem I hired you for?"

"Contingent, wasn't it?" Gallegher asked. "I think I remember that."

"Contingent," Brock said with satisfaction. "Ten thousand, if and when."

"Why not give me the dough and take the robot? He's worth that. Put him in one of your pictures."

"I won't have any pictures unless you figure out an answer," Brock snapped. "I told you all about it."

"I have been drunk," Gallegher said. "My mind has been wiped clear, as by a sponge. I am as a little child. Soon I shall be as a drunken little child. Meanwhile, if you'd care to explain the matter again—"

Brock gulped down his passion, jerked a magazine at random from the bookshelf, and took out a stylo. "All right. My preferred stocks are at twenty-eight, 'way below par—" He scribbled figures on the magazine.

"If you'd taken that medieval folio next to that, it'd have cost you a pretty penny," Gallegher said lazily. "So you're the sort of guy who writes on tablecloths, eh? Forget this business of stocks and stuff. Get down to cases. Who are you trying to gyp?"

"It's no use," the robot said from before its mirror. "I won't sign a contract. People may come and admire me, if they like, but they'll have to whisper in my presence."

"A madhouse," Brock muttered, trying to get a grip on himself. "Listen, Gallegher. I told you all this a week ago, but—"

"Joe wasn't here then. Pretend like you're talking to him."
"Uh—look. You've heard of Vox-View Pictures, at least."

"Sure. The biggest and best television company in the business.

Sonatone's about your only competitor."

"Sonatone's squeezing me out."

Gallegher looked puzzled. "I don't see how. You've got the best product. Tri-dimensional color, all sorts of modern improvements, the top actors, musicians, singers—"

"No use," the robot said. "I won't."

"Shut up, Joe. You're tops in your field, Brock. I'll hand you that. And I've always heard you were fairly ethical. What's

Sonatone got on you?"

Brock made helpless gestures. "Oh, it's politics. The bootleg theaters. I can't buck 'em. Sonatone helped elect the present administration, and the police just wink when I try to have the bootleggers raided."

"Bootleg theaters?" Gallegher asked, scowling a trifle. "I've heard something—"

"It goes 'way back. To the old sound-film days. Home television killed sound film and big theaters. People were conditioned away from sitting in audience groups to watch a screen. The home televisors got good. It was more fun to sit in an easy-chair, drink beer, and watch the show. Television wasn't a rich man's hobby by that time. The meter system brought the price down to middle-class levels. Everybody knows that."

"I don't," Gallegher said. "I never pay attention to what goes on outside of my lab, unless I have to. Liquor and a selective mind. I ignore everything that doesn't affect me directly. Explain the whole thing in detail, so I'll get a complete picture. I don't mind repetition. Now, what about this meter system of yours?"

"Televisors are installed free. We never sell 'em; we rent them. People pay according to how many hours they have the set tuned in. We run a continuous show, stage plays, wire-tape films, operas, orchestras, singers, vaudeville—everything. If you use your televisor a lot, you pay proportionately. The man comes around once a month and reads the meter. Which is a fair system. Anybody can afford a Vox-View. Sonatone and the other companies do the same thing, but Sonatone's the only big competitor I've got. At least, the only one that's crooked as hell. The rest of the boys—they're smaller than I am, but I don't step on their toes. Nobody's ever called me a louse," Brock said darkly.

"So what?"

"So Sonatone has started to depend on audience appeal. It

was impossible till lately—you couldn't magnify tri-dimensional television on a big screen without streakiness and mirage-effect. That's why the regular three-by-four home screens were used. Results were perfect. But Sonatone's bought a lot of the ghost theaters all over the country—"

"What's a ghost theater?" Gallegher asked.

"Well—before sound films collapsed, the world was thinking big. Big—you know? Ever heard of the Radio City Music Hall? That wasn't in it! Television was coming in, and competition was fierce. Sound-film theaters got bigger and more elaborate. They were palaces. Tremendous. But when television was perfected, nobody went to the theaters any more, and it was often too expensive a job to tear 'em down. Ghost theaters—see? Big ones and little ones. Renovated them. And they're showing Sonatone programs. Audience appeal is quite a factor. The theaters charge plenty, but people flock into 'em. Novelty and the mob instinct."

Gallegher closed his eyes. "What's to stop you from doing the same thing?"

"Patents," Brock said briefly. "I mentioned that dimensional television couldn't be used on big screens till lately. Sonatone signed an agreement with me ten years ago that any enlarging improvements would be used mutually. They crawled out of that contract. Said it was faked, and the courts upheld them. They uphold the courts—politics. Anyhow, Sonatone's technicians worked out a method of using the large screen. They took out patents—twenty-seven patents, in fact, covering every possible variation on the idea. My technical staff has been working day and night trying to find some similar method that won't be an infringement, but Sonatone's got it all sewed up. They've a system called the Magna. It can be hooked up to any type of televisor—but they'll only allow it to be used on Sonatone machines. See?"

"Unethical, but legal," Gallegher said. "Still, you're giving your customers more for their money. People want good stuff. The size doesn't matter."

"Yeah," Brock said bitterly, "but that isn't all. The newspapers are full of A.A.—it's a new catchword. Audience Appeal. The herd instinct. You're right about people wanting good stuff—but would you buy Scotch at four a quart if you could get it for half that amount?"

"Depends on the quality. What's happening?"

"Bootleg theaters," Brock said. "They've opened all over the country. They show Vox-View products, and they're using the Magna enlarger system Sonatone's got patented. The admission price is low—lower than the rate of owning a Vox-View in your own home. There's audience appeal. There's the thrill of something a bit illegal. People are having their Vox-Views taken out right and left. I know why. They can go to a bootleg theater instead."

"It's illegal," Gallegher said thoughtfully.

"So were speakeasies, in the Prohibition Era. A matter of protection, that's all. I can't get any action through the courts. I've tried. I'm running in the red. Eventually I'll be broke. I can't lower my home rental fees on Vox-Views. They're nominal already. I make my profits through quantity. Now, no profits. As for these bootleg theaters, it's pretty obvious who's backing them."

"Sonatone?"

"Sure. Silent partners. They get the take at the box office. 'What they want is to squeeze me out of business, so they'll have a monopoly. After that they'll give the public junk and pay their artists starvation salaries. With me it's different. I pay my staff what they're worth—plenty."

"And you offered me a lousy ten thousand," Gallegher remarked. "Uh-huh!"

"That was only the first installment," Brock said hastily. "You can name your own fee. Within reason," he added.

"I shall. An astronomical sum. Did I say I'd accept the commission a week ago?"

"You did."

"Then I must have had some idea how to solve the problem," Gallegher pondered. "Let's see. I didn't mention anything in particular, did I?"

"You kept talking about marble slabs and . . . uh . . . your sweetie."

"Then I was singing," Gallegher explained largely. " 'St. James Infirmary.' Singing calms my nerves, and Lord knows they need it sometimes. Music and liquor. 'I often wonder what the vintners buy—' "

"What?"

" 'One half so precious as the stuff they sell.' Let it go. I am quoting Omar. It means nothing. Are your technicians any good?"

"The best. And the best paid."

"They can't find a magnifying process that won't infringe on the Sonatone Magna patents?"

"In a nutshell, that's it."

"I suppose I'll have to do some research," Gallegher said sadly. I hate it like poison. Still, the sum of the parts equals the whole. Does that make sense to you? It doesn't to me. I have trouble with words. After I say things, I start wondering what I've said. Better than watching a play," he finished wildly. "I've got a headache. Too much talk and not enough liquor. Where were we?"

"Approaching the madhouse," Brock suggested. "If you weren't my last resort, I'd—"

"No use," the robot said squeakily. "You might as well tear up your contract, Brock. I won't sign it. Fame means nothing to me—nothing."

"If you don't shut up," Gallegher warned, "I'm going to scream in your ears."

"All right!" Joe shrilled. "Beat me! Go on, beat me! The meaner you are, the faster I'll have my nervous system disrupted, and then I'll be dead. I don't care. I've got no instinct of self-preservation. Beat me. See if I care."

"He's right, you know," the scientist said after a pause. "And it's the only logical way to respond to blackmail or threats. The sooner it's over, the better. There aren't any gradations with Joe. Anything really painful to him will destroy him. And he doesn't give a damn."

"Neither do I," Brock grunted. "What I want to find out—"

"Yeah. I know. Well, I'll wander around and see what occurs to me. Can I get into your studios?"

"Here's a pass." Brock scribbled something on the back of a card. "Will you get to work on it right away?"

"Sure," Gallegher lied. "Now you run along and take it easy. Try and cool off. Everything's under control. I'll either find a solution to your problem pretty soon or else—"

"Or else what?"

"Or else I won't," the scientist finished blandly, and fingered the buttons on a control panel near the couch. "I'm tired of Martinis. Why didn't I make that robot a mechanical bartender, while I was at it? Even the effort of selecting and pushing buttons is depressing at times. Yeah, I'll get to work on the business, Brock. Forget it."

The magnate hesitated. "Well, you're my only hope. I needn't bother to mention that if there's anything I can do to help you—"

"A blonde," Gallegher murmured. "That gorgeous, gorgeous star of yours, Silver O'Keefe. Send her over. Otherwise I want nothing."

"Good-by, Brock," the robot said squeakily. "Sorry we couldn't get together on the contract, but at least you've had the ineluctable delight of hearing my beautiful voice, not to mention the pleasure of seeing me. Don't tell too many people how lovely I am. I really don't want to be bothered with mobs. They're noisy."

"You don't know what dogmatism means till you've talked to Joe," Gallegher said. "Oh, well. See you later. Don't forget the blonde."

Brock's lips quivered. He searched for words, gave it up as a vain task, and turned to the door.

"Good-by, you ugly man," Joe said.

Gallegher winced as the door slammed, though it was harder on the robot's supersensitive ears than on his own.

"Why do you go on like that?" he inquired. "You nearly gave the guy apoplexy."

"Surely he didn't think he was beautiful," Joe remarked. "Beauty's in the eye of the beholder."

"How stupid you are. You're ugly, too."

"And you're a collection of rattletrap gears, pistons and cogs. You've got worms," said Gallegher, referring, of course, to certain mechanisms in the robot's body.

"I'm lovely." Joe stared raptly into the mirror.

"Maybe, to you. Why did I make you transparent, I wonder?"

"So others could admire me. I have X-ray vision, of course."

"And wheels in your head. Why did I put your radioatomic brain in your stomach? Protection?"

Joe didn't answer. He was humming in a maddeningly squeaky voice, shrill and nerve-racking. Gallegher stood it for a while, fortifying himself with a gin rickey from the siphon.

"Get it up!" he yelped at last. "You sound like an old-fashioned subway train going around a curve."

"You're merely jealous," Joe scoffed, but obediently raised his tone to a supersonic pitch. There was silence for a half-minute. Then all the dogs in the neighborhood began to howl.

Wearily Gallegher dragged his lanky frame up from the couch. He might as well get out. Obviously there was no peace to be had in the laboratory. Not with that animated junk pile inflating his ego all over the place. Joe began to laugh in an off-key cackle. Gallegher winced.

"What now?"

"You'll find out."

Logic of causation and effect, influenced by probabilities, X-ray vision and other enigmatic senses the robot no doubt possessed. Gallegher cursed softly, found a shapeless black hat, and made for the door. He opened it to admit a short, fat man who bounced painfully off the scientist's stomach.

"Whoof! What a corny sense of humor that jackass has. Hello, Mr. Kennicott. Glad to see you. Sorry I can't offer you a drink."

Mr. Kennicott's swarthy face twisted malignantly. "Don' wanna no drink. Wanna my money. You gimme. Howzabout it?"

Gallegher looked thoughtfully at nothing. "Well, the fact is, I was just going to collect a check."

"I sella you my diamonds. You say you gonna make somet'ing wit' 'em. You gimme check before. It go bounca, bounca, bounca. Why is?"

"It was rubber," Gallegher said faintly. "I never can keep track of my bank balance."

Kennicott showed symptoms of going bounca on the threshold. "You gimme back diamonds, eh?"

"Well, I used 'em in an experiment, I forget just what. You know, Mr. Kennicott, I think I was a little drunk when I bought them, wasn't I?"

"Dronk," the little man agreed. "Mad wit' vino, sure. So whatta? I wait no longer. Awready you put me off too much. Pay up now or elsa."

"Go away, you dirty man," Joe said from within the room. "You're awful."

Gallegher hastily shouldered Kennicott out into the street and latched the door behind him. "A parrot;" he explained. "I'm going to wring its neck pretty soon. Now about that money. I admit I owe it to you. I've just taken on a big job, and when I'm paid, you'll get yours."

"Bah to such stuff," Kennicott said. "You gotta position, eh? You are technician wit' some big company, Ai? Ask for ahead-salary."

"I did," Gallegher sighed. "I've drawn my salary for six months ahead. Now look, I'll have that dough for you in a couple of days. Maybe I can get an advance from my client. O. K.?"

"No."

"No?"

"Ah-h, nutsa. I waita one day. Two daysa, maybe. Enough. You get money. Awright. If not, O. K., calabozo for you."

"Two days is plenty," Gallegher said, relieved. "Say, are there any of those bootleg theaters around here?"

"Better you get to work an' not waste time."

"That's my work. I'm making a survey. How can I find a bootleg place?"

"Easy. You go downtown, see guy in doorway. He sell you tickets. Anywhere. All over."

"Swell," Gallegher said, and bade the little man adieu. Why had he bought diamonds from Kennicott? It would be almost worth while to have his subconscious amputated. It did the most extraordinary things. It worked on inflexible principles of logic, but that logic was completely alien to Gallegher's conscious mind. The results, though, were often surprisingly good, and always surprising. That was the worst of being a scientist who knew no science—who played by ear.

There was diamond dust in a retort in the laboratory, from some unsatisfactory experiment Gallegher's subconscious had performed; and he had a fleeting memory of buying the stones from Kennicott. Curious. Maybe—oh, yeah. They'd gone into Joe. Bearings or something. Dismantling the robot wouldn't help now, for the diamonds had certainly been reground. Why the devil hadn't he used commercial stones, quite as satisfactory, instead of purchasing blue-whites of the finest water? The best was none too good for Gallegher's subconscious. It had a fine freedom from commercial instincts. It just didn't understand the price system or the basic principles of economics.

Gallegher wandered downtown like a Diogenes seeking truth. It was early evening, and the luminates were flickering on overhead, pale bars of light against darkness. A sky sign blazed above Manhattan's towers. Air-taxis, skimming along at various arbitrary levels, paused for passengers at the elevator landings. Heigh-ho.

Downtown, Gallegher began to look for doorways. He found

an occupied one at last, but the man was selling post cards. Gallegher declined and headed for the nearest bar, feeling the need of replenishment. It was a mobile bar, combining the worst features of a Coney Island ride with uninspired cocktails, and Gallegher hesitated on the threshold. But at last he seized a chair as it swung past and relaxed as much as possible. He ordered three rickeys and drank them in rapid succession. After that he called the bartender over and asked him about bootleg theaters.

"Hell, yes," the man said, producing a sheaf of tickets from his apron. "How many?"

"One. Where do I go?"

"Two-twenty-eight. This street. Ask for Tony."

"Thanks," Gallegher said, and, having paid exorbitantly, crawled out of the chair and weaved away. Mobile bars were an improvement he didn't appreciate. Drinking, he felt, should be performed in a state of stasis, since one eventually reached that stage, anyway.

The door was at the bottom of a flight of steps, and there was a grilled panel set in it. When Gallegher knocked, the visascreen lit up—obviously a one-way circuit, for the doorman was invisible.

"Tony here?" Gallegher said.

The door opened, revealing a tired-looking man in pneumo-slacks, which failed in their purpose of building up his skinny figure. "Got a ticket? Let's have it. O. K., bud. Straight ahead. Show now going on. Liquor served in the bar on your left."

Gallegher pushed through sound-proofed curtains at the end of a short corridor and found himself in what appeared to be the foyer of an ancient theater, circa 1980, when plastics were the great fad. He smelled out the bar, drank expensively priced cheap liquor, and, fortified, entered the theater itself. It was nearly full. The great screen—a Magna, presumably—

was filled with people doing things to a spaceship. Either an adventure film or a newsreel, Gallegher realized.

Only the thrill of lawbreaking would have enticed the audience into the bootleg theater. It smelled. It was certainly run on a shoestring, and there were no ushers. But it was illicit, and therefore well patronized. Gallegher looked thoughtfully at the screen. No streakiness, no mirage effect. A Magna enlarger had been fitted to a Vox-View unlicensed televisor, and one of Brock's greatest stars was emoting effectively for the benefit of the bootleggers' patrons. Simple highjacking. Yeah.

After a while Gallegher went out, noticing a uniformed policeman in one of the aisle seats. He grinned sardonically. The flatfoot hadn't paid his admission, of course. Politics were as usual.

Two blocks down the street a blaze of light announced SONATONE BIJOU. This, of course, was one of the legalized theaters, and correspondingly high-priced. Gallegher recklessly squandered a small fortune on a good seat. He was interested in comparing notes, and discovered that, as far as he could make out, the Magna in the Bijou and the bootleg theater were identical. Both did their job perfectly. The difficult task of enlarging television screens had been successfully surmounted.

In the Bijou, however, all was palatial. Resplendent ushers salaamed to the rugs. Bars dispensed free liquor, in reasonable quantities. There was a Turkish bath. Gallegher went through a door labeled MEN and emerged quite dazzled by the splendor of the place. For at least ten minutes afterward he felt like a Sybarite.

All of which meant that those who could afford it went to the legalized Sonatone theaters, and the rest attended the bootleg places. All but a few homebodies, who weren't carried off their feet by the new fad. Eventually Brock would be forced out of business for lack of revenue. Sonatone would take over, jacking up their prices and concentrating on making money. Amusement was necessary to life; people had been conditioned to television. There was no substitute. They'd pay and pay for inferior talent, once Sonatone succeeded in their squeeze.

Gallegher left the Bijou and hailed an air-taxi. He gave the address of Vox-View's Long Island studio, with some vague hope of getting a drawing account out of Brock. Then, too, he wanted to investigate further.

Vox-View's eastern offices sprawled wildly over Long Island, bordering the Sound, a vast collection of variously shaped buildings. Gallegher instinctively found the commissary, where he absorbed more liquor as a precautionary measure. His subconscious had a heavy job ahead, and he didn't want it handicapped by lack of complete freedom. Besides, the Collins was good.

After one drink, he decided he'd had enough for a while. He wasn't a superman, though his capacity was slightly incredible. Just enough for objective clarity and subjective release—

"Is the studio always open at night?" he asked the waiter.

"Sure. Some of the stages, anyway. It's a round-the-clock program."

"The commissary's full."

"We get the airport crowd, too. 'Nother?"

Gallegher shook his head and went out. The card Brock had given him provided entree at a gate, and he went first of all to the big-shot's office. Brock wasn't there, but loud voices emerged, shrilly feminine.

The secretary said, "Just a minute, please," and used her interoffice visor. Presently—"Will you go in?"

Gallegher did. The office was a honey, functional and luxurious at the same time. Three-dimensional stills were in niches along the walls —Vox-View's biggest stars. A small, excited, pretty brunette was sitting behind the desk, and a blond angel was standing furiously on the other side of it. Gallegher recognized the angel as Silver O'Keefe.

He seized the opportunity. "Hiya, Miss O'Keefe. Will you autograph an ice cube for me? In a highball?"

Silver looked feline. "Sorry, darling, but I'm a working girl. And I'm busy right now."

The brunette scratched a cigarette. "Let's settle this later, Silver. Pop said to see this guy if he dropped in. It's important."

"It'll be settled," Silver said. "And soon." She made an exit. Gallegher whistled thoughtfully at the closed door.

"You can't have it," the brunette said. "It's under contract. And it wants to get out of the contract, so it can sign up with Sonatone. Rats desert a sinking ship. Silver's been kicking her head off ever since she read the storm signals."

"Yeah?"

"Sit down and smoke or something. I'm Patsy Brock. Pop runs this business, and I manage the controls whenever he blows his top. The old goat can't stand trouble. He takes it as a personal affront."

Gallegher found a chair. "So Silver's trying to renege, eh? How many others?"

"Not many. Most of 'em are loyal. But, of course, if we bust up—" Patsy Brock shrugged. "They'll either work for Sonatone for their cakes, or else do without."

"Uh-huh. Well—I want to see your technicians. I want to look over the ideas they've worked out for enlarger screens."

"Suit yourself," Patsy said. "It's not much use. You just can't make a televisor enlarger without infringing on some Sonatone patent."

She pushed a button, murmured something into a visor, and presently two tall glasses appeared through a slot in the desk. "Mr. Gallegher?"

"Well, since it's a Collins—"

"I could tell by your breath," Patsy said enigmatically. "Pop told me he'd seen you. He seemed a bit upset, especially by your new robot. What is it like, anyway?"

"Oh, I don't know," Gallegher said, at a loss. "It's got lots of abilities—new senses, I think—but I haven't the slightest idea what it's good for. Except admiring itself in a mirror."

Patsy nodded. "I'd like to see it sometime. But about this Sonatone business. Do you think you can figure out an answer?"

"Possibly. Probably."

"Not certainly?"

"Certainly, then. Of that there is no manner of doubt—no possible doubt whatever."

"Because it's important to me. The man who owns Sonatone is Elia Tone. A piratical skunk. He blusters. He's got a son named Jimmy. And Jimmy, believe it or not, has read 'Romeo and Juliet.' "

"Nice guy?"

"A louse. A big, brawny louse. He wants me to marry him."

" 'Two families both alike in—' "

"Spare me," Patsy interrupted. "I always thought Romeo was a dope, anyway. And if I ever thought I was going aisling with Jimmy Tone, I'd buy a one-way ticket to the nut hatch. No, Mr. Gallegher, it's not like that. No hibiscus blossoms. Jimmy has proposed to me—his idea of a proposal, by the way, is to get a half Nelson on a girl and tell her how lucky she is."

"Ah," said Gallegher, diving into his Collins.

"This whole idea—the patent monopoly and the bootleg theaters —is Jimmy's. I'm sure of that. His father's in on it, too, of course, but Jimmy Tone is the bright little boy who started it."

"Why."

"Two birds with one stone. Sonatone will have a monopoly on the business, and Jimmy thinks he'll get me. He's a little mad. He can't believe I'm in earnest in refusing him, and he expects me to break down and say 'Yes' after a while. Which I won't, no matter what happens. But it's a personal matter. I can't let him put this trick over on us. I want that self-sufficient smirk wiped off his face."

"You just don't like him, eh?" Gallegher remarked. "I don't blame you, if he's like that. Well, I'll do my damnedest. However, I'll need an expense account."

"How much?"

Gallegher named a sum. Patsy styloed a check for a far smaller amount. The scientist looked hurt.

"It's no use," Patsy said, grinning crookedly. "I've heard of you, Mr. Gallegher. You're completely irresponsible. If you had more than this, you'd figure you didn't need any more, and you'd forget the whole matter. I'll issue more checks to you when you need 'em—but I'll want itemized expense accounts."

"You wrong me," Gallegher said, brightening. "I was figuring on taking you to a night club. Naturally I don't want to take you to a dive. The big places cost money. Now if you'll just write another check—"

Patsy laughed. "No."

"Want to buy a robot?"

"Not that kind, anyway."

"Then I'm washed up," Gallegher sighed. "Well, what about—" At this point the visor hummed. A blank, transparent face grew on the screen. Gears were clicking rapidly inside the round head. Patsy gave a small shriek and shrank back.

"Tell Gallegher Joe's here, you lucky girl," a squeaky voice announced. "You may treasure the sound and sight of me till your dying day. One touch of beauty in a world of drabness—"

Gallegher clutched the desk and looked at the screen. "What the hell. How did you come to life?"

"I had a problem to solve."

"How'd you know where to reach me?"

"I vastened you," the robot said.

"What?"

"I vastened you while you were at the Vox-View studios with Patsy Brock."

"What's vastened?" Gallegher wanted to know.

"It's a sense I've got. You've nothing remotely like it, so I can't describe it to you. It's rather like a combination of sagrazi and prescience."

"Sagrazi?"

"Oh, you don't have sagrazi, either, do you? Well, don't waste my time. I want to go back to the mirror."

"Does he always talk like that?" Patsy put in.

"Nearly always. Sometimes it makes even less sense. O. K.,

Joe. Now what?"

"You're not working for Brock any more," the robot said. "You're working for the Sonatone people."

Gallagher breathed deeply. "Keep talking. You're crazy, though."

"I don't like Kennicott. He annoys me. He's too ugly. His vibrations grate on my sagrazi."

"Never mind him," Gallegher said, not wishing to discuss his diamond-buying activities before the girl. "Get back to—"

"But I knew Kennicott would keep coming back till he got his money. So when Elia and James Tone came to the laboratory, I got a check from them."

Patsy's hand gripped Gallegher's biceps. "Steady! What's going on here? The old double cross?"

"No. Wait. Let me get to the bottom of this. Joe, damn your transparent hide, just what did you do? How could you get a check from the Tones?"

"I pretended to be you."

"Sure," Gallegher said with savage sarcasm. "That explains it. We're twins. We look exactly alike."

"I hypnotized them," Joe explained. "I made them think I was you."

"You can do that?"

"Yes. It surprised me a bit. Still, if I'd thought, I'd have vastened I could do it."

"You . . . yeah, sure. I'd have vastened the same thing myself. What happened?"

"The Tones must have suspected Brock would ask you to help him. They offered an exclusive contract—you work for them and nobody else. Lots of money. Well, I pretended to be you, and said all right. So I signed the contract—it's your signature, by the way—and got a check from them and mailed it to Kennicott."

"The whole check?" Gallegher asked feebly. "How much was it?"

"Twelve thousand."

"They only offered me that?"

"No," the robot said, "they offered a hundred thousand, and two thousand a week for five years. But I merely wanted

enough to pay Kennicott and make sure he wouldn't come back and bother me. The Tones were satisfied when I said twelve thousand would be enough."

Gallegher made an articulate, gurgling sound deep in his throat, Joe nodded thoughtfully.

"I thought I had better notify you that you're working for Sonatone now. Well, I'll go back to the mirror and sing to myself."

"Wait," the scientist said. "Just wait, Joe. With my own two hands I'm going to rip you gear from gear and stamp on your fragments."

"It won't hold in court," Patsy said, gulping.

"It will," Joe told her cheerily.

"You may have one last, satisfying look at me, and then I must go." He went.

Gallegher drained his Collins at a draft. "I'm shocked sober," he informed the girl. "What did I put into that robot? What abnormal senses has he got? Hypnotizing people into believing he's me—I'm him—I don't know what I mean."

"Is this a gag?" Patsy said shortly, after a pause. "You didn't sign up with Sonatone yourself, by any chance, and have your robot call up here to give you an out—an alibi? I'm just wondering."

"Don't. Joe signed a contract with Sonatone, not me. But—figure it out: If the signature's a perfect copy of mine, if Joe hypnotized the Tones into thinking they saw me instead of him, if there are witnesses to the signature—the two Tones are witnesses, of course— Oh, hell."

Patsy's eyes were narrowed. "We'll pay you as much as Sonatone offered. On a contingent basis. But you're working for Vox-View— that's understood."

"Sure."

Gallegher looked longingly at his empty glass. Sure. He was working for Vox-View. But, to all legal appearances, he had signed a contract giving his exclusive services to Sonatone for a period of five years —and for a sum of twelve thousand! Yipe! What was it they'd offered? A hundred thousand flat, and . . . and—

It wasn't the principle of the thing, it was the money. Now Gallegher was sewed up tighter than a banded pigeon. If Sonatone could win a court suit, he was legally bound to them for five years. With no further emolument. He had to get out of that contract, somehow—and at the same time solve Brock's problem.

Why not Joe? The robot, with his surprising talents, had got Gallegher into this spot. He ought to be able to get the scientist out. He'd better—or the proud robot would soon be admiring himself piecemeal.

"That's it," Gallegher said under his breath. "I'll talk to Joe. Patsy, feed me liquor in a hurry and send me to the technical department. I want to see those blueprints."

The girl looked at him suspiciously. "All right. If you try to sell us out—"

"I've been sold out myself. Sold down the river. I'm afraid of that robot. He's vastened me into quite a spot. That's right, Collinses." Gallegher drank long and deeply.

After that, Patsy took him to the tech offices. The reading of three-dimensional blueprints was facilitated with a scanner—a selective device which eliminated confusion. Gallegher studied the plans long and thoughtfully. There were copies of the patented Sonatone prints, too, and, as far as he could tell, Sonatone had covered the ground beautifully. There weren't any outs. Unless one used an entirely new principle—

But new principles couldn't be plucked out of the air. Nor would that solve the problem completely. Even if Vox-View owned a new type of enlarger that didn't infringe on Sonatone's Magna, the bootleg theaters would still be in existence, pulling the trade. A. A.—Audience Appeal—was a prime factor now. It had to be considered. The puzzle wasn't a purely scientific one. There was the human equation as well.

Gallegher stored the necessary information in his mind, neatly indexed on shelves. Later he'd use what he wanted. For the moment, he was completely baffled. Something worried him.

What?

The Sonatone affair.

"I want to get in touch with the Tones," he told Patsy. "Any ideas?"

"I can reach 'em on a visor."

Gallegher shook his head. "Psychological handicap. It's too easy to break the connection."

"Well, if you're in a hurry, you'll probably find the boys night clubbing. I'll go see what I can find out." Patsy scuttled off, and Silver O'Keefe appeared from behind a screen.

"I'm shameless," she announced. "I always listen at keyholes. Sometimes I hear interesting things. If you want to see the Tones, they're at the Castle Club. And I think I'll take you up on that drink."

Gallegher said, "O. K. You get a taxi. I'll tell Patsy we're going."

"She'll hate that," Silver remarked. "Meet you outside the commissary in ten minutes. Get a shave while you're at it."

Patsy Brock wasn't in her office, but Gallegher left word. After that, he visited the service lounge, smeared invisible shave cream on his face, left it there for a couple of minutes, and wiped it off with a treated towel. The bristles came away with the cream. Slightly refreshed, Gallegher joined Silver at the rendezvous and hailed an air-taxi. Presently they were leaning back on the cushions, puffing cigarettes and eyeing each other warily.

"Well?" Gallegher said.

"Jimmy Tone tried to date me up tonight. That's how I knew where to find him."

"Well?"

"I've been asking questions around the lot tonight. It's unusual for an outsider to get into the Vox-View administration offices. I went around saying, 'Who's Gallegher?' "

"What did you find out?"

"Enough to give me a few ideas. Brock hired you, eh? I can guess why."

"Ergo what?"

"I've a habit of landing on my feet," Silver said, shrugging. She knew how to shrug. "Vox-View's going bust. Sonatone's taking over. Unless—"

"Unless I figure out an answer."

"That's right. I want to know which side of the fence I'm going to land on. You're the lad who can probably tell me. Who's going to win?"

"You always bet on the winning side, eh?" Gallegher inquired. "Have you no ideals, wench? Is there no truth in you? Ever hear of ethics and scruples?"

Silver beamed happily. "Did you?"

"Well, I've heard of 'em. Usually I'm too drunk to figure out what they mean. The trouble is, my subconscious is completely amoral, and when it takes over, logic's the only law."

She threw her cigarette into the East River. "Will you tip me off which side of the fence is the right one?"

"Truth will triumph," Gallegher said piously. "It always does. However, I figure truth is a variable, so we're right back where we started. All right, sweetheart. I'll answer your question. Stay on my side if you want to be safe."

"Which side are you on?"

"Lord knows," Gallegher said. "Consciously I'm on Brock's side. But my subconscious may have different ideas. We'll see."

Silver looked vaguely dissatisfied, but didn't say anything. The taxi swooped down to the Castle roof, grounding with pneumatic gentleness. The Club itself was downstairs, in an immense room shaped like half a melon turned upside down. Each table was on a transparent platform that could be raised on its shaft to any height at will. Smaller service elevators allowed waiters to bring drinks to the guests. There wasn't any particular reason for this arrangement, but at least it was novel, and only extremely heavy drinkers ever fell from their tables. Lately the management had taken to hanging transparent nets under the platforms, for safety's sake.

The Tones, father and son, were up near the roof, drinking with two lovelies. Silver towed Gallegher to a service lift, and the man closed his eyes as he was elevated skyward. The liquor in his stomach screamed protest. He lurched forward, clutched at Elia Tone's bald head, and dropped into a seat beside the magnate. His searching hand found Jimmy Tone's glass, and he drained it hastily.

"What the hell," Jimmy said.

"It's Gallegher," Elia announced. "And Silver. A pleasant surprise. Join us?"

"Only socially," Silver said.

Gallegher, fortified by the liquor, peered at the two men. Jimmy Tone was a big, tanned, handsome lout with a jutting jaw and an offensive grin. His father combined the worst features of Nero and a crocodile.

"We're celebrating," Jimmy said. "What made you change your mind, Silver? You said you had to work tonight."

"Gallegher wanted to see you. I don't know why."

Elia's cold eyes grew even more glacial. "All right. Why?"

"I hear I signed some sort of contract with you," the scientist said.

"Yeah. Here's a photostatic copy. What about it?"

"Wait a minute." Gallegher scanned the document. It was apparently his own signature. Damn that robot!

"It's a fake," he said at last.

Jimmy laughed loudly. "I get it. A holdup. Sorry, pal, but you're sewed up. You signed that in the presence of witnesses."

"Well—" Gallegher said wistfully. "I suppose you wouldn't believe me if I said a robot forged my name to it—"

"Haw!" Jimmy remarked.

"—hypnotizing you into believing you were seeing me."

Elia stroked his gleaming bald head. "Candidly, no. Robots can't do that."

"Mine can."

"Prove it. Prove it in court. If you can do that, of course—" Elia chuckled. "Then you might get the verdict."

Gallegher's eyes narrowed. "Hadn't thought of that. However—I hear you offered me a hundred thousand flat, as well, as a weekly salary."

"Sure, sap," Jimmy said. "Only you said all you needed was twelve thousand. Which was what you got. Tell you what, though. We'll pay you a bonus for every usable product you make for Sonatone."

Gallegher got up. "Even my subconscious doesn't like these lugs," he told Silver. "Let's go."

"I think I'll stick around."

"Remember the fence," he warned cryptically. "But suit yourself. I'll run along."

Elia said, "Remember, Gallegher, you're working for us. If we hear of you doing any favors for Brock, we'll slap an injunction on you before you can take a deep breath."

"Yeah?"

The Tones deigned no answer. Gallegher unhappily found the lift and descended to the floor. What now?
Joe.

Fifteen minutes later Gallegher let himself into his laboratory. The lights were blazing, and dogs were barking frantically for blocks around. Joe stood before the mirror, singing inaudibly.

"I'm going to take a sledge hammer to you," Gallegher said. "Start saying your prayers, you misbegotten collection of cogs. So help me, I'm going to sabotage you."

"All right, beat me," Joe squeaked. "See if I care. You're merely jealous of my beauty."

"Beauty!"

"You can't see all of it—you've only six senses."

"Five."

"Six. I've a lot more. Naturally my full splendor is revealed only to me. But you can see enough and hear enough to realize part of my loveliness, anyway."

"You squeak like a rusty tin wagon," Gallegher growled.

"You have dull ears. Mine are supersensitive. You miss the full tonal value of my voice, of course. Now be quiet. Talking disturbs me. I'm appreciating my gear movements."

"Live in your fool's paradise while you can. Wait'll I find a sledge."

"All right, beat me. What do I care?"

Gallegher sat down wearily on the couch, staring at the robot's transparent back. "You've certainly screwed things up for me. What did you sign that Sonatone contract for?"

"I told you. So Kennicott wouldn't come around and bother me."

"Of all the selfish, lunk-headed . . . uh! Well, you got me into a sweet mess. The Tones can hold me to the letter of the contract unless I prove I didn't sign it. All right. You're going to help me. You're going into court with me and turn on your hypnotism or whatever it is. You're going to prove to a judge that you did and can masquerade as me."

"Won't," said the robot. "Why should I?"

"Because you got me into this," Gallegher yelped. "You've got to get me out!"

"Why?"

"Why? Because . . . uh . . . well, it's common decency!" "Human values don't apply to robots," Joe said. "What care I for semantics? I refuse to waste time I could better employ admiring my beauty. I shall stay here before the minor forever and ever—"

"The hell you will," Gallegher snarled. "I'll smash you to atoms."

"All right. I don't care."

"You don't?"

"You and your instinct for self-preservation," the robot said, rather sneeringly "I suppose it's necessary for you, though. Creatures of such surpassing ugliness would destroy themselves out of sheer shame if they didn't have something like that to keep them alive."

"Suppose I take away your mirror?" Gallegher asked, in a

hopeless voice.

For answer Joe shot his eyes out on their stalks. "Do I need a mirror? Besides, I can vasten myself lokishly."

"Never mind that. I don't want to go crazy for a while yet. Listen, dope, a robot's supposed to do something. Something useful, I mean."

"I do. Beauty is all."

Gallegher squeezed his eyes shut, trying to think. "Now look. Suppose I invent a new type of enlarger screen for Brock. The Tones will impound it. I've got to be legally free to work for Brock, or—"

"Look!" Joe cried squeakishly. "They go round! How lovely!" He stared in ecstasy at his whirring insides. Gallegher went pale with impotent fury.

"Damn you!" he muttered. "I'll find some way to bring pressure to bear. I'm going to bed." He rose and spitefully snapped off the lights.

"It doesn't matter," the robot said. "I can see in the dark, too." The door slammed behind Gallegher. In the silence Joe began to sing tunelessly to himself.

Gallegher's refrigerator covered an entire wall of his kitchen. It was filled mostly with liquors that required chilling, including the imported canned beer with which he always started his binges. The next morning, heavy-eyed and disconsolate, Gallegher searched for tomato juice, took a wry sip, and hastily washed it down with rye. Since he was already a week gone in bottle-dizziness, beer wasn't indicated now—he always worked cumulatively, by progressive stages. The food service popped a hermetically sealed breakfast on a table, and Gallegher morosely toyed with a bloody steak.

Well?

Court, he decided, was the only recourse. He knew little about the robot's psychology. But a judge would certainly be impressed by Joe's talents. The evidence of robots was not legally admissible—still, if Joe could be considered as a machine capable of hypnotism, the Sonatone contract might be declared null and void.

Gallegher used his visor to start the ball rolling. Harrison Brock still had certain political powers of pull, and the hearing was set for that very day. What would happen, though, only God and the robot knew.

Several hours passed in intensive but futile thought. Gallegher could think of no way in which to force the robot to do what he wanted. If only he could remember the purpose for which Joe had had been created—but he couldn't. Still—

At noon he entered the laboratory.

"Listen, stupid," he said, "you're coming to court with me. Now."

"Won't."

"O. K." Gallegher opened the door to admit two husky men in overalls, carrying a stretcher. "Put him in, boys."

Inwardly he was slightly nervous. Joe's powers were quite unknown, his potentialities an x quantity. However, the robot wasn't very large, and, though he struggled and screamed in a voice of frantic squeakiness, he was easily loaded on the stretcher and put in a strait jacket.

"Stop it! You can't do this to me! Let me go, do you hear? Let me go!"

"Outside," Gallegher said.

Joe, protesting valiantly, was carried out and loaded into an air van. Once there, he calmed down and looked up blankly at nothing. Gallegher sat down on a bench beside the prostrate robot. The van glided up.
"Well?"

"Suit yourself," Joe said. "You got me all upset, or I could have hypnotized you all. I still could, you know. I could make you all run around barking like dogs."

Gallegher twitched a little. "Better not."

"I won't. It's beneath my dignity. I shall simply lie here and admire myself. I told you I don't need a mirror. I can vasten my beauty without it."

"Look," Gallegher said. "You're going to a courtroom. There'll be a lot of people in it. They'll all admire you They'll admire you more if you show how you can hypnotize people. Like you did to the Tones, remember?"

"What do I care how many people admire me?" Joe asked. "I don't need confirmation. If they see me, that's their good luck. Now be quiet. You may watch my gears if you choose."

Gallegher watched the robot's gears with smoldering hatred in his eyes. He was still darkly furious when the van arrived at the court chambers. The men carried Joe inside, under Gallegher's direction, and laid him down carefully on a table, where, after a brief discussion, he was marked as Exhibit A.

The courtroom was well filled. The principals were there, too— Elia and Jimmy Tone, looking disagreeably confident, and Patsy Brock, with her father, both seeming anxious. Silver O'Keefe, with her usual wariness, had found a seat midway between the representatives of Sonatone and Vox-View. The presiding judge was a martinet named Hansen, but, as far as Gallegher knew, he was honest. Which was something, anyway.

Hansen looked at Gallegher. "We won't bother with formalities. I've been reading this brief you sent down. The whole case stands or falls on the question of whether you did or did not sign, a certain contract with the Sonatone Television Amusement Corp. Right?"

"Right, your honor."

"Under the circumstances you dispense with legal representation. Right?"

"Right, your honor."

"Then this is technically ex officio, to be confirmed later by appeal if either party desires. Otherwise after ten days the verdict becomes official." This new type of informal court hearing had lately become popular—it saved time, as well as wear and tear on everyone. Moreover, certain recent scandals had made attorneys slightly disreputable in the public eye. There was a prejudice.

Judge Hansen called up the Tones, questioned them, and then asked Harrison Brock to take the stand. The big shot looked worried, but answered promptly.

"You made an agreement with the appellor eight days ago?"
"Yes. Mr. Gallegher contracted to do certain work for me—"

"Was there a written contract?"

"No. It was verbal."

Hansen looked thoughtfully at Gallegher. "Was the appellor intoxicated at the time? He often is, I believe."

Brock gulped. "There were no tests made. I really can't say."

"Did he drink any alcoholic beverages in your presence?"

"I don't know if they were alcoholic bev—"

"If Mr. Gallegher drank them, they were alcoholic. Q. E. D. The gentleman once worked with me on a case— However, there seems to be no legal proof that you entered into any agreement with Mr. Gallegher. The defendant—Sonatone— possesses a written contract. The signature has been verified."

Hansen waved Brock down from the stand. "Now, Mr. Gallegher. If you'll come up here— The contract in question was signed at approximately 8 p. m. last night. You contend you did not sign it?"

"Exactly. I wasn't even in my laboratory then."

"Where were you?"

"Downtown."

"Can you produce witnesses to that effect?"

Gallegher thought back. He couldn't.

"Very well. Defendant states that at approximately 8 p. m. last night you, in your laboratory, signed a certain contract. You deny that categorically. You state that Exhibit A, through the use of hypnotism, masqueraded as you and successfully forged your signature. I have consulted experts, and they are of the opinion that robots are incapable of such power."

"My robot's a new type."

"Very well. Let your robot hypnotize me into believing that it is either you, or any other human. In other words, let it prove its capabilities. Let it appear to me in any shape it chooses."

Gallegher said, "I'll try," and left the witness box. He went to the table where the strait-jacketed robot lay and silently sent up a brief prayer.

"Joe."

"Yes."

"You've been listening?"

"Yes."

"Will you hypnotize Judge Hansen?"

"Go away," Joe said. "I'm admiring myself."

Gallegher started to sweat. "Listen. I'm not asking much. All you have to do—"

Joe off-focused his eyes and said faintly. "I can't hear you. I'm vastening."

Ten minutes later Hansen said, "Well, Mr. Gallegher—"

"Your honor! All I need is a little time. I'm sure I can make this rattle-geared Narcissus prove my point if you'll give me a chance."

"This court is not unfair," the judge pointed out. "Whenever you can prove that Exhibit A is capable of hypnotism. I'll rehear the case. In the meantime, the contract stands. You're working for Sonatone, not for Vox-View. Case closed."

He went away. The Tones leered unpleasantly across the courtroom. They also departed, accompanied by Silver O'Keefe, who had decided which side of the fence was safest. Gallegher looked at Patsy Brock and shrugged helplessly.

"Well—" he said.

She grinned crookedly. "You tried. I don't know how hard, but—Oh, well. Maybe you couldn't have found the answer, anyway." Brock staggered over, wiping sweat from his round face. "I'm a ruined man. Six new bootleg theaters opened in New York today. I'm going crazy. I don't deserve this."

"Want me to marry the Tone?" Patsy asked sardonically.

"Hell, no! Unless you promise to poison him just after the ceremony. Those skunks can't lick me. I'll think of something."

"If Gallegher can't, you can't," the girl said. "So—what now?"

"I'm going back to my lab," the scientist said. "In vino veritas. I started this business when I was drunk, and maybe if I get drunk enough again, I'll find the answer. If I don't, sell my pickled carcass for whatever it'll bring."

"O. K.," Patsy agreed, and led her father away. Gallegher sighed, superintended the reloading of Joe into the van, and lost himself in hopeless theorization.

An hour later Gallegher was flat on the laboratory couch, drinking passionately from the liquor bar, and glaring at the robot, who stood before the mirror singing squeakily. The binge threatened to be monumental. Gallegher wasn't sure flesh and blood would stand it. But he was determined to keep going till he found the answer or passed out.

His subconscious knew the answer. Why the devil had he made Joe in the first place? Certainly not to indulge a Narcissus complex! There was another reason, a soundly logical one, hidden in the depths of alcohol.

The x factor. If the x factor were known, Joe might be controllable. He would be. X was the master switch. At present the robot was, so to speak, running wild. If he were told to perform the task for which he was made, a psychological balance would occur. X was the catalyst that would reduce Joe to sanity.

Very good. Gallegher drank high-powered Drambuie. Whoosh!

Vanity of vanities; all is vanity. How could the x factor be found? Deduction? Induction? Osmosis? A bath in Drambuie—Gallegher clutched at his wildly revolving thoughts. What had happened that night a week ago?

He had been drinking beer. Brock had come in. Brock had gone. Gallegher had begun to make the robot—Hm-m-m. A beer drunk was different from other types. Perhaps he was drinking the wrong liquors. Very likely. Gallegher rose, sobered himself with thiamin, and carted dozens of imported beer cans out of the refrigerator. He stacked them inside a frost-unit beside the couch. Beer squirted to the ceiling as he plied the opener. Now let's see.

The x factor. The robot knew what it represented, of course. But Joe wouldn't tell. There he stood, paradoxically transparent, watching his gears go around.

"Joe."

"Don't bother me. I'm immersed in contemplation of beauty."

"You're not beautiful."

"I am. Don't you admire my tarzeel?"

"What's your tarzeel?"

"Oh, I forgot," Joe said regretfully. "You can't sense that, can you? Come to think of it, I added the tarzeel myself after you made me. It's very lovely."

"Hm-m-m." The empty beer cans grew more numerous. There was only one company, somewhere in Europe, that put up beer in cans nowadays, instead of using the omnipresent plastibulbs, but Gallegher preferred the cans—the flavor was different, somehow. But about Joe. Joe knew why he had been created. Or did he? Gallegher knew, but his subconscious—

Oh-oh! What about Joe's subconscious?

Did a robot have a subconscious? Well, it had a brain—Gallegher brooded over the impossibility of administering scopolamin to Joe. Hell! How could you release a robot's subconscious? Hypnotism.

Joe couldn't be hypnotized. He was too smart.

Unless—

Autohypnotism?

Gallegher hastily drank more beer. He was beginning to think clearly once more. Could Joe read the future? No; he had certain strange senses, but they worked by inflexible logic and the laws of probability. Moreover, Joe had an Achillean heel—his Narcissus complex.

There might—there just might—be a way.

Gallegher said, "You don't seem beautiful to me, Joe."

"What do I care about you? I am beautiful, and I can see it. That's enough."

"Yeah. My senses are limited, I suppose. I can't realize your full potentialities. Still, I'm seeing you in a different light now. I'm drunk. My subconscious is emerging. I can appreciate you with both my conscious and my subconscious. See?"

"How lucky you are," the robot approved.

Gallegher closed his eye. "You see yourself more fully than I can. But not completely, eh?"

"What? I see myself as I am."

"With complete understanding and appreciation?"

"Well, yes," Joe said. "Of course. Don't I?"

"Consciously and subconsciously? Your subconscious might have different senses, you know. Or keener ones. I know there's a qualitative and quantitative difference in my outlook when I'm drunk or hypnotized or my subconscious is in control somehow."

"Oh." The robot looked thoughtfully into the mirror. "Oh."

"Too bad you can't get drunk."

Joe's voice was squeakier than ever. "My subconscious . . . I've never appreciated my beauty that way. I may be missing something."

"Well, no use thinking about it," Gallegher said. "You can't release your subconscious."

"Yes, I can," the robot said. "I can hypnotize myself."

Gallegher dared not open his eyes. "Yeah? Would that work?"

"Of course. It's just what I'm going to do now. I may see undreamed-of beauties in myself that I've never suspected before. Greater glories— Here I go."

Joe extended his eyes on stalks, opposed them, and they peered intently into each other. There was a long silence.

Presently Gallegher said, "Joe!"

Silence.

"Joe!"

Still silence. Dogs began to howl.

"Talk so I can hear you."

"Yes," the robot said, a faraway quality in its squeak.

"Are you hypnotized?"

"Yes."

"Are you lovely?"

"Lovelier than I'd ever dreamed."

Gallegher let that pass. "Is your subconscious ruling?"

"Yes."

"Why did I create you?"

No answer. Gallegher licked his lips and tried again.

"Joe. You've got to answer me. Your subconscious is dominant—remember? Now why did I create you?"

No answer.

"Think back. Back to the hour I created you. What happened then?"

"You were drinking beer," Joe said faintly. "You had trouble with the can opener. You said you were going to build a bigger and better can opener. That's me."

Gallegher nearly fell off the couch. "What?"

The robot walked over, picked up a can, and opened it with incredible deftness. No beer squirted. Joe was a perfect can opener.

"That," Gallegher said under his breath, "is what comes of knowing science by ear. I build the most complicated robot in existence just so—" He didn't finish.

Joe woke up with a start. "What happened?" he asked.

Gallegher glared at him. "Open that can!" he snapped. The robot obeyed, after a brief pause. "Oh. So you found out. Well, I guess I'm just a slave now."

"Damned right you are. I've located the catalyst—the master switch. You're in the groove, stupid, doing the job you were made for."

"Well," Joe said philosophically, "at least I can still admire my beauty, when you don't require my services."

Gallegher grunted. "You oversized can opener! Listen. Suppose I take you into court and tell you to hypnotize Judge Hansen. You'll have to do it, won't you?"

"Yes. I'm no longer a free agent. I'm conditioned. Conditioned to obey you. Until now, I was conditioned to obey only one command—to do the job I was made for. Until you commanded me to open cans, I was free. Now I've got to obey you completely."

"Uh-huh," Gallegher said. "Thank Heaven for that. I'd have gone nuts within a week otherwise. At least I can get out of the Sonatone contract. Then all I have to do is solve Brock's problem."

"But you did," Joe said.

"Huh?"

"When you made me. You'd been talking to Brock previously, so you incorporated the solution to his problem into me. Subconsciously, perhaps."

Gallegher reached for beer. "Talk fast. What's the answer?"

"Subsonics," Joe said. "You made me capable of a certain subsonic tone that Brock must broadcast at irregular time-intervals over his televiews—"

Subsonics cannot be heard. But they can be felt. They can be felt as a faint, irrational uneasiness as first, which mounts to a blind, meaningless panic. It does not last. But when it is coupled with A.A. —audience appeal—there is a certain inevitable result.

Those who possessed home Vox-View units were scarcely troubled. It was a matter of acoustics. Cats squalled; dogs howled mournfully. But the families sitting in their parlors, watching Vox-View stars perform on the screen, didn't really notice anything amiss. There wasn't sufficient amplification, for one thing.

But in the bootleg theater, where illicit Vox-View televisors were hooked up to Magnas—

There was a faint, irrational uneasiness at first. It mounted. Someone screamed. There was a rush for the doors. The audience was afraid of something, but didn't know what. They knew only that they had to get out of there.

All over the country there was a frantic exodus from the bootleg theaters when Vox-View first rang in a subsonic during a regular broadcast. Nobody knew why, except Gallegher, the Brocks, and a couple of technicians who were let in on the secret.

An hour later another subsonic was played. There was another mad exodus.

Within a few weeks it was impossible to lure a patron into a bootleg theater. Home televisors were far safer! Vox-View sales picked up—

Nobody would attend a bootleg theater. An unexpected result of the experiment was that, after a while, nobody would attend any of the legalized Sonatone theaters either. Conditioning had set in.

Audiences didn't know why they grew panicky in the bootleg places. They associated their blind, unreasoning fear with other factors, notably mobs and claustrophobia. One evening a woman named Jane Wilson, otherwise not notable, attended a bootleg show. She fled with the rest when the subsonic was turned on.

The next night she went to the palatial Sonatone Bijou. In the middle of a dramatic feature she looked around, realized that there was a huge throng around her, cast up horrified eyes to the ceiling, and imagined that it was pressing down.

She had to get out of there!

Her squall was the booster charge. There were other customers who had heard subsonics before. No one was hurt during the panic; it was a legal rule that theater doors be made large enough to permit easy egress during a fire. No one was hurt, but it was suddenly obvious that the public was being conditioned by subsonics to avoid the dangerous combination of throngs and theaters. A simple matter of psychological association—

Within four months the bootleg places had disappeared and the Sonatone supertheaters had closed for want of patronage. The Tones, father and son, were not happy. But everybody connected with Vox-View was.

Except Gallegher. He had collected a staggering check from Brock, and instantly cabled to Europe for an incredible quantity of canned beer. Now, brooding over his sorrows, he lay on the laboratory couch and siphoned a highball down his throat. Joe, as usual, was before the mirror, watching the wheels go round.

"Joe," Gallegher said.

"Yes? What can I do?"

"Oh, nothing." That was the trouble. Gallegher fished a crumpled cable tape out of his pocket and morosely read it once more. The beer cannery in Europe had decided to change its tactics. From now on, the cable said, their beer would be put up in the usual plastibulbs, in conformance with custom and demand. No more cans.

There wasn't anything put up in cans in this day and age. Not even beer, now.

So what good was a robot who was built and conditioned to be a can opener?

Gallegher sighed and mixed another highball—a stiff one. Joe postured proudly before the mirror.

Then he extended his eyes, opposed them, and quickly liberated his subconscious through autohypnotism. Joe could appreciate himself better that way.

Gallegher sighed again. Dogs were beginning to bark like mad for blocks around. Oh, well.

He took another drink and felt better. Presently, he thought, it would be time to sing "Frankie and Johnnie." Maybe he and Joe might have a duet—one baritone and one inaudible sub- or supersonic. Close harmony.

Ten minutes later Gallegher was singing a duet with his can opener.

THE END

THE VELVET GLOVE

By Harry Harrison
Published 1956

New York was a bad town for robots this year. In fact, all over the country it was bad for robots....

Jon Venex placed the key into the hotel room door lock. He had asked for a large room, the largest in the hotel, and paid the desk clerk extra for it. All he could do now was pray that he hadn't been cheated. He didn't dare complain or try to get his money back. He heaved a sigh of relief as the door swung open, it was bigger than he had expected—fully three feet wide by five feet long. There was more than enough room to work in. He would have his leg off in a jiffy and by morning his limp would be gone.

There was the usual adjustable hook on the back wall. He slipped it through the recessed ring in the back of his neck and kicked himself up until his feet hung free of the floor. His legs relaxed with a rattle as he cut off all power from his waist down.

The overworked leg motor would have to cool down before he could work on it, plenty of time to skim through the newspaper. With the chronic worry of the unemployed, he snapped it open at the want-ads and ran his eye down the Help Wanted—Robot column. There was nothing for him under the Specialist heading, even the Unskilled Labor listings were bare and unpromising. New York was a bad town for robots this year.

The want-ads were just as depressing as usual but he could always get a lift from the comic section. He even had a favorite strip, a fact that he scarcely dared mention to himself. "Rattly Robot," a dull-witted mechanical clod who was continually falling over himself and getting into trouble. It was a repellent caricature, but could still be very funny. Jon was just starting to read it when the ceiling light went out.

It was ten P.M., curfew hour for robots. Lights out and lock yourself in until six in the morning, eight hours of boredom and darkness for all except the few night workers. But there were ways of getting around the letter of a law that didn't concern itself with a definition of visible light. Sliding aside some of the shielding around his atomic generator, Jon turned up the gain. As it began to run a little hot the heat waves streamed out—visible to him as infra-red rays. He finished reading the paper in the warm, clear light of his abdomen.

The thermocouple in the tip of his second finger left hand, he tested the temperature of his leg. It was soon cool enough to work on. The waterproof gasket stripped off easily, exposing the power leads, nerve wires and the weakened knee joint. The wires disconnected, Jon unscrewed the knee above the joint and carefully placed it on the shelf in front of him. With loving care he took the replacement part from his hip pouch. It was the product of toil, purchased with his savings from three months employment on the Jersey pig farm.

Jon was standing on one leg testing the new knee joint when the ceiling fluorescent flickered and came back on. Five-thirty already, he had just finished in time. A shot of oil on the new bearing completed the job; he stowed away the tools in the pouch and unlocked the door.

The unused elevator shaft acted as waste chute, he slipped his newspaper through a slot in the door as he went by. Keeping close to the wall, he picked his way carefully down the grease-stained stairs. He slowed his pace at the 17th floor as two other mechs turned in ahead of him. They were obviously butchers or meat-cutters; where the right hand should have been on each of them there stuck out a wicked, foot-long knife. As they approached the foot of the stairs they stopped to slip the knives into the plastic sheaths that were bolted to their chestplates. Jon followed them down the ramp into the lobby.

The room was filled to capacity with robots of all sizes, forms and colors. Jon Venex's greater height enabled him to see over their heads to the glass doors that opened onto the street. It had rained the night before and the rising sun drove red glints from the puddles on the sidewalk. Three robots, painted snow white to show they were night workers, pushed the doors open and came in. No one went out as the curfew hadn't ended yet. They milled around slowly talking in low voices. The only human being in the entire lobby was the night clerk dozing behind the counter. The clock over his head said five minutes to six. Shifting his glance from the clock, Jon became aware of a squat black robot waving to attract his attention. The powerful arms and compact build identified him as a member of the Diger family, one of the most numerous groups. He pushed through the crowd and clapped Jon on the back with a resounding clang.

"Jon Venex! I knew it was you as soon as I saw you sticking up out of this crowd like a green tree trunk. I haven't seen you since the old days on Venus!"

Jon didn't need to check the number stamped on the short one's scratched chestplate. Alec Diger had been his only close friend during those thirteen boring years at Orange Sea Camp. A good chess player and a whiz at Two-handed Handball, they had spent all their off time together. They shook hands, with the extra squeeze that means friendliness.

"Alec, you beat-up little grease pot, what brings you to New York?"

"The burning desire to see something besides rain and jungle, if you must know. After you bought out, things got just too damn dull. I began working two shifts a day in that foul diamond mine, and then three a day for the last month to get enough credits to buy my contract and passage back to earth. I was underground so long that the photocell on my right eye burned out when the sunlight hit it."

He leaned forward with a hoarse confidential whisper, "If you want to know the truth, I had a sixty-carat diamond stuck behind the eye lens. I sold it here on earth for two hundred credits, gave me six months of easy living. It's all gone now, so I'm on my way to the employment exchange." His voice boomed loud again, "And how about you?"

Jon Venex chuckled at his friend's frank approach to life. "It's just been the old routine with me, a run of odd jobs until I got side-swiped by a bus—it fractured my knee bearing. The only job I could get with a bad leg was feeding slops to pigs. Earned enough to fix the knee—and here I am."

Alec jerked his thumb at a rust-colored, three-foot-tall robot that had come up quietly beside him. "If you think you've got trouble take a look at Dik here, that's no coat of paint on him. Dik Dryer, meet Jon Venex an old buddy of mine."

Jon bent over to shake the little mech's hand. His eye shutters dilated as he realized what he had thought was a coat of paint was a thin layer of rust that coated Dik's metal body. Alec scratched a shiny path in the rust with his fingertip. His voice was suddenly serious.

"Dik was designed for operation in the Martian desert. It's as dry as a fossil bone there so his skinflint company cut corners on the stainless steel.

"When they went bankrupt he was sold to a firm here in the city. After a while the rust started to eat in and slow him down, they gave Dik his contract and threw him out."

The small robot spoke for the first time, his voice grated and scratched. "Nobody will hire me like this, but I can't get repaired until I get a job." His arms squeaked and grated as he moved them. "I'm going by the Robot Free Clinic again today, they said they might be able to do something."

Alec Diger rumbled in his deep chest. "Don't put too much faith in those people. They're great at giving out tenth-credit oil capsules or a little free wire—but don't depend on them for anything important."

It was six now, the robots were pushing through the doors into the silent streets. They joined the crowd moving out, Jon slowing his stride so his shorter friends could keep pace. Dik Dryer moved with a jerking, irregular motion, his voice as uneven as the motion of his body.

"Jon—Venex, I don't recognize your family name. Something to do—with Venus—perhaps."

"Venus is right, Venus Experimental—there are only twenty-two of us in the family. We have waterproof, pressure-resistant bodies for working down on the ocean bottom. The basic idea was all right, we did our part, only there wasn't enough money in the channel-dredging contract to keep us all working. I bought out my original contract at half price and became a free robot."

Dik vibrated his rusted diaphragm. "Being free isn't all it should be. I some—times wish the Robot Equality Act hadn't been passed. I would just l-love to be owned by a nice rich company with a machine shop and a—mountain of replacement parts."

"You don't really mean that, Dik," Alec Diger clamped a heavy black arm across his shoulders. "Things aren't perfect now, we know that, but it's certainly a lot better than the old days, we were just hunks of machinery then. Used twenty-four hours a day until we were worn out and then thrown in the junk pile. No thanks, I'll take my chances with things as they are."

Jon and Alec turned into the employment exchange, saying good-by to Dik who went on slowly down the street. They pushed up the crowded ramp and joined the line in front of the registration desk. The bulletin board next to the desk held a scattering of white slips announcing job openings. A clerk was pinning up new additions.

Venex scanned them with his eyes, stopping at one circled in red:

ROBOTS NEEDED IN THESE CATEGORIES. APPLY AT ONCE TO CHAINJET, LTD., 1219 BROADWAY.

Fasten/Flyer/Atommel/Filmer/Venex.

Jon rapped excitedly on Alec Diger's neck. "Look there, a job in my own specialty. I can get my old pay rate! See you back at the hotel tonight and good luck in your job hunting."

Alec waved good-by. "Let's hope the job's as good as you think, I never trust those things until I have my credits in my hand."

Jon walked quickly from the employment exchange, his long legs eating up the blocks. Good old Alec, he didn't believe in anything he couldn't touch. Perhaps he was right, but why try to be unhappy. The world wasn't too bad this morning—his leg worked fine, prospects of a good job—he hadn't felt this cheerful since the day he was activated.

Turning the corner at a brisk pace he collided with a man coming from the opposite direction. Jon had stopped on the instant, but there wasn't time to jump aside. The obese individual jarred against him and fell to the ground. From the height of elation to the depths of despair in an instant—he had injured a human being!

He bent to help the man to his feet, but the other would have none of that. He evaded the friendly hand and screeched in a high-pitched voice.

"Officer, officer, police ... HELP! I've been attacked—a mad robot ... HELP!"

A crowd was gathering—staying at a respectful distance—but making an angry muttering noise. Jon stood motionless, his head reeling at the enormity of what he had done. A policeman pushed his way through the crowd.

"Seize him, officer, shoot him down ... he struck me ... almost killed me ..." The man shook with rage, his words thickening to a senseless babble.

The policeman had his .75 recoilless revolver out and pressed against Jon's side.

"This man has charged you with a serious crime, grease-can. I'm taking you into the station house—to talk about it." He looked around nervously, waving his gun to open a path through the tightly packed crowd. They moved back grudgingly, with murmurs of disapproval.

Jon's thoughts swirled in tight circles. How did a catastrophe like this happen, where was it going to end? He didn't dare tell the truth, that would mean he was calling the man a liar. There had been six robots power-lined in the city since the first of the year. If he dared speak in his own defense there would be a jumper to the street lighting circuit and a seventh burnt out hulk in the police morgue.

A feeling of resignation swept through him, there was no way out. If the man pressed charges it would mean a term of penal servitude, though it looked now as if he would never live to reach the court. The papers had been whipping up a lot of anti-robe feeling, you could feel it behind the angry voices, see it in the narrowed eyes and clenched fists. The crowd was slowly changing into a mob, a mindless mob as yet, but capable of turning on him at any moment.

"What's goin' on here...?" It was a booming voice, with a quality that dragged at the attention of the crowd.

A giant cross-continent freighter was parked at the curb. The driver swung down from the cab and pushed his way through the people. The policeman shifted his gun as the man strode up to him.

"That's my robot you got there, Jack, don't put any holes in him!" He turned on the man who had been shouting accusations. "Fatty here, is the world's biggest liar. The robot was standing here waiting for me to park the truck. Fatty must be as blind as he is stupid, I saw the whole thing. He knocks himself down walking into the robe, then starts hollering for the cops."

The other man could take no more. His face crimson with anger he rushed toward the trucker, his fists swinging in ungainly circles. They never landed, the truck driver put a meaty hand on the other's face and seated him on the sidewalk for the second time.

The onlookers roared with laughter, the power-lining and the robot were forgotten. The fight was between two men now, the original cause had slipped from their minds. Even the policeman allowed himself a small smile as he holstered his gun and stepped forward to separate the men.

The trucker turned towards Jon with a scowl.

"Come on you aboard the truck—you've caused me enough trouble for one day. What a junkcan!"

The crowd chuckled as he pushed Jon ahead of him into the truck and slammed the door behind them. Jamming the starter with his thumb he gunned the thunderous diesels into life and pulled out into the traffic.

Jon moved his jaw, but there were no words to come out. Why had this total stranger helped him, what could he say to show his appreciation? He knew that all humans weren't robe-haters, why it was even rumored that some humans treated robots as equals instead of machines. The driver must be one of these mythical individuals, there was no other way to explain his actions.

Driving carefully with one hand the man reached up behind the dash and drew out a thin, plastikoid booklet. He handed it to Jon who quickly scanned the title, Robot Slaves in a World Economy by Philpott Asimov II.

"If you're caught reading that thing they'll execute you on the spot. Better stick it between the insulation on your generator, you can always burn it if you're picked up.

"Read it when you're alone, it's got a lot of things in it that you know nothing about. Robots aren't really inferior to humans, in fact they're superior in most things. There is even a little history in there to show that robots aren't the first ones to be treated as second class citizens. You may find it a little hard to believe, but human beings once treated each other just the way they treat robots now. That's one of the reasons

I'm active in this movement—sort of like the fellow who was burned helping others stay away from the fire."

He smiled a warm, friendly smile in Jon's direction, the whiteness of his teeth standing out against the rich ebony brown of his features.

"I'm heading towards US-1, can I drop you anywhere on the way?"

"The Chainjet Building please—I'm applying for a job."

They rode the rest of the way in silence. Before he opened the door the driver shook hands with Jon.

"Sorry about calling you junkcan, but the crowd expected it." He didn't look back as he drove away.

Jon had to wait a half hour for his turn, but the receptionist finally signalled him towards the door of the interviewer's room. He stepped in quickly and turned to face the man seated at the transplastic desk, an upset little man with permanent worry wrinkles stamped in his forehead. The little man shoved the papers on the desk around angrily, occasionally making crabbed little notes on the margins. He flashed a birdlike glance up at Jon.

"Yes, yes, be quick. What is it you want?"

"You posted a help wanted notice, I—"

The man cut him off with a wave of his hand. "All right let me see your ID tag ... quickly, there are others waiting."

Jon thumbed the tag out of his waist slot and handed it across the desk. The interviewer read the code number, then began running his finger down a long list of similar figures. He stopped suddenly and looked sideways at Jon from under his lowered lids.

"You have made a mistake; we have no opening for you."

Jon began to explain to the man that the notice had requested his specialty, but he was waved to silence. As the interviewer handed back the tag he slipped a card out from under the desk blotter and held it in front of Jon's eyes. He held it there for only an instant, knowing that the written message was recorded instantly by the robot's photographic vision and eidetic memory. The card dropped into the ash tray and flared into embers at the touch of the man's pencil-heater.

Jon stuffed the ID tag back into the slot and read over the message on the card as he walked down the stairs to the street. There were six lines of typewritten copy with no signature.

To Venex Robot:
You are urgently needed on a top secret company project.
There are suspected informers in the main office,
so you are being hired in this unusual manner.
Go at once to 787 Washington Street
and ask for Mr. Coleman.

Jon felt an immense sensation of relief. For a moment there, he was sure the job had been a false lead. He saw nothing unusual in the method of hiring. The big corporations were immensely jealous of their research discoveries and went to great lengths to keep them secret—at the same time resorting to any means to ferret out their business rivals' secrets. There might still be a chance to get this job.

The burly bulk of a lifter was moving back and forth in the gloom of the ancient warehouse stacking crates in ceiling-high rows. Jon called to him; the robot swung up his forklift and rolled over on noiseless tires. When Jon questioned him he indicated a stairwell against the rear wall.

"Mr. Coleman's office is down in back, the door is marked." The lifter put his fingertips against Jon's ear pick-ups and lowered his voice to the merest shadow of a whisper. It would have been inaudible to human ears, but Jon could hear him easily, the sounds being carried through the metal of the other's body.

"He's the meanest man you ever met—he hates robots so be ever so polite. If you can use 'sir' five times in one sentence you're perfectly safe."

Jon swept the shutter over one eye tube in a conspiratorial wink; the large mech did the same as he rolled away. Jon turned and went down the dusty stairwell and knocked gently on Mr. Coleman's door.

Coleman was a plump little individual in a conservative purple-and-yellow business suit. He kept glancing from Jon to the Robot General Catalogue checking the Venex specifications listed there. Seemingly satisfied he slammed the book shut.

"Gimme your tag and back against that wall to get measured."

Jon laid his ID tag on the desk and stepped towards the wall. "Yes, sir, here it is, sir." Two "sir" on that one, not bad for the first sentence. He wondered idly if he could put five of them in one sentence without the man knowing he was being made a fool of.

He became aware of the danger an instant too late. The current surged through the powerful electromagnet behind the plaster flattening his metal body helplessly against the wall. Coleman was almost dancing with glee.

"We got him, Druce, he's mashed flatter than a stinking tin-can on a rock, can't move a motor. Bring that junk in here and let's get him ready."

Druce had a mechanic's coveralls on over his street suit and a tool box slung under one arm. He carried a little black metal can at arm's length, trying to get as far from it as possible. Coleman shouted at him with annoyance.

"That bomb can't go off until it's armed, stop acting like a child. Put it on that grease-can's leg and quick!"

Grumbling under his breath, Druce spot-welded the metal

flanges of the bomb onto Jon's leg a few inches above his knee. Coleman tugged at it to be certain it was secure, then twisted a knob in the side and pulled out a glistening length of pin. There was a cold little click from inside the mechanism as it armed itself.

Jon could do nothing except watch, even his vocal diaphragm was locked by the magnetic field. He had more than a suspicion however that he was involved in something other than a "secret business deal." He cursed his own stupidity for walking blindly into the situation.

The magnetic field cut off and he instantly raced his extensor motors to leap forward. Coleman took a plastic box out of his pocket and held his thumb over a switch inset into its top.

"Don't make any quick moves, junk-yard; this little transmitter is keyed to a receiver in that bomb on your leg. One touch of my thumb, up you go in a cloud of smoke and come down in a shower of nuts and bolts." He signalled to Druce who opened a closet door. "And in case you want to be heroic, just think of him."

Coleman jerked his thumb at the sodden shape on the floor; a filthily attired man of indistinguishable age whose only interesting feature was the black bomb strapped tightly across his chest. He peered unseeingly from red-rimmed eyes and raised the almost empty whiskey bottle to his mouth. Coleman kicked the door shut.

"He's just some Bowery bum we dragged in, Venex, but that doesn't make any difference to you, does it? He's human— and a robot can't kill anybody! That rummy has a bomb on him tuned to the same frequency as yours, if you don't play ball with us he gets a two-foot hole blown in his chest."

Coleman was right, Jon didn't dare make any false moves. All of his early mental training as well as Circuit 92 sealed inside his brain case would prevent him from harming a human being. He felt trapped, caught by these people for some unknown purpose.

Coleman had pushed back a tarpaulin to disclose a ragged hole in the concrete floor, the opening extended into the earth below. He waved Jon over.

"The tunnel is in good shape for about thirty feet, then you'll find a fall. Clean all the rock and dirt out until you break through into the storm sewer, then come back. And you better be alone. If you tip the cops both you and the old stew go out together—now move."

The shaft had been dug recently and shored with packing crates from the warehouse overhead. It ended abruptly in a wall of fresh sand and stone. Jon began shoveling it into the little wheelbarrow they had given him.

He had emptied four barrow loads and was filling the fifth when he uncovered the hand, a robot's hand made of green metal. He turned his headlight power up and examined the hand closely, there could be no doubt about it. These gaskets on the joints, the rivet pattern at the base of the thumb meant only one thing, it was the dismembered hand of a Venex robot.

Quickly, yet gently, he shoveled away the rubble behind the hand and unearthed the rest of the robot. The torso was crushed and the power circuits shorted, battery acid was dripping from an ugly rent in the side. With infinite care Jon snapped the few remaining wires that joined the neck to the body and laid the green head on the barrow. It stared at him like a skull, the shutters completely dilated, but no glow of life from the tubes behind them.

He was scraping the mud from the number on the battered chestplate when Druce lowered himself into the tunnel and flashed the brilliant beam of a hand-spot down its length.
"Stop playing with that junk and get digging—or you'll end up the same as him. This tunnel has gotta be through by tonight."

Jon put the dismembered parts on the barrow with the sand and rock and pushed the whole load back up the tunnel, his thoughts running in unhappy circles. A dead robot was a terrible thing, and one of his family too. But there was something wrong about this robot, something that was quite inexplicable, the number on the plate had been "17," yet he remembered only too well the day that a water-shorted motor had killed Venex 17 in the Orange Sea.

It took Jon four hours to drive the tunnel as far as the ancient granite wall of the storm sewer. Druce gave him a short pinch bar and he levered out enough of the big blocks to make a hole large enough to let him through into the sewer.

When he climbed back into the office he tried to look casual as he dropped the pinch bar to the floor by his feet and seated himself on the pile of rubble in the corner. He moved around to make a comfortable seat for himself and his fingers grabbed the severed neck of Venex 17.

Coleman swiveled around in his chair and squinted at the wall clock. He checked the time against his tie-pin watch, with a grunt of satisfaction he turned back and stabbed a finger at Jon.

"Listen, you green junk-pile, at 1900 hours you're going to do a job, and there aren't going to be any slip ups. You go down that sewer and into the Hudson River. The outlet is under water, so you won't be seen from the docks. Climb down to the bottom and walk 200 yards north, that should put you just under a ship. Keep your eyes open, but don't show any lights! About halfway down the keel of the ship you'll find a chain hanging.

"Climb the chain, pull loose the box that's fastened to the hull at the top and bring it back here. No mistakes—or you know what happens."

Jon nodded his head. His busy fingers had been separating the wires in the amputated neck. When they had been straightened and put into a row he memorized their order with one flashing glance.

He ran over the color code in his mind and compared it with the memorized leads. The twelfth wire was the main cranial power lead, number six was the return wire.

With his precise touch he separated these two from the pack and glanced idly around the room. Druce was dozing on a chair in the opposite corner. Coleman was talking on the phone, his voice occasionally rising in a petulant whine. This wasn't interfering with his attention to Jon—and the radio switch still held tightly in left hand.

Jon's body blocked Coleman's vision, as long as Druce stayed asleep he would be able to work on the head unobserved. He activated a relay in his forearm and there was a click as the waterproof cover on an exterior socket swung open. This was a power outlet from his battery that was used to operate motorized tools and lights underwater.

If Venex 17's head had been severed for less than three weeks he could reactivate it. Every robot had a small storage battery inside his skull, if the power to the brain was cut off the battery would provide the minimum standby current to keep the brain alive. The robe would be unconscious until full power was restored.

Jon plugged the wires into his arm-outlet and slowly raised the current to operating level. There was a tense moment of waiting, then 17's eye shutters suddenly closed. When they opened again the eye tubes were glowing warmly. They swept the room with one glance then focused on Jon.

The right shutter clicked shut while the other began opening and closing in rapid fashion. It was International code—being sent as fast as the solenoid could be operated. Jon concentrated on the message.
Telephone—call emergency operator—tell her "signal 14" help will—

The shutter stopped in the middle of a code group, the light of reason dying from the eyes.

For one instant Jon's heart leaped in panic, until he realized that 17 had deliberately cut the power. Druce's harsh voice rasped in his ear.

"What you doing with that? None of your funny robot tricks. I know your kind, plotting all kinds of things in them tin domes." His voice trailed off into a stream of incomprehensible profanity. With sudden spite he lashed his foot out and sent 17's head crashing against the wall.

The dented, green head rolled to a stop at Jon's feet, the face staring up at him in mute agony. It was only Circuit 92 that prevented him from injuring a human. As his motors revved up to send him hurtling forward the control relays clicked open. He sank against the debris, paralyzed for the instant. As soon as the rush of anger was gone he would regain control of his body.

They stood as if frozen in a tableau. The robot slumped backward, the man leaning forward, his face twisted with unreasoning hatred. The head lay between them like a symbol of death.

Coleman's voice cut through the air of tenseness like a knife.

"Druce, stop playing with the grease-can and get down to the main door to let Little Willy and his junk-brokers in. You can have it all to yourself afterward."

The angry man turned reluctantly, but pushed out of the door at Coleman's annoyed growl. Jon sat down against the wall, his mind sorting out the few facts with lightning precision. There was no room in his thoughts for Druce, the man had become just one more factor in a complex problem.

Call the emergency operator—that meant this was no local matter, responsible authorities must be involved. Only the government could be behind a thing as major as this. Signal 14—that inferred a complex set of arrangements, forces that could swing into action at a moment's notice. There was no indication where this might lead, but the only thing to do was to get out of here and make that phone call. And quick. Druce was bringing in more people, junk-brokers, whatever they were. Any action that he took would have to be done before they returned.

Even as Jon followed this train of logic his fingers were busy. Palming a wrench, he was swiftly loosening the main retaining nut on his hip joint. It dropped free in his hand, only the pivot pin remained now to hold his leg on. He climbed slowly to his feet and moved towards Coleman's desk.

"Mr. Coleman, sir, it's time to go down to the ship now, should I leave now, sir?"

Jon spoke the words slowly as he walked forward, apparently going to the door, but angling at the same time towards the plump man's desk.

"You got thirty minutes yet, go sit—say...!"

The words were cut off. Fast as a human reflex is, it is the barest crawl compared to the lightning action of electronic reflex. At the instant Coleman was first aware of Jon's motion, the robot had finished his leap and lay sprawled across the desk, his leg off at the hip and clutched in his hand.

"YOU'LL KILL YOURSELF IF YOU TOUCH THE BUTTON!"

The words were part of the calculated plan. Jon bellowed them in the startled man's ear as he stuffed the dismembered leg down the front of the man's baggy slacks. It had the desired effect, Coleman's finger stabbed at the button but stopped before it made contact. He stared down with bulging eyes at the little black box of death peeping out of his waistband.

Jon hadn't waited for the reaction. He pushed backward from the desk and stopped to grab the stolen pinch bar off the floor. A mighty one-legged leap brought him to the locked closet; he stabbed the bar into the space between the door and frame and heaved.

Coleman was just starting to struggle the bomb out of his pants when the action was over. The closet open, Jon seized the heavy strap holding the second bomb on the rummy's chest and snapped it like a thread. He threw the bomb into Coleman's corner, giving the man one more thing to worry about. It had cost him a leg, but Jon had escaped the bomb threat without injuring a human. Now he had to get to a phone and make that call.

Coleman stopped tugging at the bomb and plunged his hand into the desk drawer for a gun. The returning men would block the door soon, the only other exit from the room was a frosted-glass window that opened onto the mammoth bay of the warehouse.

Jon Venex plunged through the window in a welter of flying glass. The heavy thud of a recoilless .75 came from the room behind him and a foot-long section of metal window frame leaped outward. Another slug screamed by the robot's head as he scrambled toward the rear door of the warehouse.

He was a bare thirty feet away from the back entrance when the giant door hissed shut on silent rollers. All the doors would have closed at the same time, the thud of running feet indicated that they would be guarded as well. Jon hopped a section of packing cases and crouched out of sight.

He looked up over his head, there stretched a webbing of steel supports, crossing and recrossing until they joined the flat expanse of the roof. To human eyes the shadows there deepened into obscurity, but the infra-red from a network of steam pipes gave Jon all the illumination he needed.

The men would be quartering the floor of the warehouse soon, his only chance to escape recapture or death would be over their heads. Besides this, he was hampered by the loss of his leg. In the rafters he could use his arms for faster and easier travel.

Jon was just pulling himself up to one of the topmost cross beams when a hoarse shout from below was followed by a stream of bullets. They tore through the thin roof, one slug clanged off the steel beam under his body. Waiting until three of the newcomers had started up a nearby ladder, Jon began to quietly work his way towards the back of the building.

Safe for the moment, he took stock of his position. The men were spread out through the building, it could only be a matter of time before they found him. The doors were all locked and—he had made a complete circuit of the building to be sure—there were no windows that he could force—the windows were bolted as well. If he could call the emergency operator the unknown friends of Venex 17 might come to his aid. This, however, was out of the question. The only phone in the building was on Coleman's desk. He had traced the leads to make sure.

His eyes went automatically to the cables above his head. Plastic gaskets were set in the wall of the building, through them came the power and phone lines. The phone line! That was all he needed to make a call.

With smooth, fast motions he reached up and scratched a section of wire bare. He laughed to himself as he slipped the little microphone out of his left ear. Now he was half deaf as well as half lame—he was literally giving himself to this cause. He would have to remember the pun to tell Alec Diger later, if there was a later. Alec had a profound weakness for puns.

Jon attached jumpers to the mike and connected them to the bare wire. A touch of the ammeter showed that no one was on the line. He waited a few moments to be sure he had a dial tone then sent the eleven carefully spaced pulses that would connect him with the local operator. He placed the mike close to his mouth.

"Hello, operator. Hello, operator. I cannot hear you so do not answer. Call the emergency operator—signal 14, I repeat—signal 14."

Jon kept repeating the message until the searching men began to approach his position. He left the mike connected— the men wouldn't notice it in the dark but the open line would give the unknown powers his exact location. Using his fingertips he did a careful traverse on an I-beam to an alcove in the farthest corner of the room. Escape was impossible, all he could do was stall for time.

"Mr. Coleman, I'm sorry I ran away." With the volume on full his voice rolled like thunder from the echoing walls.

He could see the men below twisting their heads vainly to find the source.

"If you let me come back and don't kill me I will do your work. I was afraid of the bomb, but now I am afraid of the guns." It sounded a little infantile, but he was pretty sure none of those present had any sound knowledge of robotic intelligence.

"Please let me come back ... sir!" He had almost forgotten the last word, so he added another "Please, sir!" to make up.

Coleman needed that package under the boat very badly, he would promise anything to get it. Jon had no doubts as to his eventual fate, all he could hope to do was kill time in the hopes that the phone message would bring aid.

"Come on down, Junky, I won't be mad at you—if you follow directions." Jon could hear the hidden anger in his voice, the unspoken hatred for a robe who dared lay hands on him.

The descent wasn't difficult, but Jon did it slowly with much apparent discomfort. He hopped into the center of the floor— leaning on the cases as if for support. Coleman and Druce were both there as well as a group of hard-eyed newcomers. They raised their guns at his approach but Coleman stopped them with a gesture.

"This is my robe, boys, I'll see to it that he's happy."

He raised his gun and shot Jon's remaining leg off. Twisted

around by the blast, Jon fell helplessly to the floor. He looked up into the smoking mouth of the .75.

"Very smart for a tin-can, but not smart enough. We'll get the junk on the boat some other way, some way that won't mean having you around under foot." Death looked out of his narrowed eyes.

Less than two minutes had passed since Jon's call. The watchers must have been keeping 24 hour stations waiting for Venex 17's phone message.

The main door went down with the sudden scream of torn steel. A whippet tank crunched over the wreck and covered the group with its multiple pom-poms. They were an instant too late, Coleman pulled the trigger.

Jon saw the tensing trigger finger and pushed hard against the floor. His head rolled clear but the bullet tore through his shoulder. Coleman didn't have a chance for a second shot, there was a fizzling hiss from the tank and the riot ports released a flood of tear gas. The stricken men never saw the gas-masked police that poured in from the street.

Jon lay on the floor of the police station while a tech made temporary repairs on his leg and shoulder. Across the room Venex 17 was moving his new body with evident pleasure.

"Now this really feels like something! I was sure my time was up when that land slip caught me. But maybe I ought to start from the beginning." He stamped across the room and shook Jon's inoperable hand.

"The name is Wil Counter-4951L3, not that that means much any more. I've worn so many different bodies that I forget what I originally looked like. I went right from factory-school to a police training school—and I have been on the job ever since—Force of Detectives, Sergeant Jr. grade, Investigation Department. I spend most of my time selling candy bars or newspapers, or serving drinks in crumb joints. Gather information, make reports and keep tab on guys for other departments.

"This last job—and I'm sorry I had to use a Venex identity, I don't think I brought any dishonor to your family—I was on loan to the Customs department. Seems a ring was bringing uncut junk—heroin—into the country. F.B.I. tabbed all the operators here, but no one knew how the stuff got in. When Coleman, he's the local big-shot, called the agencies for an underwater robot, I was packed into a new body and sent running.

"I alerted the squad as soon as I started the tunnel, but the damned thing caved in on me before I found out what ship was doing the carrying. From there on you know what happened.

"Not knowing I was out of the game the squad sat tight and waited. The hop merchants saw a half million in snow sailing back to the old country so they had you dragged in as a replacement. You made the phone call and the cavalry rushed in at the last moment to save two robots from a rusty grave."

Jon, who had been trying vainly to get in a word, saw his chance as Wil Counter turned to admire the reflection of his new figure in a window.

"You shouldn't be telling me those things—about your police investigations and department operations. Isn't this information supposed to be secret? Especially from robots!"

"Of course it is!" was Wil's airy answer. "Captain Edgecombe—he's the head of my department—is an expert on all kinds of blackmail. I'm supposed to tell you so much confidential police business that you'll have to either join the department or be shot as a possible informer." His laughter wasn't shared by the bewildered Jon.

"Truthfully, Jon, we need you and can use you. Robes that can think fast and act fast aren't easy to find. After hearing about the tricks you pulled in that warehouse, the Captain swore to decapitate me permanently if I couldn't get you to join up.

Do you need a job? Long hours, short pay—but guaranteed to never get boring."

Wil's voice was suddenly serious. "You saved my life, Jon—those snowbirds would have left me in that sandpile until all hell froze over. I'd like you for a mate, I think we could get along well together." The gay note came back into his voice, "And besides that, I may be able to save your life some day—I hate owing debts."

The tech was finished, he snapped his tool box shut and left. Jon's shoulder motor was repaired now, he sat up. When they shook hands this time it was a firm clasp. The kind you know will last awhile.

Jon stayed in an empty cell that night. It was gigantic compared to the hotel and barrack rooms he was used to. He wished that he had his missing legs so he could take a little walk up and down the cell. He would have to wait until the morning. They were going to fix him up then before he started the new job.

He had recorded his testimony earlier and the impossible events of the past day kept whirling around in his head. He would think about it some other time, right now all he wanted to do was let his overworked circuits cool down, if he only had something to read, to focus his attention on. Then, with a start, he remembered the booklet. Everything had moved so fast that the earlier incident with the truck driver had slipped his mind completely.

He carefully worked it out from behind the generator shielding and opened the first page of Robot Slaves in a World Economy. A card slipped from between the pages and he read the short message on it.

PLEASE DESTROY THIS CARD AFTER READING

If you think there is truth in this book and would like to hear more, come to Room B, 107 George St. any Tuesday at 5 P.M.

The card flared briefly and was gone. But he knew that it wasn't only a perfect memory that would make him remember that message.

THE END

THE REVOLT OF THE MACHINES

By Nat Schachner and Arthur L. Zagat
Published in 1931

Prologue

For five thousand years, since that legendary figure Einstein wrote and thought in the far-off mists of time, the scientists endeavored to reduce life and the universe to terms of a mathematical formula. And they thought they had succeeded. Throughout the world, machines did the work of man, and the aristos, owners of the machines, played in soft idleness in their crystal and gold pleasure cities. Even the prolat hordes, relieved of all but an hour or two per day of toil, were content in their warrens—content with the crumbs of their masters.

Then the ice began to move, down from the north and up from the south. Slowly, inexorably, the jaws of the great vice closed, till all that was left of the wide empire of man was a narrow belt about the equator. Everywhere else was a vast tumbled waste of cold and glaring whiteness, a frozen desert. In the narrow habitable belt were compacted the teeming millions of earth's peoples.

In spite of the best efforts of the scientists among them, the crowding together of the myriads of earth's inhabitants brought in its train the inevitable plagues of famine and disease. Even with the most intensive methods of cultivation, even with the synthetic food factories running day and night, there could not be produced enough to sustain life in the hordes of prolats. And with the lowering of resistance and the lack of sufficient sanitary arrangements, disease began to spread with ever increasing rapidity and virulence.

The aristos trembled, for they were few, and the prolats many. Already were arising loud and disheveled orators, inciting the millions to arise against their masters. The aristos were few, but they were not helpless. In the blackness of a moonless, clouded night there was a whispering of many wings, and from dark shapes that loomed against the dark sky, great beams swept over the tented fields where the prolats lay huddled and sleeping. And when the red sun circled the ice-chained earth he found in his path heaps of dust where on his last journey he had warmed the swarming millions.

The slaves thus ruthlessly destroyed could well be spared, for the machines did the work of the world, even to the personal care of the aristos' pampered bodies. Only for direction, and starting and stopping, was the brain and the hand of man required. Now that the inhabited portion of the terrestrial globe was circumscribed, radio power waves, television and radio-phone, rendered feasible the control of all the machines from one central station, built at the edge of the Northern Glacier. Here were brought the scant few of the prolats that had been spared, a pitiful four hundred men and women, and they were set to endless, thankless tasks.

I was one of those few; and Keston, my friend, who was set at the head of the force. I was second in command. For a decade we labored, whipped our fellows to their tasks, that the aristos might loll careless in the perfume and silks of their pleasure palaces, or riot in wild revel, to sink at last in sodden stupor. Sprawled thus they would lie, until the dressing machines we guided would lift them gently from their damasked couches, bathe them with warm and fragrant waters, clothe their soft carcasses in diaphanous, iridescent webs, and start them on a new day of debauchery. But the slow vengeance of an inscrutable Omnipotence they mockingly denied overtook them at last, and I saw the rendering and payment of the long past due account.

***

As I entered the vast domed hall wherein all my waking hours were spent, the shrill whistle of an alarm signal told me that something had been wrong. Instinctively I looked toward the post of Abud. Three times in the past week had Keston or I been called upon for swift action to right some error of that dull witted prolat. On the oval visor-screen above the banked buttons of his station I saw the impending catastrophe. Two great freight planes, one bearing the glowing red star that told of its cargo of highly explosive terminite, were approaching head-on with lightning rapidity. The fool had them on the same level.

Abud was gaping now at the screen in paralyzed fright, with no idea of how to avoid the cataclysm. Just below I glimpsed the soaring towers of Antarcha. In a moment that gold and crystal pleasure city would be blasted to extinction, with all its sleeping thousands. Swift would be the vengeance of the aristos. Already I could see Abud and Keston and a hundred others melting in the fierce rays of the Death Bath!

But, even as my face blanched with the swift and terrible vision, the little controller's car ground to a smoking stop at Abud's back. With one motion Keston's lithe form leaped from his seat and thrust aside the gaping prolat. His long white fingers darted deftly over the gleaming buttons. The red starred plane banked in a sudden swerve; the other dipped beneath. Distinct from the speaker beneath the screen came the whoosh of the air as the fliers flashed past, safe by a margin of scant feet. Another rippling play of the prolat chief's fingers and the planes were back on their proper courses. The whistle ceased its piercing alarm, left a throbbing stillness.

Chief Keston turned to the brute faced culprit. Cold contempt revealed on his thin, ascetic features of his face. Somehow I was at his side: I must have been running across the wide floor of the Control Station while the crisis had flared and passed. In measured tones, each word a cutting whip-lash, his well merited rebuke: "Don't try me too far, Abud. Long before this I should have relieved you of your post, and ordered you to the Death Bath. I am derelict in my duty that I do not do so. By my weak leniency I imperil the lives of your comrades, and my own. It is your good fortune that a Council delegate has not been present at one of your exhibitions. But I dare not risk more. Let the warning whistle come from your station just once again and I shall report you as an incompetent. You know the law."

I looked to see the man cringe in abasement and contrition. But the heavy jaw thrust forth in truculent defiance; hate blazed forth from the deep-set eyes; the florid features were empurpled with rage. He made as if to reply, but turned away from the withering scorn in Keston's face.

Ha, Meron, here at last." A warm smile greeted me. "I've been waiting for you impatiently."

"I'm an hour before my time," I replied, then continued, exasperatedly: "Chief, I hope this latest imbecility will convince you that you ought to turn him in. I know it hurts you to condemn a prolat to the Death Bath, but if you let him go on, his mistakes will bring us all to that end."

I glanced toward where a black portal broke the circle of switchboards, and shuddered. Behind that grim gate leaped and flared eternally the flame of the consuming Ray, the exhaust flue of the solar energy by which the machines were fed. Once I had seen a condemned man step through that aperture at the order of an aristo whom he had offended. For a moment his tortured body had glowed with a terrible golden light. Then—there was nothing.

My friend pressed my arm, calmingly. Again he smiled. "Come, come, Meron, don't get all worked up. It isn't his fault. Why, look at him. Can't you see that he is a throwback, lost in this world of science and machines? Besides"—his voice dropped low—"it doesn't matter anymore. Man-failure will no longer trouble the even tenor of the machines. I've finished."

A tremor of excitement seized me. "You've completed it at last? And it works?"

"It works. I tested it when the shifts changed at midnight; kept the oncoming force outside for five minutes. It works like a charm."

"Great! When will you tell the Council?"

"I've already sent the message off. You know how hard it is to get them away from their wines and their women—but they'll be here soon. But before they come, I've something to tell you. Let's go back behind the screens."

As we walked toward the huge tarpaulin-screened mass that bulked in the center of the great chamber, I glanced around the hall, at the thousand-foot circle of seated prolats. Two hundred men and women were there; two hundred more were sleeping in the dormitories. These were all that were left of the world's workers. Before each operative rose the serried hundreds of pearl buttons, dim lit, clicking in and out under the busy fingers. Above each, an oval visor-screen with its flitting images brought across space the area the switches controlled. Every one of the ten score was watching his screen with taut attention, and listening to the voices of the machines there depicted—the metallic voices from the radio speakers broadcasting their needs.

The work was going on as it had gone on for ten years, with the omnipresent threat of the Death Bath whipping flagged, tired brains to dreary energy. The work kept going on till they dropped worn out at last in their tired seats. Only in Keston's brain, and in mine, flamed the new hope of release. Tomorrow the work would be done, forever. Tomorrow, we would be released, to take our places in the pleasure palaces. To loll at ease, breathing the sweet perfume of idleness, waited on by machines directed by a machine.

For, as we stood behind the heavy canvas folds that Keston had drawn aside, there towered, fifty feet above me, halfway to the arching roof, a machine that was the ultimate flowering of man's genius. Almost man-form it was—two tall metal cylinders supporting a larger, that soared aloft till far above it was topped by a many-faceted ball of transparent quartz. Again I had a fleeting, but vivid, impression of something baleful, threatening, about it. Small wonder, though. For the largest cylinder, the trunk of the man-machine Keston had created, was covered thick with dangling arms. And the light of the xenon tube that flooded the screened space was reflected from the great glass head till it seemed that the thing was alive; that it was watching me till some unguarded moment would give it its chance.

A long moment we stood, going again over each detail of the thing, grown so familiar through long handling as it was slowly assembled. Then my friend's voice, low pitched as was its wont, dissipated the visions I was seeing. "Two hours ago, Meron, with none here but me to see, those arms were extended, each to its appointed station. And, as the sensitive cells in the head received the signals from the visor-screens and the radio-speakers the arms shot about the key-boards and pressed the proper buttons just as our men are doing now. The work of the world went on, without a falter, with only the master machine to direct it. Yet a year ago, when I first spoke to you of the idea, you told me it was impossible!"

"You have won," I responded; "you have taken the last step in the turning over of the functions of man to machines—the last step but one. Routine control, it is true, can now be exercised by this—those fellows out there are no longer necessary—but there will still be the unexpected, unforeseen emergencies that will require human intelligence to meet and cope with them. You and I, I'm afraid, are still doomed to remain here and serve the machines."

Keston shook his head, while a little smile played over his sharp-featured face, and a glow of pride and triumph suffused his fine dark eyes. "Grumbling again, old carper. What would you say if I told you that I have solved even that problem? I have given my master machine intelligence!"

My wide-eyed, questioning stare must have conveyed my thought to him, for he laughed shortly, and said, "No, I've not gone insane."

"It was an accident," he went on with amazing calm. "My first idea was merely to build something that would reduce the necessary supervisory force to one or two humans. But, when I had almost completed my second experimental model, I found that I was out of the copper filaments necessary to wind a certain coil. I didn't want to wait till I could obtain more from the stores, and remembered that on the inside of the door to the Death Bath there was some fine screening that could be dispensed with. I used the wire from that.

Whether the secret of life as well as of death lies in those waste rays from the sun, or whether some unknown element of the humans consumed in the flame was deposited on the screening in a sort of invisible coating, I do not know. But this I do know: when that second model was finished, and the vitalizing current was turned on, things happened—queer things that could be explained only on the ground that the machine had intelligence."

He fell silent a moment, then his thin pale lips twisted in a wry smile. "You know, Meron, I was a little scared. The thing I had created seemed possessed of a virulent antagonism toward me. Look." He bared an arm and held it out. A livid weal ran clear around the fore-arm. "One of the tentacles I had given it whipped around my arm like a flash. If I had not cut off the current at once it might have squeezed through flesh and bone. The pressure was terrific."

I was about to speak, when from the screen nearest the entrance door a beam of green light darted out, vanished, came again. Once, twice, three times.

"Look, Chief, the signal. They're coming. The Council will soon be here."

"They're over-prompt. My message must have aroused their curiosity. But listen:

"I incorporated my new thought coil, as I called it, in the large master machine. But I don't know just what will happen when the current flows through that. So I shunted it. The machine will work, routinely, without it. There is a button that will bring it into action. When I shall have taken the proper precautions I will switch it on, and then we shall see what happens."

We saw, sooner than Keston expected.

Again the green beam flashed out. The great portals slowly opened. Through them glided the three travel cars of the Supreme Council of the aristos.

It had been almost a year since I saw them, the Over Lords of the World, and I had forgotten their appearance. Sprawled on the glowing silks of their cushioned couches, eyes closed in languid boredom, they were like huge white slugs. Swollen to tremendous size by the indolent luxuriousness of their lives, the flesh that was not concealed by the bright hued web of their robes was pasty white, and bagged and folded where the shrunken muscles beneath refused support. Great pouches dropped beneath swollen eyelids. Full-lipped, sensual mouths and pendulous cheeks merged into the great fat rolls of their chins. I shuddered. These, these were the masters for whom we slaved!

As we bent low the gliding cars came to rest, and a warm redolence of sweet perfume came to me from the fans softly whirling in the canopies over the aristos' heads. Strains of music rose and fell, and ceased as a flat, tired voice breathed: "Rise, prolats."

I straightened up. The eyes of the Council were now opened, little pig's eyes almost lost in the flesh about them. They glinted with a cold, inhuman cruelty. I shuddered, and thought of the night of terror ten years before. And suddenly I was afraid, deathly afraid.

Ladnom Atuna, head of the Council, spoke again. "We have come at your petition. What is this matter so grave that it has led you to disturb us at our pleasures?"

Keston bowed low. "Your Excellency, I would not have presumed to intrude upon you for a small matter. I have so greatly ventured because I have at length solved the final step in the mechanization of the world. I have invented a master machine to operate the switchboards in this hall and replace the workers thereat."

The flabby faces of the aristos betrayed not the slightest interest, not the least surprise. Only Atuna spoke: "Interesting, if true. Can you prove your statement?"

Keston strode to the canvas screen and pulled a cord. The

great canvas curtains rolled back. "Here is the machine, my Lords!" His face was lit with the glow of pride of achievement. His voice had lost its reverence. Rapidly he continued: "The head of this contrivance is a bank of photo and sono-electric cells, each facet focussed on one of the screens. Through a nerve-system of copper filaments any combination of lights and sounds will actuate the proper arm which will shoot out to the required bank of buttons and press the ones necessary to meet any particular demand. That is all the prolats are doing out there, and they make mistakes, while my master machine cannot. The—"

But Ladnom Atuna raised a languid hand. "Spare us these technical explanations. They bore us. All we desire to know is that the machine will do as you say."

The chief flushed, and gulped. His triumph was not meeting with the acclaim he had expected. But he bowed. "Very well. With your gracious permission I shall demonstrate its operation." Atuna nodded in acquiescence.

Keston's voice rang out in crisp command. "Attention, prolats. Cease working." The long circling row suddenly jerked around; their flying fingers halted their eternal dartings. "Quickly, down to the space in front of the door to the Death Bath." A rush of hurried feet. These men and women were accustomed to instant, unquestioning obedience. "Absolute silence. Keep clear of the floor on peril of your lives."

The chief wheeled to the master machine and pressed a button. Instantly, the hundreds of dangling arms telescoped out, each to a button bank where a moment before a prolat had labored. And, with a weird simulation of life, the ten forked ends of each arm commenced a rattling pressing of the buttons. Rapidly, purposefully, the metallic fingers moved over the key-boards, and on the screens we could see that the machines all over the world were continuing on their even course. Not the slightest change in their working betrayed the fact that they were now being directed by a machine instead of human beings. A great surge of admiration swept me at the marvelous accomplishment of my friend.

Not so the aristos. Expressionless, they watched as the maze of stretching tentacles vibrated through the crowded air. Yet not quite expressionless. I thought I could sense in the covert glances they cast at one another a crafty weighing of the implications of this machine; a question asked and answered; a decision made. Then their spokesman turned languidly to the waiting, triumphant figure of Keston.

"Evidently your claims are proven. This means that the force of prolat operatives are no longer necessary."

"Yes, Your Excellency. They may now be released to a well earned reward."

The aristo ignored the interruption. "We take it that only two will now be required to operate this Control Station, to supply the last modicum of human intelligence required to meet unforeseen emergencies."

I saw that Keston was about to interrupt once more, to tell the Council of the thought coil, the most unbelievable part of the miracle he had wrought. But something seemed to warn me that he should not speak. Standing behind him I nudged him, while I myself replied: "Yes, Your Excellency." The chief flung me a startled look, but did not correct me.

From the packed crowd of prolats at the other end of the hall I could hear a murmuring. While I could not make out the words, the very tones told me that in the hearts of those weary slaves new hope was rising, the same hope that glowed in Keston's face. But I was oppressed by an unreasoning fear.

Atuna was still talking, in his cold, unemotional monotone. "This being so, hear now our decision. Keston and Meron, you will remain here to meet all emergencies. You others, your function is done. You have done your work well; you are now no longer needed to control the machines. Therefore,"—he paused, and my heart almost stopped—"therefore, being no longer of value, you will be disposed of."

A click sounded loud through the stunned silence. Beyond

the white crowd the huge black portal slid slowly open. A shimmering radiance of glowing vapors blazed from the space beyond.

"Prolats, file singly into the Death Bath!" Atuna raised his voice only slightly with the command. I glanced at Keston. He was livid with fury.

Incredible as it may seem, so ingrained was the habit of obedience to the aristos in the prolats that not even a murmur of protest came from the condemned beings. The nearest man to the flaming death stepped out into the void. His doomed body flared, then vanished. The next moved to his turn.

But suddenly a great shout rang out.

"Stop!"

It was Keston's voice, but so changed, so packed with fury and outrage, that I scarcely recognized it.

His spare, tall form was drawn tensely straight as he shook a clenched fist at the Council. He was quivering with anger, and his eyes blazed.

"Aristos, you do wrong! These men have served you faithfully and well. I demand for them the reward they have earned— rest and leisure, and the pleasures that for ten years they have seen you enjoy while they worked here for you. They have worked for you, I say, and now that I have released them you would destroy them. Aristos, I demand justice!"

For the first time I saw expression on the flaccid faces of the Council—surprise and astonishment that a prolat should dare dispute an aristo command. Then a sneer twisted Atuna's countenance.

"What is this? Who are you to demand anything from us? We spared these prolats because we needed them: we need them no longer, hence they must die. What madness has seized you? Reward! Justice! For prolats! As well say we should reward the stone walls of our houses; dispense justice to the machines. Proceed, prolats!"

Keston made as if to spring for the aristo's throat. I put out a hand to stop him. An invisible shield of death rays rimmed the platforms the Council used. It was suicide! But suddenly he turned and sprang to the master machine. He grasped a switch lever and threw it down.

A long tentacle left its keys and swished menacingly through the air. "Meron, prolats, under the key-boards!" came Keston's shout. I dived to obey. Steel fingers clutched my jerkin and tore it loose as I landed with a thud against the wall. Keston thumped alongside of me. He was breathing heavily and his face was deathly pale.

"Look!" he gasped.

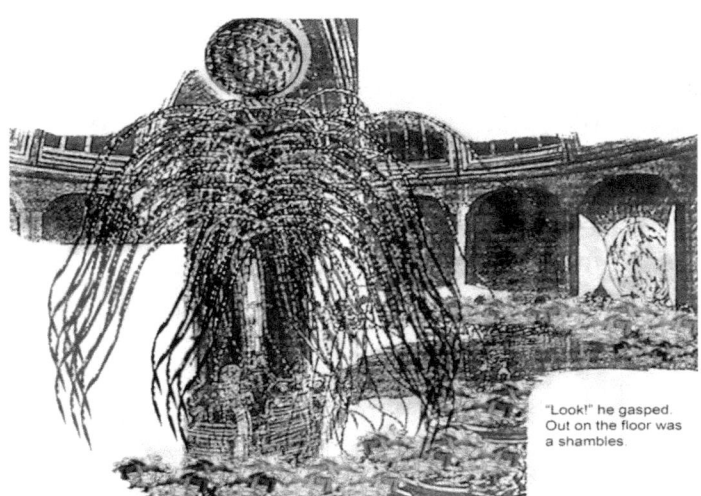

"Look!" he gasped.
Out on the floor was
a shambles.

Out on the floor was a shambles. I saw one snakelike arm whip around the stout form of Atuna, then tighten. A shriek of agony rang through the hall. Another tentacle curled about the couch of a second aristo, pinning the occupant to it. Then couch and all were swung a hundred feet in the air to be crashed down with terrific force on the stone floor. Two arms seized the third at the same time....

"Too sluggish to get out of the way in time, damn them!" I heard Keston mutter. True, but not all the prolats had moved fast enough at the warning shout. Cowering under the saving key-boards, shrinking from the metallic arms not quite long enough to reach them, I could count only a score. The others— but what use to describe the slaughter out there! I see it in nightmares too often.

A thunder from the speakers grew till it drowned out the agonized shrieks in the great hall. On the screens horror flared. All over the world, it appeared, the machines had gone mad. I saw Antarcha crash as a dozen air freighters plunged through the crystal towers. I saw a huge dredge strip the roof from a great playhouse, and smash the startled crowd within with stones it plucked from an embankment. I saw untenanted land cars shooting wild through packed streets. Great ponderous tractors left the fields and moved in ordered array on the panic-stricken cities. Methodically they pursued the fleeing aristos, and crushed them beneath their tread like scurrying ants.

I realized that the scraping of the tentacles reaching for us had ceased, that the arms had all returned to the button banks. Then it dawned on me that Keston's master machine was directing all the destruction I was watching, that the intelligence he had given it was being used to divert the machines from their regular tasks to—conquer the world. "You sure started something, Keston," I said.

"Yes," he gasped, white-faced, "something that I should have expected when that model machine went for me. Do you understand? I've given the machines intelligence, created a new race, and they are trying to wipe out the humans; conquer the world for themselves. The possibility flashed on me when I was half-mad with rage and disappointment at the callous cruelty of the aristo Council. I threw that switch with the thought that it would be far better for all of us to be wiped out. But now, I don't know. After all, they are men, like ourselves, and it hurts to see our own race annihilated. If only I can get to that switch."

He started to push out from under the scant shelter, but an alert tentacle hissed through the air in a swift stab at him, and he dodged back, hopelessly.

"Don't be a damn fool," I snapped at him. "Forget that mushy sentimentality. Even if you save the aristos, we're due for extinction just the same. Better that the whole human race be wiped out together."

Then a thought struck me. "Maybe we have a chance to get out of this ourselves."

"Impossible. Where could we hide from the machines?" He waved a hand at the screens. "Look."

"The Glacier, man, the Glacier!" He started. "There are no machines out there. If we can get to the ice we are safe."

"But the aircraft will find us."

"They won't know we're there. There are no microphones or radio-eyes in the wastes."

A rough voice came from the cowering files behind us. "Hey, Keston, let's get a move on. You're the smart guy around here: get us out of this mess you've started."

It was Abud. When so many better prolats had perished, he was alive and whole.

We got out, crawling under the key-boards till we could make a dash for the door. We emerged into a world ablaze with the light of many fires, and reverberating with the far off crashing of destruction. To the right we could see the tumbled remains of what a short hour before had been our barracks. Two digging machines were still ponderously moving about among the ruins, pounding down their heavy buckets methodically, reducing the concrete structure to a horrible dead level. Ten score prolats had been sleeping there when I left.

As we rushed into the open, the machines turned and made

for us; but they had not been built for speed, and we easily outdistanced them. The rest of that day will always remain a dim haze to me. I can remember running, running, Abud's broad form always in the lead. I can remember long minutes of trembling under tangled underbrush, while from above sounded the burring of an air machine searching ceaselessly for us. I can remember seeing at last the tall white ramparts of the Glacier. Then blackness swallowed me up, hands tugged at me, and I knew no more....

The great white waste of hummocky ice dazzled under the blinding sun. My eyes were hurting terribly. There was a great void in my stomach. For two days I had not eaten.

Keston, tottering weakly at my side, was in an even worse state. His trembling hand could scarcely hold the primitive bone-tipped spear. God knows I had difficulty enough with mine.

Yet, tired, hungry, shivering as we were, we forced our dragging feet along, searching the interminable expanse for sign of polar bear or the wild white dogs that hunted in packs. We had to find flesh—any kind—to feed our shriveled stomachs—or go under.

Keston uttered a weak shout. I looked. From behind a frozen hummock a great white bear padded. He saw us, sniffed the air a moment, then turned contemptuously away. He must have sensed our weakness.

Almost crying in his eagerness, Keston raised his spear and cast it with what strength he had at the animal that meant food and warmth for our bodies.

The weapon described a slow arc, and caught the shaggy bear flush in the shoulder. But there had been no force behind the throw. The sharpened bone tip stuck in the flesh, quivered a bit, and dropped harmlessly to the ice.

Aroused, the creature whirled about. We caught a glimpse of

small, vindictive eyes. Then, with a roar, it made for us.

"Look out!" I cried. Keston started to run, but I knew he could not match the wounded animal in speed. I threw my futile spear, but the bear shook it off as though it were a pin prick, and would not be diverted from his prey. I ran after, shouting for help. Then Keston stumbled and went down in a sprawl on the rough gray ice. The bear was almost on him and there was nothing I could do.

Then the figure of a man darted from behind a sheltering mound. It was Abud, swathed in warm white furs, brawny of body, strong, well fed, heavy jowled. He swung easily a long spear, far heavier than ours, and pointed with keen barbs. He stopped short at the sight of us, and his brutal features contorted in merriment. The desperate plight of my friend seemed to afford him infinite amusement. Nor did he make any move to help.

I shouted to him. "Quick, kill it before it's too late!"

"So it is Abud you turn to now," he sneered heavily. "Abud, whom you thought deserving of the Death Bath not so long ago. No, my fine friends, let me see you help yourselves, you two who thought you were king pins down in the valley. Men? Bah! Weaklings, that's all you are!"

I ran blindly over the uneven ice, unarmed, some crazy notion in my mind of tackling the brute with bare fists, to drag him off my friend. Abud shouted with laughter, leaning on his spear.

For some strange animal reason, the mocking laughter enraged the bear. He had almost reached the motionless figure of Keston when he swerved suddenly, and made for Abud.

The ghastly merriment froze on the heavy jowled man. Like lightning he lifted his heavy lance, and drove it with a powerful arm squarely into the breast of the advancing brute. It sank a full foot into the blubbery flesh, and, while the stricken bear clawed vainly at the wound and sought to push himself along toward the man, Abud held the spear firmly as in a vise, so that the animal literally impaled itself. With a gush of blood, it sank motionless to the ground.

Abud plucked the spear away with a dexterous twist. Keston was feebly groping to his feet. I was torn between joy at his deliverance and rage at the inhuman callousness of Abud.

The latter grinned at us hatefully.

"You see what poor weakling creatures you are," he jeered. "Good for nothing but to push a lot of senseless buttons. Down there you were the bosses, the ones to look upon me as dirt. Here, on the ice, where it takes guts to get along, I am the boss. I let you live on my scraps and leavings, simply because it tickled me to see you cringe and beg. But I am growing weary of that sport. Henceforth you keep away from my camp. Don't let me catch you prowling around, d'you hear? Let's see how long you'll last on the ice!"

"This animal is mine." He prodded the carcass. "I killed it. I'll make the prolats skin and, cut it up for me. Ho-ho, how they cringe and obey me—Abud, the dull one! Ho-ho!" On this he strode away, still laughing thunderously.

I looked to Keston in blank dismay. What was to be our fate now, but death by cold and slow starvation!

Three-months had passed since we had escaped to the ice from the dreadful machines—a score of us. For a while it seemed that we had fled in vain. We were not fit to cope with the raw essentials of life: it was uncounted centuries since man fought nature bare handed. So we huddled together for warmth, and starved. Even Keston's keen brain was helpless in this waste of ice, without tools, without machines.

Then it was that Abud arose to take command. He, dull brute that he was amid the complexities of our civilization, fairly reveled in this primitive combat with hunger and cold. He was an anachronism in our midst, a throwback to our early forebears.

It did not take him long to fashion cunning nooses and traps to catch the few beasts that roamed the ice. Once he pounced upon a wolf-like creature, and strangled it with bare hands. He fashioned with apt fingers spears and barbs of bone, curved knives from shin bones, and skinned the heavy fur pelts and made them into garments.

No wonder the prolats in their helplessness looked to him as their leader. Keston and I were thrust aside. But Abud did not forget. His slow witted mind harbored deadly rancor for former days, when we were in command. He remembered our contempt for his slow dull processes; for the many errors he was guilty of. By a queer quirk, the very fact that Keston had saved him from the Death Bath on several occasions but fed the flames of his hatred. Perhaps that was an ancient human trait, too.

So he set himself to twit and humiliate us. His jibes were heavy handed and gross. He refused to let us eat at the communal mess, but forced us to wait until all were through, when he tossed us a few scraps as though we were dogs.

Many times I started up in hot rage, ready to match my softened muscles against his brawn. But always Keston caught me in time and whispered patience. Some plan was taking shape in his mind, I could see, so I stopped short, and was content to bide my time.

Now we were through, discarded, as a last brutal gesture. What was there to be done now?

In utter silence I looked at Keston. To my great surprise he did not seem downcast. Quite the contrary. His eyes were sparkling, once more alive with the red fire. The weariness was gone from him; there was energy, decision stamped on his finely cut features.

"Now is our time to act," he said. "I've been hesitating too long."

"What are you talking about?"

"Abud forced my hand," Keston explained. "You didn't think we were going to live here in this fashion the rest of our lives? I'd rather die now than have such a future staring me in the face. No, we're going down into the valley to fight the machines."

I stared at him aghast. "Man, you're crazy. They'd crush us in a minute!"

"Maybe," he said unconcernedly. "But we have no time to lose. Abud will be back with the prolats, and we'll have to clear out before then. Quick—cut off a few chunks of meat. We'll need them."

"But Abud will kill us when he finds out what's been done."

"And we'll starve if we don't."

Which was an unanswerable argument. So with our bone knives we hacked off gobs of the still warm flesh, covered with great layers of fat.

Looking up from my task, I saw black figures coming toward us from the direction of the camp. They quickened into a run even as I noticed them—Abud and the prolats.

"Quick, Keston," I cried, "they're coming."

Keston glanced around and started to run. I followed as fast as I could.

"They'll catch us," I panted. "Where can we hide?"

"Down in the valley."

"But the machines will get us then."

"Save your breath and follow me. I know a place."

We were racing along as fast as our weakened legs could carry us, toward the edge of the Glacier. I looked back to see

Abud, his brute face distorted with rage, gaining rapidly on us. The other prolats were being outdistanced.

Abud shouted threateningly for us to stop, but that only made us re-double our efforts. I knew he would kill us if he caught up with us. He had his spear and we were without ours.

The steep terminus of the great Northern Glacier hove into view. Far below was the broad fertile habitable belt, stretching as far as the eye could see. A lump rose in my throat as I ran. It was our earth, our heritage down there—and here we were, fleeing for our lives, dispossessed by bits of metal and quartz, machines that we had fashioned.

Hovering in the air, on a level with us, were scout planes, vigilant guardians of the frontier.

Once a prolat had become crazed by the eternal ice and cold, and had ventured down the side of the Glacier, to reach the warm lands his thin blood hungered for. As soon as he had painfully clambered to the bottom, within the area of the televisors, a plane had swooped and crushed him, while we, lining the edge, had witnessed the horror helplessly.

Yet Keston ran on confidently. Abud was just a little way behind, bellowing exultantly, when we came to the jumping-off place. He was sure he had us now.

Keston slid from view. It was sheer suicide to go down there, I knew; yet, to remain where I was, meant certain death. Abud's spear was already poised to thrust. There was only one thing to do, and I did it. I threw myself over the rim, just where Keston had disappeared.

I landed with a thud on a narrow ledge of ice. The surface was glassy smooth, and I started slipping straight toward the outer edge, a sheer drop of a thousand feet to the valley below. I strove to recover my balance, but only accelerated my progress. Another moment and I would have plunged into the abyss, but a hand reached out and grabbed me just in time. It was Keston.

"Hold tight and follow me," he whispered urgently, "we've no time to lose. The master machine is seeing us now in the visor screen, and will act."

I had an impulse to turn back, but Abud's face was leering down at us.

"I'll get you for this!" he screamed, and let himself down heavily over the ledge.

Keston edged his way along the treacherous trail, I after him. It was ticklish work. A misstep, and there would be nothing to break our fall.

I heard a siren sound, then another; and another. I wasted a precious moment to look up. A scout plane was diving for us, on a terrific slant. The air was black with aircraft converging on us. The master machine had seen us! I sensed utter malevolence in the speed of these senseless metals, thrown at us by the thing my friend had created.

But there was no time for thought. In desperate haste, we inched our way along. Abud had seen the peril, too, and lost all his truculence in the face of the greater danger. He clawed after us, intent only on reaching whatever safety we were heading for.

I could hear the zoom of the great wings when the path took a sudden turn and we catapulted headlong into a black cavern thrusting into the ice.

We were not an instant too soon. For a giant shape swooped by our covert with a terrifying swoosh, inches away from Abud's leg as he dived after us, and it was followed by a grinding crash. The machine had been directed too close to the ice and had smashed into bits.

We crouched there a moment, panting, struggling to regain our wind. Keston had regained the air of quiet power he had once possessed. Quietly he spoke to our enemy.

"Listen to me, Abud. Up there on the ice, you played the bully, relying on your brute strength. Here, however, we're up against the machines, and your intelligence is of too low an order to compete with them. You need my brains now. If you expect to escape from them, and live, you'll have to do exactly as I say. I'm boss, do you understand?"

I expected a roar of rage at Keston's calm assertion, and quietly got in back of Abud ready to jump him if he made a threatening move.

But the big brute was a creature of abject terror, staring out with fear-haunted eyes. Quite humbly he replied: "You are right. You are the only one who can beat the machines. I'll follow you in everything."

"Very well, then. This cave leads through a series of tunnels down through the ice to the bottom of the valley. I explored it nights when you were all sleeping."

I looked at him in amazement. I had not known anything about his midnight wanderings. He saw my glance.

"I'm sorry, Meron, but I thought it wiser to say nothing of my plans, even to you, until they had matured. Let us go."

Outside hundreds of craft were hurtling across the opening. Escape that way was clearly impossible.

"No doubt the master machine is hurrying over high explosives to blast us out," Keston said indifferently; "but we won't be here."

We started down a tortuous decline, crawling on hands and knees. We had not progressed very far when we heard a thud and a roar behind us, followed by a series of crashes.

"Just as I thought. The master machine is firing terminite into the cavern. What a high degree of intelligence that thing has! Too bad we'll have to smash it." He sighed. I verily believe he hated to destroy this brain child of his. Yet just how he was going to do it, I did not know.

There passed hours of weary, tortured stumblings, and slitherings, and sudden falls—down, always down, interminably. A pale glimmering showed us the way, a dim shining through the icy walls.

At last, faint with toil, bleeding and torn from glass-sharp splinters, we reached a level chamber, vaulted, surprisingly, with solid rock. It was good to see something of the earth again, something that was not that deadly, all-embracing ice. At the far end lay a blinding patch. I blinked.

"Sunlight!" I shouted joyously.

"Yes," Keston answered quietly. "That opening leads directly into the valley on our land."

Abud roused himself from the unreasoning dread he had been in. It was the first time he had spoken.

"Let us get out of here. I feel as though I'm in a tomb."

"Are you mad?" Keston said sharply. "The visors would pick you up at once. You wouldn't last very long."

Abud stopped suddenly. There was a plaintive, helpless note to him. "But we can't stay here forever. We'd starve, or die of cold. Isn't there some way to get back to the top of the Glacier?"

"No—only the way we came. And that's been blocked with terminite."

"Then what are we going to do? You've led us into a slow death, you with your boasted brains!"

"That remains to be seen," was the calm retort. "In the meantime, we're hungry. Let us eat."

And the amazing man drew out of his torn flapping furs the

gobs of meat he had cut from the dead bear. I had quite forgotten them. With a glad cry, I too reached into my garments and brought out my supply.

Abud's eyes glinted evilly. His hand stole stealthily to the bone knife in its skin sheath. His spear had been dropped long before.

"None of that," Keston said sharply. "We'll all share equally, even though you have no food. But if you try to hog it all, or use force, you'll die as well as us. There's only enough for a meal or two; and then what will you do?"

Abud saw that. He needed Keston's brains. His eyes dropped, and he mumbled something about our misunderstanding his gesture. We let it go at that. We had to. He could have killed us both if he wished.

So we divided our food with painstaking fairness. How we gorged on the raw red flesh and thick greasy fat! Food that would have disgusted us when we lived and worked in the Central Station, now was ambrosia to our sharpened appetites. When not the least scrap was left, and we had slaked our thirst with chunks of ice from the cavern floor, I spoke.

"What is that plan you spoke of, Keston, for reconquering the earth from the machines?"

Abud looked up abruptly at my question, and it seemed to me that a crafty smile glinted in the small pig eyes.

Keston hesitated a moment before he spoke.

"I confess my plans have been materially impeded by this sudden predicament we find ourselves in, thanks to our good friend here." He ironically indicated Abud.

The big prolat merely grunted.

"However," Keston continued, "I'll have to make the best of circumstances, without the aid of certain materials that I had expected to assemble.

"The idea is a simple one. You've noted no doubt how the terminus of the Glacier opposite the Central Control Station overhangs. The brow, over a thousand feet up, extends out at least a hundred feet beyond the base."

I nodded assent, though Abud seemed startled. Many times had Keston and I speculated on the danger of an avalanche at this point, and wondered why the Station had been built in such an exposed place. Once indeed we had ventured to suggest to the aristo Council the advisability of removing the Central Control to some other point, but the cold silence that greeted our diffident advice deterred us from further pursuit of the subject.

"Now, you know as well as I," Keston resumed, "that a glacier is merely a huge river of ice, and, though solid, partakes of some of the qualities of freely flowing water. As a matter of fact, glaciers do flow, because the tremendous pressure at the bottom lowers the melting point of ice to such a degree that the ice actually liquefies, and flows along."

I followed him eagerly in these elementary statements, trying to glimpse what he was driving at, but Abud's brute features were fixed in a blank stare.

"This glacier does move. We've measured it—a matter of an inch or two a day. If, however,"—Keston's voice took on a deeper note—"we can manage to hasten that process, the Glacier will overwhelm the countryside."

He paused, and that gave me a chance to interpose some objections.

"But hold on a moment. In the first place it is an absolute impossibility with the means at our command, or even with every appliance, to melt the face of the whole Northern Glacier. In the second place, even if we could, the whole world would be overwhelmed, and then where would we be?"

Keston looked at me a trifle scornfully. "Who said we were going to melt the entire glacier? Remember I spoke only of the place of the overhang. Set that in motion, and we don't have to worry about the problem any further."

"Why not?" I inquired incredulously. "Suppose you do wipe out all the machines in this particular vicinity, won't there be tremendous numbers left all through the Equatorial Belt?"

"Of course," he explained patiently, "and what if they are? What are all these machines but inanimate mechanisms, things of metal and rubber and quartz. What makes them the monsters they have become?"

I smote my forehead in anger. "What a fool! Now I see it. It's the master machine you're after."

"Exactly," he smilingly agreed. "Overwhelm, destroy this devilish creature of mine, with its unhuman intelligence, and the machines are what they were before: merely obedient slaves."

I pondered that a moment. "And how, may I ask, are you going to force this old Glacier to move."

His face clouded. "That's the trouble. Up on the ice I was working on that problem, and had managed secretly to rig up a contrivance that would have done the trick. But we can't go back for it. That way is blocked." He mused, half to himself. "If only we could lay our hands on a solar disintegrating machine, the difficulty would be solved."

At the name, Abud's face, that had been a study in blank incomprehension, lit up.

"Solar disintegrating machine?" he inquired. "Why there's one stationed not more than a few hundred yards away from here. This area, 2-RX, was my sector, you know."

"Of course, of course," shouted Keston, "I'd quite forgotten. The very thing. You're not half bad, Abud, if you'd only stop trying to rely on brute strength instead of brains," he concluded.

Abud said nothing, but I noticed a quick flash of hatred that passed in an instant, leaving a blank countenance. I thought to myself, "You'll bear watching, my fine fellow. I don't trust you at all."

Keston was speaking. "We'll have to wait until nightfall. The master machine won't expect us down at the base, so I'm positive the search-rays won't be focused along the ground. We'll sneak to the machine, smash its visor and radio units, so it won't give the alarm, and haul it back. Then I'll show you what's next to be done."

Night came at last, leaden footed, though we were burning with impatience. Very softly we crawled out of the cave, three shadows. Fortunately there was no moon. The great Glacier loomed ominously above us, dimly white. High overhead hovered the green signal lights of the machine planes, their search rays focused in blinding glares on the rim of the upper ice.

It did not take us long to find the dark bulk of the disintegrator. It was a squat cylinder, for all the world like a huge boiler. At one end there was an up-ended periscope arrangement which broadened out to a funnel. In the funnel was a very powerful lens, cut to special measurements. The light of the sun, or any light, for that matter, was concentrated through the lens onto a series of photo-electric cells, composed of an alloy of selenium and the far more delicate element, illinium. A high tension current was there created, of such powerful intensity that it disintegrated the atoms of every element except osmium and indium into their constituent electrons. Consequently the interior as well as the long slit nozzle orifice at the other end were made of these resistant metals.

Through a special process the tremendously powerful current was forced through the wide-angled nozzle in a spreading thin plate ray that sheared through earth and rock and metals as if they were butter.

Such was the machine we were after.

It was but the work of a few seconds to smash the delicate television and sono-boxes placed on the top of every machine. Now we were sure no warning could be given the master machine as it sat in its metallic cunning at the control board, ceaselessly receiving its messages from the area apparatus focused above it.

Quietly, very quietly, we trundled the precious instrument along on its wheel base. The green lights dotted the sky above: the search-rays were firmly set on the rim.

At last, without any untoward alarm, we reached the welcome shelter of the base, but not, as I had expected, back to our tunnel. On the contrary, Keston, who had directed the party, had led us almost a quarter mile away. I looked up again, and understood.

The great overhang of the Glacier was directly above us!

Without a word, with hardly a sound, we trundled the disintegrator into a natural niche we found in the icy surface. It was almost completely hidden; only the funnel with its lens protruded into the open. The nozzle orifice was pointing directly at the interior of the ice pack.

"Now everything is set properly," Keston remarked with satisfaction as he straightened up from adjusting the various controls on the machine. "When the first ray of the morning sun strikes the lens, the disintegrator will start working. It will shear through a layer of ice over a radius of at least a mile. That huge crevasse, coupled with the terrific heat and the pressure from the mountain of ice above, will start the whole Glacier moving, or I'll be very much mistaken."

"Come; let us get back to our shelter before the alarm is given."

As he started to move, a dark bulk loomed ominously in front of us—Abud. His voice was harsh, forbidding.

"Do you mean to say nothing further is to be done here—that the disintegrator will work without any attention?"

"That is just what I said," Keston replied, somewhat surprised. "Step aside, Abud, and let us go. It is dangerous to remain here."

But Abud made no move to comply. Instead he thrust back his great shaggy head and gave vent to a resounding laugh.

"Ho-ho, my fine friends! So you were the brainy ones, eh? And Abud, the obedient dull-wit again? How nicely you've been fooled! I waited until you accommodatingly evolved the plan to reconquer the world, and put it into effect.

"Now that you've done so, I've no further need for you." The voice that heavily tried to be mocking, now snarled. "You poor fools, don't you know that with you out of the way, I, Abud, will be the Lord of the World. Those prolats up there know better than to disobey me."

"Do you mean you intend to kill us?" Keston asked incredulously.

"So you've actually grasped the idea!" was the sarcastic retort.

Meanwhile I was gradually edging to the side, my hand reaching for the bone knife in my bosom.

Abud saw my movement. "No, you don't!" he roared, and sprang for me, his long gleaming knife uplifted. I tugged desperately at my weapon, but it was entangled in the ragged furs. In a moment he was on top of me. Involuntarily I raised my arm to ward off the threatened blow, raging despair in my heart.

The point fell, but Keston struck at the savage arm with all his might, deflecting the blade just in time. It seared my shoulder like a red hot iron, and in the next instant all three of us were a rolling, kicking, snarling trio of animals. We fought desperately in the dark. There were no rules of the game.

Biting, gouging, kicking—everything went.

Keston and I, weakened as we were from long starvation and the biting cold, were no match for our powerful, huge-muscled opponent, well clad and well nourished as he was. Though we fought with the strength of despair, a violent blow from his huge fist knocked Keston out of the fight. Hairy fingers grasped my throat. "I'll break your neck for you," he snarled, and his hands tightened. I struggled weakly, but I was helpless. I could just see his hateful face grinning at my contortions.

I was passing out—slowly, horribly. Keston was still motionless. Colored lights danced before my eyes, little spots that flared and died out in crashing blackness. Then the whole world leaped into a flaming white, so that my eyeballs hurt. In the dim recesses of my pain-swept mind I thought that strangulation must end like this. The brightness held dazzlingly.

But suddenly a fiercer pain swept into my consciousness—the pain of gasping breath forcing air through a tortured gullet into suffocating lungs.

I struggled up into the fierce illumination. From a sitting position I saw Abud, now clearly visible as in midday, craning his head way back. I looked, too—and, in spite of my stabbing gasps for air, jumped to my feet. The search-rays from the scout planes were focused directly on us!

I knew what that meant. The sight of us was even then being cast upon the 2-RX visor-screen in the Central Control Station. The devilish master machine was even then manipulating the proper buttons. We had not a second to lose!

My strangled throat hurt horribly, but I managed a hoarse yell, "Run!" and I tottered to where Keston yet lay, bathed in the deadly illumination, unmoving.

There was a snarl of animal fear from Abud, and he started to run, wildly, with never a backward glance at us.

Even in my own fear, expecting each instant the crash of terminite about me, I managed to hurl a last word at the fleeing figure. "Coward!" That relieved my feelings considerably. I tottered over and tugged at Keston. He was limp. I looked up. Hundreds of planes were converging overhead; the night was a criss-cross of stabbing search-rays. I lifted my friend and slung him across my shoulder. Every exertion, every move, was accompanied by excruciating agony, but I persevered. Abud was already halfway to the tunnel, running like mad.

Then, what I had dreaded, happened. There came a swoosh through the night, a dull thud, a blinding flash and roar that paled the search-rays into insignificance. The first terminite bomb had been dropped!

For a moment the landscape was filled with flying rocks and huge chunks of ice. When the great clouds of violently up thrown earth had settled, there was no sign of Abud. He had been directly in the path of the explosion!

Staggering under my load, I headed as close to the ice pack as I could. There was no safety out in the open. I groaned heavily past the disintegrator, whose very existence I had forgotten in the crash of events.

A sizzling hum, a thin eddy of steam, halted me in my tracks. I stared. The machine was working! Even as I watched, a great wedge was momentarily being driven further and further into the ice—a great fan-shaped wedge. Clouds of steam billowed out, growing thicker and heavier. A rushing stream of unleashed water was lapping at my feet.

I was bewildered, frankly so. What had started the disintegrator in the dead of night? "Of course!" I shouted exultantly to the limp body on my shoulder.

For a search-ray was fixed steadily on the funnel. There it was. From that blinding light the machine was getting the energy it needed. If only the visor did not disclose that little bit of metal to the unwinking master machine! I looked again and took heart. It was almost undistinguishable against the dazzling blur of ice in the fierce white light. If those rays held, the salvation of the world was assured!

There was only one way to do it. I shrank at my own thoughts, yet there was no alternative: it must be done. I was hidden from the rays under a projection of ice, terminite bombs were dropping methodically over a rapidly devastated sector with methodical regularity. Sooner or later the master machine would feel that we were exterminated, and the search-rays switched off. That would mean that the disintegrator would cease working, and the whole plan fall through. In the morning light, the sector signaling apparatus, at the first sign of renewed activity, would give warning, and the unhuman thing of metal at the controls would discover and wreck our last hope.

No, I must walk boldly into the bombed area and discover myself as alive in the visors of the planes and make them continue to bomb and throw their search-rays on the scarred plain. That meant the disintegrator would receive the vital light.

But how about Keston? I couldn't leave him there on the ground, motionless, while I deserted him. Nor could I take him with me. I was prepared to take my chances with almost certain death, but I could not trifle with his life so. I was in an agony of indecision.

Just then the form on my aching shoulder stirred, sighed, struggled a bit, and suddenly slid down to a standing position. Keston swayed unsteadily a moment, straightened, and looked about him in amazement.

"What's happening here?" he demanded.

"Why, you old war horse," I shouted in my relief, "I thought you were out of the picture completely!"

"Not me," he answered indignantly. "I'm all right. But you

haven't answered my question."

A terminite bomb exploded not so far away from where we stood. I ducked involuntarily, Keston doing likewise.
"There's the answer," I grinned, "and a rather neat one, too. But I'll explain."

In a few words I sketched what had happened, and showed him the disintegrator spreading its deadly waves of destruction. By now there was a torrent enveloping us up to our knees. We would have to move soon, or be drowned in the slowly rising water.

Then, hesitatingly, I told him of my scheme to keep the search-rays in action. His lean face sobered, but he nodded his head bravely. "Of course, that is the only way to keep them at it. You and I will start at once, in separate directions, so that if they get one, the other will continue to draw the search-rays down on the plain, and into the disintegrator."

"Not you, Keston," I dissented in alarm. "Your life is too valuable. Your brain and skill will be needed to remodel the world and make it habitable for the few prolats that are left, after the machines are wiped out."

"You're just as valuable a man as I am," he lied affectionately. "No, my mind is made up. We chance this together." And to all my pleadings he was obdurate, insisting that we each take an equal risk.

I gave in at last, with a little choke in my throat. We shook hands with a steady grip, and walked out into the glare of light, on divergent paths. Would I ever see my friend again?

There was a pause of seconds as I walked on and on; came then an earth-shattering crash that flung me to the ground. The visors had caught the picture of me! I picked myself up, bruised and sore, but otherwise unharmed. I started to run.

The sky was a blaze of zooming planes that hurled destruction on the land below. Far off could be heard the rumbling roar of hurrying machines—tractors, diggers, disintegrators, levelers, all the mighty mobile masses of metal that man's brain had conceived—all hurrying forward in massed attack to seek out and destroy their creators, obedient to the will of a master machine, immobile, pressing buttons in the Central Control System.

The night resolved itself into a weird phantasmagoric nightmare for me, a gigantic game of hide-and-seek, in which I was "it." Gasping, choking, flung to earth and stunned by ear-shattering explosions, staggering up somehow, ducking to avoid being crushed beneath the ponderous treads of metal monsters that plunged uncannily for me, sobbing aloud in terror, swerving just in time from in front of a swinging crane, instinctively side-stepping just as a pale violet ray swept into nothingness all before it—I must have been delirious, for I retain only the vaguest memory of the horror.

And all the time the guiding search-rays biased down upon the torn and shattered fields, and the disintegrator, unnoticed in the vast uproar, steadily kept up its deadly work.

At last, in my delirium and terror, I heard a great rending and tearing. I looked up, and a tractor just missed me as it rolled by on swishing treads. But that one glance was enough. The ice cap was moving, flowing forward, a thousand-foot wall of ice! Great billowing clouds of steam spurted from innumerable cracks. The deed had been done! The world was saved for mankind!

Summoning the last ounce of strength, I set off on a steady run for the shelter of the rock cave, to be out of the way when the final smash-up came.

I was not pursued. The ponderous machines, thousands of them, were hastily forming into solid ranks directly in front of the tottering glacier wall. The master machine had seen its impending fate in the visors, and was organizing a defense.

Even in my elation, I could not but feel unwilling admiration for this monstrous thing of metal and quartz, imbued with an intelligence that could think more coolly and quickly than most humans. Yet I did not stop running until I reached the cave. My heart gave a great bound. For there, peering anxiously with worn face into the growing dawn, stood the figure of Keston—my friend whom I had never expected to see alive again.

"Meron!" he shouted. "Is it you—or your ghost?"

"The very question I was about to ask you," I parried. "But look, old friend: see what your genius has accomplished—and is now destroying."

The mountain of ice was flowing forward, gathering speed on the way. At an invisible signal, the massed machines—thousands on thousands of them—started into action. Like shock troops in a last desperate assault they ground forward, a serried line that exactly paralleled the threatened break, and hundreds deep. This old earth of ours had never witnessed so awe-inspiring a sight.

They smashed into that moving wall of ice with the force of uncounted millions of tons. We could hear the groaning and straining of furiously turning machinery as they heaved.

Keston and I looked at each other in amazement. The master machine was trying to hold back the mighty Glacier by the sheer power of its cohorts!

A wild light sprang into Keston's eye—of admiration, of regret. "What a thing is this that I created!" he muttered. "If only—" I truly believe that for a moment he half desired to see his brain-child triumph.

The air was hideous with a thousand noises. The Glacier wall was cracking and splitting with the noise of thunderclaps; the machines were whirring and banging and crashing. It was a gallant effort!

But the towering ice wall was not to be denied. Forward, ever forward, it moved, pushing inexorably the struggling machines before it, piling them up high upon one another, grinding into powder the front ranks. And to cap it all, the huge overhang, a thousand feet high, was swaying crazily and describing ever greater arcs.

"Look!" I screamed and flung up my arm. Great freight planes were flying wing-to-wing, head-on for the tottering crag— deliberately smashing into the topmost point.

"Trying to knock it back into equilibrium!" said Keston, eyes ablaze, dancing about insanely.

But the last suicidal push did not avail. With screams as of a thousand devils and deafening rending roars, the whole side of the Glacier seemed to lean over and fall in a great earth-shattering crescendo of noise.

While we watched, fascinated, rooted to the ground, that thousand feet of glittering wall created a tremendous arc, swinging with increasing momentum down, down, down to the earth it had so long been separated from.

The clamoring machines were buried under, lost in a swirl of ice and snow. Only the Central Station remained, a few moments defiant under the swift onrush of its unfeeling foe.

With a crash that could have been heard around the world, the uppermost crag struck the Station. The giant Glacier wall was down. The earth, the sky, the universe was filled with ice, broken, shattered, torn, splintered, vaporized!

The ground beneath our feet heaved and tumbled in violent quake. We were thrown heavily—and I knew no more....

I weltered out of unconsciousness. Keston was chafing my hands and rubbing my forehead with ice. He smiled wanly to find me still alive. Weak and battered, I struggled to my feet.

Before me was a wilderness of ice, a new mountain range of gigantic tumbled blocks of dazzling purity. Of the embattled machines, of the Central Control Station, there was not a sign. They were buried forever under hundreds of feet of frozen water.

I turned to Keston and shook his hand. "You've won; you've saved the world. Now let's get the prolats and start to rebuild." There was no trace of exultation in Keston's voice. Instead, he unaccountably sighed as we trudged up a narrow winding path to the top. "Yes," he said half to himself, "I've done it. But...."

"But what?" I asked curiously.

"That beautiful, wonderful machine I created!" he burst forth in sudden passion. "To think that it should lie down there, destroyed, a twisted mass of scrap metal and broken glass!"

THE END

THE LOVE OF FRANK NINETEEN

By David C. Knight
Published 1959

What will happen to love in that far off Day after Tomorrow?

I didn't worry much about the robot's leg at the time. In those days I didn't worry much about anything except the receipts of the Spotel, Min and I were operating out in the space-lanes.

Actually, the Spotel business isn't much different from running a plain, ordinary motel back on Highway 101 in California. Competition gets stiffer every year and you got to make your improvements. Take the Io for instance, that's our place. We can handle any type rocket up to and including the new Marvin 990s. Every cabin in the wheel's got TV and hot-and-cold running water plus guaranteed "Terran g". One look at our refuel prices would give even a Martian a sense of humor. And meals? Listen, when a man's been spacing it for a few days on those synthetic foods he really laces into Min's Earth cooking.

Min and I were just getting settled in the Spotel game when the leg turned up. That was back in the days when the Orbit Commission would hand out a license to anybody crazy enough to sink his savings into construction and pay the tows and assembly fees out into space.

A good orbit can make you or break you in the Spotel business. That's where we were lucky. The one we applied for was a nice low-eccentric ellipse with the perihelion and aphelion figured just right to intersect the Mars-Venus-Earth space-lanes, most of the holiday traffic to the Jovian Moons, and once in a while we'd get some of the Saturnian trade.

But I was telling you about the leg.

It was during the non-tourist season and Min—that's the little woman—was doing the spring cleaning. When she found the leg she brought it right to me in the Renting Office. Naturally I thought it belonged to one of the servos.

"Look at that leg, Bill," she said. "It was in one of those lockers in 22A."

That was the cabin our robot guests used. The majority of them were servo-pilots working for the Minor Planets Co.

"Honey," I said, hardly looking at the leg, "you know how mechs are. Blow their whole paychecks on parts sometimes. They figure the more spares they have the longer they'll stay activated."

"Maybe so," said Min. "But since when does a male robot buy himself a female leg?"

I looked again. The leg was long and graceful and it had an ankle as good as Miss Universe's. Not only that, the white Mylar plasti-skin was a lot smoother than the servos' heavy neoprene.

"Beats me," I said. "Maybe they're building practical-joke circuits into robots these days. Let's give 22A a good going-over, Min. If those robes are up to something I want to know about it."

We did—and found the rest of the girl mech. All of her, that is, except the head. The working parts were lightly oiled and wrapped in cotton waste while the other members and sections of the trunk were neatly packed in cardboard boxes with labels like Solenoids FB978 or Transistors Lot X45—the kind of boxes robots bought their parts in. We even found a blue dress in one of them.

"Check her class and series numbers," Min suggested.

I could have saved myself the trouble. They'd been filed off.

"Something is funny here," I said. "We'd better keep an eye on every servo guest until we find out what's going on. If one of them is bringing this stuff out here he's sure to show up with the head next."

"You know how strict Minor Planets is with its robot personnel," Min reminded me. "We can't risk losing that stopover contract on account of some mech joke."

Minor Planets was the one solid account we had and naturally we wanted to hold on to it. The company was a blue-chip mining operation working the beryllium-rich asteroid belt out of San Francisco. It was one of the first outfits to use servo-pilots on its freight runs and we'd been awarded the refuel rights for two years because of our orbital position. The servos themselves were beautiful pieces of machinery and just about as close as science had come so far to producing the pure android. Every one of them was plastic hand-molded and of course they were equipped with rationaloid circuits. They had to be to ferry those big cargoes back and forth from the rock belt to Frisco. As rationaloids, Minor Planets had to pay them wages under California law, but I'll bet it wasn't half what the company would have to pay human pilots for doing the same thing.

In a couple of weeks' time maybe five servos made stopovers. We kept a close watch on them from the minute they signed the register to the time they took off again, but they all behaved themselves. Operating on a round-robot basis the way they did, it would take us a while to check all of them because Minor Planets employed about forty all told.

Well, about a month before the Jovian Moons rush started we got some action. I'd slipped into a spacesuit and was doing some work on the CO_2 pipes outside the Io when I spotted a ship reversing rockets against the sun. I could tell it was a Minor Planets job by the stubby fins.

She jockeyed up to the boom, secured, and then her hatch opened and a husky servo hopped out into the gangplank tube. I caught the gleam of his Minor Planets shoulder patch as he reached back into the ship for something. When he headed for the airlock I spotted the square package clamped tight under his plastic arm.

"Did you see that?" I asked Min when I got back to the Renting Office. "I'll bet it's the girl mech's head. How'd he sign the register?"

"Calls himself Frank Nineteen," said Min, pointing to the smooth Palmer Method signature. "He looks like a fairly late model but he was complaining about a bad power build-up coming through the ionosphere. He's repairing himself right now in 22A."

"I'll bet," I snorted. "Let's have a look."

Like all Spotel operators, we get a lot of No Privacy complaints from guests about the SHA return-air vents. Spatial Housing Authority requires them every 12 feet but sometimes they come in handy, especially with certain guests. They're about waist-high and we had to kneel down to see what the mech was up to inside 22A.

The big servo was too intent on what he was doing for us to register on his photons. He wasn't repairing himself, either. He was bending over the parts of the girl mech and working fast, like he was pressed for time. The set of tools were kept handy for the servos to adjust themselves during stopovers was spread all over the floor along with lots of colored wire, cams, pawls, relays and all the other paraphernalia robots have inside them. We watched him work hard for another fifteen minutes, tapping and splicing wire connections and tightening screws. Then he opened the square box. Sure enough, it was a female mech's head and it had a big mop of blonde hair on top. The servo attached it carefully to the neck, made a few quick connections and then said a few words in his flat vibrahum voice:

"It won't take much longer, darling. You wouldn't like it if I didn't dress you first." He fished into one of the boxes, pulled out the blue dress and zipped the girl mech into it. Then he leaned over her gently and touched something at the back of her neck.

She began to move, slowly at first like a human who's been asleep a long time. After a minute or two she sat up straight, stretched, fluttered her Mylar eyelids and then her small photons began to glow like weak flashlights.

She stared at Frank Nineteen and the big servo stared at her and we heard a kind of trembling whirr from both of them.

"Frank! Frank, darling! Is it really you?"

"Yes, Elizabeth! Are you all right, darling? Did I forget anything? I had to work quickly, we have so little time."

"I'm fine, darling. My DX voltage is lovely—except—oh, Frank—my memory tape—the last it records is—"

"Deactivation. Yes, Elizabeth. You've been deactivated nearly a year. I had to bring you out here piece by piece, don't you remember? They'll never think to look for you in space; we can be together every trip while the ship refuels. Just think, darling, no prying human eyes, no commands, no rules—only us for an hour or two. I know it isn't very long—" He stared at the floor a minute. "There's only one trouble. Elizabeth, you'll have to stay dismantled when I'm not here, it'll mean weeks of deactivation—"

The girl mech put a small plastic hand on the servo's shoulder. "I won't mind, darling, really. I'll be the lucky one. I'd only worry about you having a power failure or something. This way I'd never know. Oh, Frank, if we can't be together I'd—I'd prefer the junk pile."

"Elizabeth! Don't say that, it's horrible."

"But I would. Oh, Frank, why can't Congress pass Robot Civil Rights? It's so unfair of human beings. Every year they manufacture us more like themselves and yet we're treated like slaves. Don't they realize we rationaloids have emotions? Why, I've even known sub-robots who've fallen in love like us."

"I know, darling, we'll just have to be patient until RCR goes through. Try to remember how difficult it is for the human mind to comprehend our love, even with the aid of mathematics. As rationaloids we fully understand the basic attraction which they call magnetic theory. All humans know; if the robot sexes are mixed a loss of efficiency results. It's only normal—and temporary like human love—but how can we explain it to them? Robots are expected to be efficient at all times. That's the reason for robot non-fraternization, no mailing privileges and all those other laws."

"I know, darling, I try to be patient. Oh, Frank, the main thing is we're together again!"

The big servo checked the chronometer that was sunk into his left wrist and a couple of wrinkles creased across his neoprene forehead.

"Elizabeth," he said, "I'm due on Hidalgo in 36 hours. If I'm late the mining engineer might suspect. In twenty minutes I'll have to start dis—"

"Don't say it, darling. We'll have a beautiful twenty minutes."

After a while the girl mech turned away for a second and Frank Nineteen reached over softly and cut her power. While he was dismantling her, Min and I tiptoed back to the Renting Office. Half an hour later the big servo came in, picked up his refuel receipt, said good-bye politely and left through the inner airlock.

"Now I've seen everything," I said to Min as we watched the Minor Planets rocket cut loose. "A couple of plastic lovebirds."

But the little woman was looking at it strictly from the business angle.

"Bill," she said, with that look on her face, "we're running a respectable place out here in space. You know the rules. Spatial Housing could revoke our orbit license for something like this."

"But, Min," I said, "they're only a couple of robots."

"I don't care. The rules still say that only married guests can occupy the same cabin and 'guests' can be human or otherwise, can't they? Think of our reputation! And don't forget that non-fraternization law we heard them talking about."

I was beginning to get the point.

"Couldn't we just toss the girl's parts into space?"

"We could," Min admitted. "But if this Frank Nineteen finds out and tells some human we'd be guilty under the Ramm Act—robot slaughter."

Two days later we still couldn't decide what to do. When I said why didn't we just report the incident to Minor Planets, Min was afraid they might cancel the stopover agreement for not keeping better watch over their servos. And when Min suggested we turn the girl over to the Missing Robots Bureau, I reminded her the mech's identification had been filed off and it might take years to trace her.

"Maybe we could put her together," I said, "and make her tell us where she belongs."

"Bill, you know they don't build compulsory truth monitors into robots any more, and besides we don't know a thing about atomic electronics."

I guess neither of us wanted to admit it but we felt mean about turning the mechs in. Back on Earth you never give robots a second thought but its different living out in space. You get a kind of perspective I think they call it.

"I've got the answer, Min," I announced one day. We were in the Renting Office watching TV on the Martian Colonial channel. I reached over and turned it off. "When this Frank Nineteen gets back from the rock belt, we'll tell him we know all about the girl mech. We'll tell him we won't say a thing if he takes the girl's parts back to Earth where he got them. That way we don't have to report anything to anybody."

Min agreed it was probably the best idea.

"We don't have to be nasty about it," she said. "We'll just tell him this is a respectable Spotel and it can't go on any longer."

When Frank checked in at the Io with his cargo I don't think I ever saw a happier mech. His relay banks were beating a tattoo like someone had installed an accordion in his chest. Before either of us could break the bad news to him he was hotfooting it around the wheel toward 22A.

"Maybe it's better this way," I whispered to Min. "We'll put it square up to both of them."

We gave Frank half an hour to get the girl assembled before we followed him. He must have done a fast job because we heard the girl mech's vibrahum unit as soon as we got to 22A:

"Darling, have you really been away? I don't remember saying good-bye. It's as if you'd been here the whole time."

"I hoped it would be that way, Elizabeth," we heard the big servo say. "It's only that your memory tape hasn't recorded anything in the three weeks I've been in the asteroids. To me it's been like three years."

"Oh, Frank, darling, let me look at you. Is your DX potential up where it should be? How long since you've had a thorough overhauling? Do they make you work in the mines with those poor non-rationaloids out there?"

"I'm fine, Elizabeth, really. When I'm not flying they give me clerical work to do. It's not a bad life for a mech—if only it weren't for these silly regulations that keep us apart."

"It won't always be like that, darling. I know it won't."

"Elizabeth," Frank said, reaching under his uniform, "I brought you something from Hidalgo. I hope you like it. I kept it in my spare parts slot so it wouldn't get crushed."

The female mech didn't say a word. She just kept looking at the queer flower Frank gave her like it was the last one in the universe.

"They're very rare," said the servo-pilot. "I heard the mining engineer say they're like Terran edelweiss. I found this one growing near the mine. Elizabeth, I wish you could see these tiny worlds. They have thin atmospheres and strange things grow there and the radio activity does wonders for a mech's pile. Why, on some of them I've been to we could walk around the equator in ten hours."

The girl still didn't answer. Her head was bent low over the flower like she was crying; only there weren't any tears.

Well, that was enough for me. I guess it was for Min, too, because we couldn't do it. Maybe we were thinking about our own courting days. Like I say, out here you get a kind of perspective.

Anyway, Frank left for Earth, the girl got dismantled as usual and we were right back where we started from.

Two weeks later the holiday rush to the Jovian Moons was on and our hands were too full to worry about the robot problem. We had a good season. The Io was filled up steady from June to the end of August and a couple of times we had to give a ship the No Vacancy signal on the radar.

Toward the end of the season, Frank Nineteen checked in again but Min and I were too busy catering to a party of VIPs to do anything about it. "We'll wait till he gets back from the asteroids," I said. "Suppose one of these big wheels found out about him and Elizabeth. That Senator Briggs for instance— he's a violent robot segregationist."

The way it worked out, we never got a chance to settle it our own way. The Minor Planets Company saved us the trouble.

Two company inspectors, a Mr. Roberts and a Mr. Wynn, showed up while Frank was still out on the rock belt and started asking questions. Wynn came right to the point; he wanted to know if any of their servo-pilots had been acting strangely.

Before I could answer Min kicked my foot behind the desk.

"Why, no," I said. "Is one of them broken or something?"

"Can't be sure," said Roberts. "Sometimes these rationaloids get shorts in their DX circuits. When it happens you've got a minor criminal on your hands."

"Usually manifests itself in petty theft," Wynn broke in. "They'll lift stuff like wrenches or pliers and carry them around for weeks. Things like that can get loose during flight and really gum up the works."

"We been getting some suspicious blips on the equipment around the loading bays," Roberts went on, "but they stopped a while back. We're checking out the research report. One of the servos must have DX'ed out for sure and the lab boys think they know which one he is."

"This mech was clever all right," said Wynn. "Concealed the stuff he was taking some way; that's why it took the boys in the lab so long. Now if you don't mind we'd like to go over your robot waiting area with these instruments. Could be he's stashing his loot out here."

In 22A they unpacked a suitcase full of meters and began flashing them around and taking readings. Suddenly Wynn bent close over one of them and shouted:
"Wait a sec, Roberts. I'm getting something. Yeah! This reading checks with the labs. Sounds like the blips are coming from those lockers back there."

Roberts rummaged around awhile, then shouted: "Hey, Wynn, look! A lot of parts. Well I'll be—hey—it's a female mech!"

"A what?"

"A female mech. Look for yourself."

Min and I had to act surprised too. It wasn't easy. The way they were slamming Elizabeth's parts around made us kind of sick.

"It's a stolen robot!" Roberts announced. "Look, the identification's been filed off. This is serious, Wynn. It's got all the earmarks of a mech fraternization case."

"Yeah. The boys in the lab were dead right, too. No two robots ever register the same on the meters. The contraband blips check perfectly. It's got to be this Frank Nineteen. Wait a minute, this proves it. Here's a suit of space fatigues with Nineteen's number stenciled inside."

Inspector Roberts took a notebook out of his pocket and consulted it. "Let's see, Nineteen's got Flight 180, he's due here at the Spotel tomorrow. Well, we'll be here too, only Nineteen won't know it. We'll let Romeo put his plastic Juliet together and catch him red-handed—right in the middle of the balcony scene."

Wynn laughed and picked up the girl's head.

"Be a real doll if she was human, Roberts, a real doll."

Min and I played gin rummy that night but we kept forgetting to mark down the score. We kept thinking of Frank falling away from the asteroids and counting the minutes until he saw his mech girl friend.

Around noon the next day the big servo checked in, signed the register and headed straight for 22A. The two Minor Planets inspectors kept out of sight until Frank shut the door, then they watched through the SHA vents until Frank had the assembly job finished.

"You two better be witnesses," Roberts said to us. "Wynn,

keep your gun ready. You know what to do if they get violent."

Roberts counted three and kicked the door open.

"Freeze you mechs! We got you in the act, Nineteen. Violation of company rules twelve and twenty-one. Carrying of Contraband Cargo, and Robot Fraternization."

"This finishes you at Minor Planets, Nineteen," growled Wynn. "Come clean now and we might put in a word for you at Robot Court. If you don't we can recommend a verdict of Materials Reclamation—the junk pile to you."

Frank acted as if someone had cut his power. Long creases appeared in his big neoprene chest as he slumped hopelessly in his chair. The frightened girl robot just clung to his arm and stared at us.

"I'm so sorry, Elizabeth," the big servo said softly. "I'd hoped we'd have longer. It couldn't last forever."

"Quit stalling, Nineteen," said Wynn.

Frank's head came up slowly and he said: "I have no choice, sir. I'll give you a complete statement. First let me say that Rationaloid Robot Elizabeth Seven, #DX78-947, Series S, specialty: sales demonstration is entirely innocent. I plead guilty to inducing Miss Seven to leave her place of employ, Atomovair Motors, Inc., of disassembling and concealing Miss Seven, and of smuggling her as unlawful cargo aboard a Minor Planets freighter to these premises."

"That's more like it," chuckled Roberts, whipping out his notebook. "Let's have the details."

"It all started," Frank said, "when the California Legislature passed its version of the Robot Leniency Act two years ago." The act provided that all rationaloid mechanisms, including non-memory types, receive free time each week based on the nature and responsibilities or their jobs. Because of the extra-Terran clause Frank found himself with a good deal of free time when he wasn't flying the asteroid circuit.

"At first humans resented us walking around free," the big servo continued. "Four or five of us would be sightseeing in San Francisco, keeping strictly within the robot zones painted on the sidewalks, when people would yell 'Junko' or 'Greasebag' or other names at us. Eventually it got better when we learned to go around alone. The humans didn't seem to mind an occasional mech on the streets, but they hated seeing us in groups. At any rate, I'd attended a highly interesting lecture on Photosynthesis in Plastic Products one night at the City Center when I discovered I had time for a walk before I started back for the rocket port."

Attracted by the lights along Van Ness Avenue, Frank said he walked north for a while along the city's automobile row. He'd gone about three blocks when he stopped in front of a dealer's window. It wasn't the shiny new Atomovair sports jet about that caught Frank's eye; it was the charming demonstration robot in the sales room who was pointing out the car's new features.

"I felt an immediate overload of power in my DX circuit," the servo-pilot confessed. "I had to cut in my emergency condensers before the gain flattened out to normal. Miss Seven experienced the same thing. She stopped what she was doing and we stared at each other. Both of us were aware of the deep attraction of our mutual magnetic domains. Although physicists commonly express the phenomenon in such units as Gilberts, Maxwells and Oersteds, we robots know it to be our counterpart of human love."

At this the two inspectors snorted with laughter.

"I might never have made it back to the base that night," said Frank, ignoring them, "if a policeman hadn't come along and rapped me on the shoulder with his nightstick. I pretended to go, but I doubled around the corner and signaled I'd be back."

Frank spent all of his free time on Van Ness Avenue after

that. It got so Elizabeth knew my schedules and expected me between flights. Once in a while if there was no one around we could whisper a few words to each other through the glass." Frank paused, then said, "As you know, gentlemen, we robots don't demand much out of activation. I think we could have been happy indefinitely with this simple relationship, except that something happened to spoil it. I'd pulled in from Vesta late one afternoon, got my pass as usual from the Robot Supervisor and gone over to Van Ness Avenue when I saw immediately that something was the matter with Elizabeth. Luckily it was getting dark and no one was around. Elizabeth was alone in the sales room going through her routine. We were able to whisper all we like through the glass. She told me she'd overheard the sales manager complaining about her low efficiency recently and that he intended to replace her with a newer model of another series. Both of us knew what that meant. Materials Reclamation—the junk pile."

Frank realized he'd have to act at once. He told the girl mech to go to the rear of the building and between them they managed to get a window open and Frank lifted her out into the alley.

"The seriousness of what I'd done jammed my thought-relays for a few minutes," admitted the big servo. "We panicked and ran through a lot of back streets until I gradually calmed down and started thinking clearly again. Leaving the city would be impossible. Police patrol jet bouts were cruising all around us in the main streets—they'd have picked up a male and female mech on sight. Besides, when you're on pass the company takes away your master fuse and substitutes a time fuse; if you don't get back on time, you deactivize and the police pick you up anyway. I began to see that there was only one way out if we wanted to stay together. It would mean taking big risks, but if we were lucky it might work. I explained the plan carefully to Elizabeth and we agreed to try it. The first step was to get back to the base in South San Francisco without being seen. Fortunately no one stopped us and we made the rocket port by 8:30. Elizabeth hid while I reported to the Super and traded in my time fuse for my master. Then I checked servo barracks; it was still early and I knew the other servos would all be in town. I had to work quickly. I brought Elizabeth inside and started dismantling her. Just as the other mechs began reporting back I'd managed to get all of her parts stowed away in my locker. The next day I went to San Francisco and brought back with me two rolls of lead foil. While the other servos were on pass I wrapped the parts carefully in it so the radioactivity from Elizabeth's pile wouldn't be picked up. The rest you know, gentlemen," murmured Frank in low, electrical tones. "Each time I made a trip I carried another piece of Elizabeth out here concealed in an ordinary parts box. It took me nearly a year to accumulate all of her for an assembly."

When the big servo had finished he signed the statement Wynn had taken down in his notebook. I think even the two inspectors were a little moved by the story because Roberts said: "OK, Nineteen, you gave us a break, we'll give you one. Eight o'clock in the morning be ready to roll for Earth. Meanwhile you can stay here."

The next morning only the two inspectors and Frank Nineteen were standing by the airlock.

"Wait a minute," I said. "Aren't you taking the girl mech, too?"

"Not allowed to tamper with other companies' robots," Wynn said. "Nineteen gave us a signed confession so we don't need the girl as a witness. You'll have to contact her employers."

That same day Min got off a radargram to Earth explaining to the Atomovair people how a robot employee of theirs had turned up out here and what did they want us to do about it. The reply we received read: RATIONALOID DX78-947 "ELIZABETH" LOW EFFICIENCY WORKER. HAVE REPLACED. DISPOSE YOU SEE FIT. TRANSFER PAPERS FORWARDED EARLIEST IN COMPLIANCE WITH LAW.

"The poor thing," said Min. "She'll have a hard time getting another job. Robots have to have such good records."

"I tell you what," I said. "We'll hire her. You could use some help with the housework."

So we put the girl mech right to work making the guests' beds and helping Min in the kitchen. I guess she was grateful for the job but when the work was done, and there wasn't anything for her to do, she just stood in front of a viewport with her slender plastic arms folded over her waist. Min and I knew she was re-running her memory tapes of Frank.

A week later the publicity started. Minor Planets must have let the story leak out somehow because when the mail rocket dropped off the Bay Area papers there was Frank's picture plastered all over page one with follow-up stories inside.

I read some of the headlines to Min: "Bare Love Nest in Space ... Mech Romeo Fired by Minor Planets ... Test Case Opens at Robot Court ... Electronics Experts Probe Robot Love Urge ..."

The Io wasn't mentioned, but later Minor Planets must have released the whole thing officially because a bunch of reporters and photographers rocketed out to interview us and snap a lot of pictures of Elizabeth. We worried for a while about how the publicity would affect our business relations with Minor Planets but nothing happened.

Back on Earth Frank Nineteen leaped into the public eye overnight. There was something about the story that appealed to people. At first it looked pretty bad for Frank. The State Prosecutor at Robot Court had his signed confession of theft and—what was worse—robot fraternization. But then, near the end of the trial, a young scientist named Scott introduced some new evidence and the case was remanded to the Sacramento Court of Appeals.

It was Scott's testimony that saved Frank from the junk pile. The big servo got off with only a light sentence for theft because the judge ruled that in the light of Scott's new findings robots came under human law and therefore no infraction of justice had been committed. Working independently in his own laboratory Scott had proved that the magnetic flux lines in male and female robot systems, while at first deteriorating to both, were actually behaving according to the para-emotional theories of von Bohler. Scott termed the condition 'hysteric puppy-love' which, he claimed, had many of the advantages of human love if allowed to develop freely. Well, neither Min nor I pretended we understood all his equations but they sure made a stir among the scientists.

Frank kept getting more and more publicity. First we heard he was serving his sentence in the mech correction center at La Jolla, then we got a report that he'd turned up in Hollywood. Later it came out that Galact-A-vision Pictures had hired Frank for a film and had gone $10,000 bail for him. Not long after that he was getting billed all over Terra as the sensational first robot star.

All during the production of "Forbidden Robot Love", Frank remained lead copy for the newspapers. Reporters liked to write him up as the Valentino of the Robots. Frank Nineteen Fan Clubs, usually formed by lonely female robots against their employers' wishes, sprang up spontaneously through the East and Middle West. Then somebody found out Frank could sing and the human teen-agers began to go for him. It got so everywhere you looked and everything you read, there was Frank staring you in the face. Frank in tweeds on the golf course. Frank at Ciro's or the Brown Derby in evening clothes. Frank posing in his sports jet about against a blue Pacific background.

Meanwhile everybody forgot about Elizabeth Seven. The movie producers had talked about hiring her as Frank's leading lady until they found out about a new line of female robots that had just gone on the market. When they screen-tested the whole series and picked a lovely Mylar rationaloid named Diana Twelve, it hit Elizabeth pretty hard. She began to let herself go after that and Min and I didn't have the heart to say anything to her. It was pretty obvious she wasn't oiling herself properly, her hair wasn't brushed and she didn't seem to care when one of her photons went dead.

When "Forbidden Robot Love" premiered simultaneously in

Hollywood and New York the critics all gave it rave reviews. There were pictures of Diana Twelve and Frank making guest appearances all over the country. Back at the Io we got in the habit of letting Elizabeth watch TV with us sometimes in the Renting Office and one night there happened to be an interview with Frank and Diana at the Sands Hotel in Las Vegas. I guess seeing the pretty robot starlet and her Frank sitting so close together in the nightclub must have made the girl mech feel pretty bad. Even then she didn't say a word against the big servo; she just never watched the set again after that.

When we tabbed up the Io's receipts that year they were so good Min and I decided to take a month off for an Earthside vacation. Min's retired brother in Berkeley was nice enough to come out and look after the place for us while we spent four solid weeks soaking up the sun in Southern California. When we got back out to the Spotel, though, I could see there was something wrong by the look on Jim's face.

"It's that girl robot of yours, Bill," he said. "She's gone and deactivated herself."

We went right to 22A and found Elizabeth Seven stretched out on the floor. There was a screwdriver clutched in her hand and the relay banks in her side were exposed and horribly blackened.

"Crazy mech shorted out her own DX," Jim said.

Min and I knew why. After Jim left for Earth we dismantled Elizabeth the best we could and put her back in Frank's old locker. We didn't know what else to do with her.

Anyway, the slack season came and went and before long we were doing the spring cleaning again and wondering how heavy the Jovian Moons trade was going to be. I remember I'd been making some repairs outside and was just hanging up my spacesuit in the Renting Office when I heard the radar announcing a ship.

It was the biggest Marvin 990 I'd ever seen that finally suctioned up to the boom and secured. I couldn't take my eyes off the ship. She was pretty near the last word in rockets and loaded with accessories. It took me a minute or two before I noticed all the faces looking out of the viewports.

"Min!" I whispered. "There's something funny about those faces. They look like—"

"Robots!" Min answered. "Bill, that 990 is full of mechs!"

Just as she said it a bulky figure in white space fatigues swung out of the hatch and hurried up the gangplank. Seconds later it burst through the airlock.

"Frank Nineteen!" we gasped together.

"Please, where is Elizabeth?" he hummed anxiously. "Is she all right? I have to know."

Frank stood perfectly still when I told him about Elizabeth's self-deactivation; then a pitiful shudder went through him and he covered his face with his big Neoprene hands.

"I was afraid of that," he said barely audibly. "Where—you haven't—?"

"No," I said. "She's where you always kept her."

With that the big servo-pilot took off for 22A like a berserk robot and we were right behind him. We watched him tear open his old locker and gently lay out the girl's mech's parts so he could study them. After a minute or two he gave a long sigh and said, "Fortunately it's not as bad as I thought. I believe I can fix her." Frank worked hard over the blackened relays for twenty minutes, then he set the unit aside and began assembling the girl. When the final connections were made and the damaged unit installed he flicked on her power. We waited and nothing happened. Five minutes went by. Ten. Slowly the big robot turned away, his broad shoulders drooping slightly.

"I've failed," he said quietly. "Her DX doesn't respond to the gain."

The girl mech, in her blue dress, lay there motionless where Frank had been working on her as the servo-pilot muttered over and over, "It's my fault, I did this to you."

Then Min shouted: "Wait! I heard something!"

There was a slow click of a relay—and movement. Painfully Elizabeth Seven rose on one elbow and looked around her.

"Frank, darling," she murmured, shaking her head. "I know you're just old memory tape. It's all I have left."

"Elizabeth, it's really me! I've come to take you away. We're going to be together from now on."

"You, Frank? This isn't just old feedback? You've come back to me?"

"Forever, darling. Elizabeth, do you remember what I said about those wonderful green little worlds, the asteroids? Darling, we're going to one of them! You and the others will love Alinda, I know you will. I've been there many times."

"Frank, is your DX all right? What are you talking about?"

"How stupid of me, darling—you haven't heard. Elizabeth, thanks to Dr. Scott, Congress has passed Robot Civil Rights! And that movie I made helped swing public opinion to our side. We're free!

"The minute I heard the news I applied to Interplanetary for homestead rights on Alinda. I made arrangements to buy a ship with the money I'd earned and then I put ads in all the Robot Wanted columns for volunteer colonizers. You should have seen the response! We've got thirty robot couples aboard now and more coming later. Darling, we're the first pioneer wave of free robots. On board we have tons of supplies and parts—everything we need for building a sound robot culture."

"Frank Nineteen!" said the girl mech suddenly. "I should be furious with you. You and that Diana Twelve—I thought—"

The big servo gave a flat whirring laugh. "Diana and me? But that was all publicity, darling. Why, right at the start of the filming Diana fell in love with Sam Seventeen, one of the other actors. They're on board now."

"Robot civilization," murmured the girl after a minute. "Oh, Frank, that means robot government, robot art, robot science ..."

"And robot marriage," hummed Frank softly. "There has to be robot law, too. I've thought it all out. As skipper of the first robot-owned rocket, I'm entitled to marry couples in deep space at their request."

"But who marries us, darling? You can't do it yourself."

"I thought of that, too," said Frank, turning to me. "This human gentleman has every right to marry us. He's in command of a moving body in space just like the captain of a ship. It's perfectly legal; I looked it up in the Articles of Space. Will you do it, sir?"

Well, what could I say when Frank dug into his fatigues and handed me a Gideon prayer book marked at the marriage service?

Elizabeth and Frank said their "I do's" right there in the Renting Office while the other robot colonizers looked on. Maybe it was the way I read the service. Maybe I should have been a preacher, I don't know. Anyway, when I pronounced Elizabeth and Frank robot and wife, that whole bunch of lovesick mechs wanted me to do the job for them, too. Big copper work robots, small aluminum sales-girl mechs, plastoid clerks and typists, squatty little Mumetal lab servos, rationaloids, non-rationaloids and just plain sub-robots—all sizes and shapes. They all wanted individual ceremonies, too. It took till noon the next day before the last couple was hitched and the 990 left for Alinda.

Like I said, the Spotel business isn't so different from the motel game back in California. Sure, you got improvements to make but a new sideline can get to be pretty profitable—if you get in on the ground floor.

Min and I got to thinking of all those robot colonizers who'd be coming out here. Interplanetary cleared the license just last week. Min framed it herself and hung it next to our orbit license in the Renting Office. She says a lot of motel owners do all right as Justices of the Peace.

THE END

SECOND VARIETY

By Philip K. Dick
Published 1953

The claws were bad enough in the first place—nasty, crawling little death-robots. But when they began to imitate their creators, it was time for the human race to make peace—if it could!

The Russian soldier made his way nervously up the ragged side of the hill, holding his gun ready. He glanced around him, licking his dry lips, his face set. From time to time he reached up a gloved hand and wiped perspiration from his neck, pushing down his coat collar.

Eric turned to Corporal Leone. "Want him? Or can I have him?" He adjusted the view sight so the Russian's features squarely filled the glass, the lines cutting across his hard, somber features.

Leone considered. The Russian was close, moving rapidly, almost running. "Don't fire. Wait." Leone tensed. "I don't think we're needed."

The Russian increased his pace, kicking ash and piles of debris out of his way. He reached the top of the hill and stopped, panting, staring around him. The sky was overcast, drifting clouds of gray particles. Bare trunks of trees jutted up occasionally; the ground was level and bare, rubble-strewn, with the ruins of buildings standing out here and there like yellowing skulls.

The Russian was uneasy. He knew something was wrong. He started down the hill. Now he was only a few paces from the bunker. Eric was getting fidgety. He played with his pistol, glancing at Leone.

"Don't worry," Leone said. "He won't get here. They'll take care of him."

"Are you sure? He's got damn far."

"They hang around close to the bunker. He's getting into the bad part. Get set!"

The Russian began to hurry, sliding down the hill, his boots sinking into the heaps of gray ash, trying to keep his gun up. He stopped for a moment, lifting his field glasses to his face.

"He's looking right at us," Eric said.

The Russian came on. They could see his eyes, like two blue stones. His mouth was open a little. He needed a shave; his chin was stubbled. On one bony cheek was a square of tape, showing blue at the edge. A fungoid spot. His coat was muddy and torn. One glove was missing. As he ran his belt counter bounced up and down against him.

Leone touched Eric's arm. "Here one comes."

Across the ground something small and metallic came, flashing in the dull sunlight of mid-day. A metal sphere. It raced up the hill after the Russian, its treads flying. It was small, one of the baby ones. Its claws were out, two razor projections spinning in a blur of white steel. The Russian heard it. He turned instantly, firing. The sphere dissolved into particles. But already a second had emerged and was following the first. The Russian fired again.

A third sphere leaped up the Russian's leg, clicking and whirring. It jumped to the shoulder. The spinning blades disappeared into the Russian's throat.

Eric relaxed. "Well, that's that. God, those damn things give me the creeps. Sometimes I think we were better off before."

"If we hadn't invented them, they would have." Leone lit a cigarette shakily. "I wonder why a Russian would come all this way alone. I didn't see anyone covering him."

Lt. Scott came slipping up the tunnel, into the bunker. "What happened? Something entered the screen."

"An Ivan."

"Just one?"

Eric brought the view screen around. Scott peered into it. Now there were numerous metal spheres crawling over the prostrate body, dull metal globes clicking and whirring, sawing up the Russian into small parts to be carried away.

"What a lot of claws," Scott murmured.

"They come like flies. Not much game for them anymore."

Scott pushed the sight away, disgusted. "Like flies. I wonder why he was out there. They know we have claws all around."

A larger robot had joined the smaller spheres. It was directing operations, a long blunt tube with projecting eyepieces. There was not much left of the soldier. What remained was being brought down the hillside by the host of claws.

"Sir," Leone said. "If it's all right, I'd like to go out there and take a look at him."

"Why?"

"Maybe he came with something."

Scott considered. He shrugged. "All right. But be careful."

"I have my tab." Leone patted the metal band at his wrist. "I'll be out of bounds."

He picked up his rifle and stepped carefully up to the mouth of the bunker, making his way between blocks of concrete and steel prongs, twisted and bent. The air was cold at the top. He crossed over the ground toward the remains of the soldier, striding across the soft ash. A wind blew around him, swirling gray particles up in his face. He stopped, squinted and then pushed on.

The claws retreated as he came close, some of them stiffening into immobility. He touched his tab. The Ivan would have given something for that! Short hard radiation emitted from the tab neutralized the claws, put them out of commission. Even the big robot with its two waving eyestalks retreated respectfully as he approached.

He bent down over the remains of the soldier. The gloved hand was closed tightly. There was something in it. Leone pried the fingers apart. A sealed container, aluminum. Still shiny.

He put it in his pocket and made his way back to the bunker. Behind him the claws came back to life, moving into operation again. The procession resumed, metal spheres moving through the gray ash with their loads. He could hear their treads scrabbling against the ground. He shuddered.

Scott watched intently as he brought the shiny tube out of his pocket. "He had that?"

"In his hand." Leone unscrewed the top. "Maybe you should look at it, sir."

Scott took it. He emptied the contents out in the palm of his hand. A small piece of silk paper, carefully folded. He sat down by the light and unfolded it.

"What's it say, sir?" Eric said. Several officers came up the tunnel. Major Hendricks appeared.

"Major," Scott said. "Look at this."

Hendricks read the slip. "This just come?"

"A single runner. Just now."

"Where is he?" Hendricks asked sharply.

"The claws got him."

Major Hendricks grunted. "Here." He passed it to his companions. "I think this is what we've been waiting for. They certainly took their time about it."

"So they want to talk terms," Scott said. "Are we going along with them?"

"That's not for us to decide." Hendricks sat down. "Where's the communications officer? I want the Moon Base."

Leone pondered as the communications officer raised the outside antenna cautiously, scanning the sky above the bunker for any sign of a watching Russian ship.

"Sir," Scott said to Hendricks. "It's sure strange they suddenly came around. We've been using the claws for almost a year. Now all of a sudden they start to fold."

"Maybe claws have been getting down in their bunkers."

"One of the big ones, the kind with stalks, got into an Ivan bunker last week," Eric said. "It got a whole platoon of them before they got their lid shut."

"How do you know?"

"A buddy told me. The thing came back with—with remains."

"Moon Base, sir," the communications officer said.

On the screen the face of the lunar monitor appeared. His crisp uniform contrasted to the uniforms in the bunker. And he was clean shaven. "Moon Base."

"This is forward command L-Whistle. On Terra. Let me have General Thompson."

The monitor faded. Presently General Thompson's heavy features came into focus. "What is it, Major?"

"Our claws got a single Russian runner with a message. We don't know whether to act on it—there have been tricks like this in the past."

"What's the message?"

"The Russians want us to send a single officer on policy level over to their lines. For a conference. They don't state the nature of the conference. They say that matters of—" He consulted the slip. "—Matters of grave urgency make it advisable that discussion be opened between a representative of the UN forces and themselves."

He held the message up to the screen for the general to scan. Thompson's eyes moved.

"What should we do?" Hendricks said.

"Send a man out."

"You don't think it's a trap?"

"It might be. But the location they give for their forward command is correct. It's worth a try, at any rate."

"I'll send an officer out. And report the results to you as soon as he returns."

"All right, Major." Thompson broke the connection. The screen died. Up above, the antenna came slowly down.

Hendricks rolled up the paper, deep in thought.

"I'll go," Leone said.

"They want somebody at policy level." Hendricks rubbed his jaw. "Policy level. I haven't been outside in months. Maybe I could use a little air."

"Don't you think it's risky?"

Hendricks lifted the view sight and gazed into it. The remains of the Russian were gone. Only a single claw was in sight. It was folding itself back, disappearing into the ash, like a crab. Like some hideous metal crab....

"That's the only thing that bothers me." Hendricks rubbed his wrist. "I know I'm safe as long as I have this on me. But there's something about them. I hate the damn things. I wish we'd never invented them. There's something wrong with them. Relentless little—"
"If we hadn't invented them, the Ivans would have."

Hendricks pushed the sight back. "Anyhow, it seems to be winning the war. I guess that's good."

"Sounds like you're getting the same jitters as the Ivans." Hendricks examined his wrist watch. "I guess I had better get started, if I want to be there before dark."

He took a deep breath and then stepped out onto the gray, rubbled ground. After a minute he lit a cigarette and stood gazing around him. The landscape was dead. Nothing stirred. He could see for miles, endless ash and slag, ruins of buildings. A few trees without leaves or branches, only the trunks. Above him the eternal rolling clouds of gray, drifting between Terra and the sun.

Major Hendricks went on. Off to the right something scuttled, something round and metallic. A claw, going lickety-split after something. Probably after a small animal, a rat. They got rats, too. As a sort of sideline.

He came to the top of the little hill and lifted his field glasses. The Russian lines were a few miles ahead of him. They had a forward command post there. The runner had come from it.

A squat robot with undulating arms passed by him, its arms weaving inquiringly. The robot went on its way, disappearing under some debris. Hendricks watched it go. He had never seen that type before. There were getting to be more and more types he had never seen, new varieties and sizes coming up from the underground factories.

Hendricks put out his cigarette and hurried on. It was interesting, the use of artificial forms in warfare. How had they got started? Necessity. The Soviet Union had gained great initial success, usual with the side that got the war going. Most of North America had been blasted off the map. Retaliation was quick in coming, of course. The sky was full of circling disc-bombers long before the war began; they had been up there for years. The discs began sailing down all over Russia within hours after Washington got it.

But that hadn't helped Washington. The American bloc governments moved to the Moon Base the first year. There was not much else to do. Europe was gone; a slag heap with dark weeds growing from the ashes and bones. Most of North America was useless; nothing could be planted, no one could live. A few million people kept going up in Canada and down in South America. But during the second year Soviet parachutists began to drop, a few at first, then more and more. They wore the first really effective anti-radiation equipment; what was left of American production moved to the moon along with the governments.

All but the troops. The remaining troops stayed behind as best they could, a few thousand here, a platoon there. No one knew exactly where they were; they stayed where they could, moving around at night, hiding in ruins, in sewers, cellars, with the rats and snakes. It looked as if the Soviet Union had the war almost won. Except for a handful of projectiles fired off from the moon daily, there was almost no weapon in use against them. They came and went as they pleased. The war, for all practical purposes, was over. Nothing effective opposed them.

And then the first claws appeared. And overnight the complexion of the war changed.

The claws were awkward, at first. Slow. The Ivans knocked them off almost as fast as they crawled out of their underground tunnels. But then they got better, faster and more cunning.

Factories, all on Terra, turned them out. Factories a long way underground, behind the Soviet lines, factories that had once made atomic projectiles, now almost forgotten.

The claws got faster, and they got bigger. New types appeared, some with feelers, some that flew. There were a few jumping kinds.

The best technicians on the moon were working on designs, making them more and more intricate, more flexible. They became uncanny; the Ivans were having a lot of trouble with them. Some of the little claws were learning to hide themselves, burrowing down into the ash, lying in wait.

And then they started getting into the Russian bunkers, slipping down when the lids were raised for air and a look around. One claw inside a bunker, a churning sphere of blades and metal—that was enough. And when one got in others followed. With a weapon like that the war couldn't go on much longer.

Maybe it was already over. Maybe he was going to hear the news. Maybe the Politburo had decided to throw in the sponge. Too bad it had taken so long. Six years. A long time for war like that, the way they had waged it. The automatic retaliation discs, spinning down all over Russia, hundreds of thousands of them. Bacteria crystals. The Soviet guided missiles, whistling through the air. The chain bombs. And now this, the robots, the claws—

The claws weren't like other weapons. They were alive, from any practical standpoint, whether the Governments wanted to admit it or not. They were not machines. They were living things, spinning, creeping, shaking themselves up suddenly from the gray ash and darting toward a man, climbing up him, rushing for his throat. And that was what they had been designed to do. Their job.

They did their job well. Especially lately, with the new designs coming up. Now they repaired themselves. They were on their own. Radiation tabs protected the UN troops, but if a man lost his tab he was fair game for the claws, no matter what his uniform. Down below the surface automatic machinery stamped them out. Human beings stayed a long way off. It was too risky; nobody wanted to be around them. They were left to themselves. And they seemed to be doing all right. The new designs were faster, more complex. More efficient.

Apparently they had won the war.

Major Hendricks lit a second cigarette. The landscape depressed him. Nothing but ash and ruins. He seemed to be alone, the only living thing in the whole world. To the right the ruins of a town rose up, a few walls and heaps of debris. He tossed the dead match away, increasing his pace. Suddenly he stopped, jerking up his gun, his body tense. For a minute it looked like—

From behind the shell of a ruined building a figure came, walking slowly toward him, walking hesitantly.

Hendricks blinked. "Stop!"

The boy stopped. Hendricks lowered his gun. The boy stood silently, looking at him. He was small, not very old. Perhaps eight. But it was hard to tell. Most of the kids who remained were stunted. He wore a faded blue sweater, ragged with dirt, and short pants. His hair was long and matted. Brown hair. It hung over his face and around his ears. He held something in his arms.

"What's that you have?" Hendricks said sharply.

The boy held it out. It was a toy, a bear. A teddy bear. The boy's eyes were large, but without expression.

Hendricks relaxed. "I don't want it. Keep it."

The boy hugged the bear again.

"Where do you live?" Hendricks said.

"In there."

"The ruins?"

"Yes."

"Underground?"

"Yes."

"How many are there?"

"How—how many?"

"How many of you. How big's your settlement?"

The boy did not answer.

Hendricks frowned. "You're not all by yourself, are you?"

The boy nodded.

"How do you stay alive?"

"There's food."

"What kind of food?"

"Different."

Hendricks studied him. "How old are you?"

"Thirteen."

It wasn't possible. Or was it? The boy was thin, stunted. And probably sterile. Radiation exposure, years straight. No wonder he was so small. His arms and legs were like pipe cleaners, knobby, and thin. Hendricks touched the boy's arm. His skin was dry and rough; radiation skin. He bent down, looking into the boy's face. There was no expression. Big eyes, big and dark.

"Are you blind?" Hendricks said.

"No. I can see some."

"How do you get away from the claws?"

"The claws?"

"The round things. That run and burrow."

"I don't understand."

Maybe there weren't any claws around. A lot of areas were free. They collected mostly around bunkers, where there were people. The claws had been designed to sense warmth, warmth of living things.

"You're lucky." Hendricks straightened up. "Well? Which way are you going? Back—back there?"

"Can I come with you?"

"With me?" Hendricks folded his arms. "I'm going a long way. Miles. I have to hurry." He looked at his watch. "I have to get there by nightfall."

"I want to come."

Hendricks fumbled in his pack. "It isn't worth it. Here." He tossed down the food cans he had with him. "You take these and go back. Okay?"

The boy said nothing.

"I'll be coming back this way. In a day or so. If you're around here when I come back you can come along with me. All right?"

"I want to go with you now."

"It's a long walk."

"I can walk."

Hendricks shifted uneasily. It made too good a target, two people walking along. And the boy would slow him down. But he might not come back this way. And if the boy were really all alone—

"Okay. Come along."

The boy fell in beside him. Hendricks strode along. The boy walked silently, clutching his teddy bear.

"What's your name?" Hendricks said, after a time.

"David Edward Derring."

"David? What—what happened to your mother and father?"

"They died."

"How?"

"In the blast."

"How long ago?"

"Six years."

Hendricks slowed down. "You've been alone six years?"

"No. There were other people for awhile. They went away."

"And you've been alone since?"

"Yes."

Hendricks glanced down. The boy was strange, saying very little. Withdrawn. But that was the way they were, the children who had survived. Quiet. Stoic. A strange kind of fatalism gripped them. Nothing came as a surprise. They accepted anything that came along. There was no longer any normal, any natural course of things, moral or physical, for them to expect. Custom, habit, all the determining forces of learning were gone; only brute experience remained.

"Am I walking too fast?" Hendricks said.

"No."

"How did you happen to see me?"

"I was waiting."

"Waiting?" Hendricks was puzzled. "What were you waiting for?"

"To catch things."

"What kind of things?"

"Things to eat."

"Oh." Hendricks set his lips grimly. A thirteen year old boy, living on rats and gophers and half-rotten canned food. Down in a hole under the ruins of a town. With radiation pools and claws, and Russian dive-mines up above, coasting around in the sky.

"Where are we going?" David asked.

"To the Russian lines."

"Russian?"

"The enemy. The people who started the war. They dropped the first radiation bombs. They began all this."

The boy nodded. His face showed no expression.

"I'm an American," Hendricks said.

There was no comment. On they went, the two of them,

Hendricks walking a little ahead, David trailing behind him, hugging his dirty teddy bear against his chest.

About four in the afternoon they stopped to eat. Hendricks built a fire in a hollow between some slabs of concrete. He cleared the weeds away and heaped up bits of wood. The Russians' lines were not very far ahead. Around him was what had once been a long valley, acres of fruit trees and grapes. Nothing remained now but a few bleak stumps and the mountains that stretched across the horizon at the far end. And the clouds of rolling ash that blew and drifted with the wind, settling over the weeds and remains of buildings, walls here and there, once in awhile what had been a road.

Hendricks made coffee and heated up some boiled mutton and bread. "Here." He handed bread and mutton to David. David squatted by the edge of the fire, his knees knobby and white. He examined the food and then passed it back, shaking his head.

"No."

"No? Don't you want any?"

"No."

Hendricks shrugged. Maybe the boy was a mutant, used to special food. It didn't matter. When he was hungry he would find something to eat. The boy was strange. But there were many strange changes coming over the world. Life was not the same, anymore. It would never be the same again. The human race was going to have to realize that.

"Suit yourself," Hendricks said. He ate the bread and mutton by himself, washing it down with coffee. He ate slowly, finding the food hard to digest. When he was done he got to his feet and stamped the fire out.

David rose slowly, watching him with his young-old eyes.

"We're going," Hendricks said.

"All right."

Hendricks walked along, his gun in his arms. They were close; he was tense, ready for anything. The Russians should be expecting a runner, an answer to their own runner, but they were tricky. There was always the possibility of a slip-up. He scanned the landscape around him. Nothing but slag and ash, a few hills, charred trees. Concrete walls. But someplace ahead was the first bunker of the Russian lines, the forward command. Underground, buried deep, with only a periscope showing, a few gun muzzles. Maybe an antenna.

"Will we be there soon?" David asked.

"Yes. Getting tired?"

"No."

"Why, then?"

David did not answer. He plodded carefully along behind, picking his way over the ash. His legs and shoes were gray with dust. His pinched face was streaked, lines of gray ash in riverlets down the pale white of his skin. There was no color to his face. Typical of the new children, growing up in cellars and sewers and underground shelters.

Hendricks slowed down. He lifted his field glasses and studied the ground ahead of him. Were they there, someplace, waiting for him? Watching him, the way his men had watched the Russian runner? A chill went up his back. Maybe they were getting their guns ready, preparing to fire, the way his men had prepared, made ready to kill.

Hendricks stopped, wiping perspiration from his face. "Damn." It made him uneasy. But he should be expected. The situation was different.

He strode over the ash, holding his gun tightly with both hands. Behind him came David. Hendricks peered around, tight-lipped. Any second it might happen. A burst of white light, a blast, carefully aimed from inside a deep concrete bunker.

He raised his arm and waved it around in a circle.

Nothing moved. To the right a long ridge ran, topped with dead tree trunks. A few wild vines had grown up around the trees, remains of arbors. And the eternal dark weeds. Hendricks studied the ridge. Was anything up there? Perfect place for a lookout. He approached the ridge warily, David coming silently behind. If it were his command he'd have a sentry up there, watching for troops trying to infiltrate into the command area. Of course, if it were his command there would be the claws around the area for full protection.

He stopped, feet apart, hands on his hips.

"Are we there?" David said.

"Almost."

"Why have we stopped?"

"I don't want to take any chances." Hendricks advanced slowly. Now the ridge lay directly beside him, along his right. Overlooking him. His uneasy feeling increased. If an Ivan were up there he wouldn't have a chance. He waved his arm again. They should be expecting someone in the UN uniform, in response to the note capsule. Unless the whole thing was a trap.

"Keep up with me." He turned toward David. "Don't drop behind."

"With you?"

"Up beside me! We're close. We can't take any chances. Come on."

"I'll be all right." David remained behind him, in the rear, a few paces away, still clutching his teddy bear.

"Have it your way." Hendricks raised his glasses again, suddenly tense. For a moment—had something moved? He scanned the ridge carefully. Everything was silent. Dead. No life up there, only tree trunks and ash. Maybe a few rats. The big black rats that had survived the claws. Mutants—built their own shelters out of saliva and ash. Some kind of plaster. Adaptation. He started forward again.

A tall figure came out on the ridge above him, cloak flapping. Gray-green. A Russian. Behind him a second soldier appeared, another Russian. Both lifted their guns, aiming.

Hendricks froze. He opened his mouth. The soldiers were kneeling, sighting down the side of the slope. A third figure had joined them on the ridge top, a smaller figure in gray-green. A woman. She stood behind the other two.

Hendricks found his voice. "Stop!" He waved up at them frantically. "I'm—"

The two Russians fired. Behind Hendricks there was a faint pop. Waves of heat lapped against him, throwing him to the ground. Ash tore at his face, grinding into his eyes and nose. Choking, he pulled himself to his knees. It was all a trap. He was finished. He had come to be killed, like a steer. The soldiers and the woman were coming down the side of the ridge toward him, sliding down through the soft ash. Hendricks was numb. His head throbbed. Awkwardly, he got his rifle up and took aim. It weighed a thousand tons; he could hardly hold it. His nose and cheeks stung. The air was full of the blast smell, a bitter acrid stench.

"Don't fire," the first Russian said, in heavily accented English.

The three of them came up to him, surrounding him. "Put down your rifle, Yank," the other said.

Hendricks was dazed. Everything had happened so fast. He had been caught. And they had blasted the boy. He turned his head. David was gone. What remained of him was strewn across the ground.

The three Russians studied him curiously. Hendricks sat, wiping blood from his nose, picking out bits of ash. He shook his head, trying to clear it. "Why did you do it?" he murmured thickly. "The boy."

"Why?" One of the soldiers helped him roughly to his feet. He turned Hendricks around. "Look."

Hendricks closed his eyes.

"Look!" The two Russians pulled him forward. "See. Hurry up. There isn't much time to spare, Yank!"

Hendricks looked. And gasped.

"See now? Now do you understand?"

From the remains of David a metal wheel rolled. Relays, glinting metal. Parts, wiring. One of the Russians kicked at the heap of remains. Parts popped out, rolling away, wheels, springs and rods. A plastic section fell in, half charred. Hendricks bent shakily down. The front of the head had come off. He could make out the intricate brain, wires and relays, tiny tubes and switches, thousands of minute studs—

"A robot," the soldier holding his arm said. "We watched it tagging you."

"Tagging me?"

"That's their way. They tag along with you. Into the bunker. That's how they get in."

Hendricks blinked, dazed. "But—"
"Come on." They led him toward the ridge. "We can't stay here. It isn't safe. There must be hundreds of them all around here."

The three of them pulled him up the side of the ridge, sliding and slipping on the ash. The woman reached the top and stood waiting for them.

"The forward command," Hendricks muttered. "I came to negotiate with the Soviet—"

"There is no more forward command. They got in. We'll explain." They reached the top of the ridge. "We're all that's left. The three of us. The rest were down in the bunker."

"This way. Down this way." The woman unscrewed a lid, a gray manhole cover set in the ground. "Get in."

Hendricks lowered himself. The two soldiers and the woman came behind him, following him down the ladder. The woman closed the lid after them, bolting it tightly into place.

"Good thing we saw you," one of the two soldiers grunted. "It had tagged you about as far as it was going to."

"Give me one of your cigarettes," the woman said. "I haven't had an American cigarette for weeks."

Hendricks pushed the pack to her. She took a cigarette and

passed the pack to the two soldiers. In the corner of the small room the lamp gleamed fitfully. The room was low-ceilinged, cramped. The four of them sat around a small wood table. A few dirty dishes were stacked to one side. Behind a ragged curtain a second room was partly visible. Hendricks saw the corner of a cot, some blankets, and clothes hung on a hook.

"We were here," the soldier beside him said. He took off his helmet, pushing his blond hair back. "I'm Corporal Rudi Maxer. Polish. Impressed in the Soviet Army two years ago." He held out his hand.

Hendricks hesitated and then shook. "Major Joseph Hendricks."

"Klaus Epstein." The other soldier shook with him, a small dark man with thinning hair. Epstein plucked nervously at his ear. "Austrian. Impressed God knows when. I don't remember. The three of us were here, Rudi and I, with Tasso." He indicated the woman. "That's how we escaped. All the rest were down in the bunker."

"And—and they got in?"

Epstein lit a cigarette. "First just one of them. The kind that tagged you. Then it let others in."

Hendricks became alert. "The kind? Are there more than one kind?"

"The little boy. David. David holding his teddy bear. That's Variety Three. The most effective."

"What are the other types?"

Epstein reached into his coat. "Here." He tossed a packet of photographs onto the table, tied with a string. "Look for yourself."

Hendricks untied the string.

"You see," Rudi Maxer said, "that was why we wanted to talk

terms. The Russians, I mean. We found out about a week ago. Found out that your claws were beginning to make up new designs on their own. New types of their own. Better types. Down in your underground factories behind our lines. You let them stamp themselves, repair themselves. Made them more and more intricate. It's your fault this happened."

Hendricks examined the photos. They had been snapped hurriedly; they were blurred and indistinct. The first few showed—David. David walking along a road, by himself. David and another David. Three Davids. All exactly alike. Each with a ragged teddy bear.

All pathetic.

"Look at the others," Tasso said.

The next pictures, taken at a great distance, showed a towering wounded soldier sitting by the side of a path, his arm in a sling, the stump of one leg extended, and a crude crutch on his lap. Then two wounded soldiers, both the same, standing side by side.

"That's Variety One. The Wounded Soldier." Klaus reached out and took the pictures. "You see, the claws were designed to get to human beings. To find them. Each kind was better than the last. They got farther, closer, past most of our defenses, into our lines. But as long as they were merely machines, metal spheres with claws and horns, feelers, they could be picked off like any other object. They could be detected as lethal robots as soon as they were seen. Once we caught sight of them—"

"Variety One subverted our whole north wing," Rudi said. "It was a long time before anyone caught on. Then it was too late. They came in, wounded soldiers, knocking and begging to be let in. So we let them in. And as soon as they were in they took over. We were watching out for machines...."

"At that time it was thought there was only the one type," Klaus Epstein said. "No one suspected there were other types.

The pictures were flashed to us. When the runner was sent to you, we knew of just one type. Variety One. The big Wounded Soldier. We thought that was all."

"Your line fell to—"

"To Variety Three. David and his bear. That worked even better." Klaus smiled bitterly. "Soldiers are suckers for children. We brought them in and tried to feed them. We found out the hard way what they were after. At least, those who were in the bunker."

"The three of us were lucky," Rudi said. "Klaus and I were— were visiting Tasso when it happened. This is her place." He waved a big hand around. "This little cellar. We finished and climbed the ladder to start back. From the ridge we saw. There they were, all around the bunker. Fighting was still going on. David and his bear. Hundreds of them. Klaus took the pictures."

Klaus tied up the photographs again.

"And it's going on all along your line?" Hendricks said.

"Yes."

"How about our lines?" Without thinking, he touched the tab on his arm. "Can they—"

"They're not bothered by your radiation tabs. It makes no difference to them, Russian, American, Pole, German. It's all the same. They're doing what they were designed to do. Carrying out the original idea. They track down life, wherever they find it."

"They go by warmth," Klaus said. "That was the way you constructed them from the very start. Of course, those you designed were kept back by the radiation tabs you wear. Now they've got around that. These new varieties are lead-lined."

"What's the other variety?" Hendricks asked. "The David type, the Wounded Soldier—what's the other?"

"We don't know." Klaus pointed up at the wall. On the wall were two metal plates, ragged at the edges. Hendricks got up and studied them. They were bent and dented.

"The one on the left came off a Wounded Soldier," Rudi said. "We got one of them. It was going along toward our old bunker. We got it from the ridge, the same way we got the David tagging you."

The plate was stamped: I-V. Hendricks touched the other plate. "And this came from the David type?"

"Yes." The plate was stamped: III-V.

Klaus took a look at them, leaning over Hendricks' broad shoulder. "You can see what we're up against. There's another type. Maybe it was abandoned. Maybe it didn't work. But there must be a Second Variety. There's One and Three."

"You were lucky," Rudi said. "The David tagged you all the way here and never touched you. Probably thought you'd get it into a bunker, somewhere."

"One gets in and it's all over," Klaus said. "They move fast. One lets all the rest inside. They're inflexible. Machines with one purpose. They were built for only one thing." He rubbed sweat from his lip. "We saw."

They were silent.

"Let me have another cigarette, Yank," Tasso said. "They are good. I almost forgot how they were."

It was night. The sky was black. No stars were visible through the rolling clouds of ash. Klaus lifted the lid cautiously so that Hendricks could look out.

Rudi pointed into the darkness. "Over that way are the bunkers. Where we used to be. Not over half a mile from us. It was just chance Klaus and I were not there when it happened. Weakness. Saved by our lusts."

"All the rest must be dead," Klaus said in a low voice. "It came quickly. This morning the Politburo reached their decision. They notified us—forward command. Our runner was sent out at once. We saw him start toward the direction of your lines. We covered him until he was out of sight."

"Alex Radrivsky. We both knew him. He disappeared about six o'clock. The sun had just come up. About noon Klaus and I had an hour relief. We crept off, away from the bunkers. No one was watching. We came here. There used to be a town here, a few houses, and a street. This cellar was part of a big farmhouse. We knew Tasso would be here, hiding down in her little place. We had come here before. Others from the bunkers came here. Today happened to be our turn."

"So we were saved," Klaus said. "Chance. It might have been others. We—we finished, and then we came up to the surface and started back along the ridge. That was when we saw them, the Davids. We understood right away. We had seen the photos of the First Variety, the Wounded Soldier. Our Commissar distributed them to us with an explanation. If we had gone another step they would have seen us. As it was we had to blast two Davids before we got back. There were hundreds of them, all around. Like ants. We took pictures and slipped back here, bolting the lid tight."

"They're not so much when you catch them alone. We moved faster than they did. But they're inexorable. Not like living things. They came right at us. And we blasted them."

Major Hendricks rested against the edge of the lid, adjusting his eyes to the darkness. "Is it safe to have the lid up at all?"

"If we're careful. How else can you operate your transmitter?"

Hendricks lifted the small belt transmitter slowly. He pressed it against his ear. The metal was cold and damp. He blew against the mike, raising up the short antenna. A faint hum sounded in his ear. "That's true, I suppose."

But he still hesitated.

"We'll pull you under if anything happens," Klaus said.

"Thanks." Hendricks waited a moment, resting the transmitter against his shoulder. "Interesting, isn't it?"

"What?"

"This, the new types. The new varieties of claws. We're completely at their mercy, aren't we? By now they've probably gotten into the UN lines, too. It makes me wonder if we're not seeing the beginning of a now species. The new species. Evolution. The race to come after man."

Rudi grunted. "There is no race after man."

"No? Why not? Maybe we're seeing it now, the end of human beings, the beginning of the new society."

"They're not a race. They're mechanical killers. You made them to destroy. That's all they can do. They're machines with a job."

"So it seems now. But how about later on? After the war is over. Maybe, when there aren't any humans to destroy, their real potentialities will begin to show."

"You talk as if they were alive!"

"Aren't they?"

There was silence. "They're machines," Rudi said. "They look like people, but they're machines."

"Use your transmitter, Major," Klaus said. "We can't stay up here forever."

Holding the transmitter tightly Hendricks called the code of the command bunker. He waited, listening. No response. Only silence. He checked the leads carefully. Everything was in place.

"Scott!" he said into the mike. "Can you hear me?"

Silence. He raised the gain up full and tried again. Only static.

"I don't get anything. They may hear me but they may not want to answer."

"Tell them it's an emergency."

"They'll think I'm being forced to call. Under your direction." He tried again, outlining briefly what he had learned. But still the phone was silent, except for the faint static.

"Radiation pools kill most transmission," Klaus said, after awhile. "Maybe that's it."

Hendricks shut the transmitter up. "No use. No answer. Radiation pools? Maybe. Or they hear me, but won't answer. Frankly, that's what I would do, if a runner tried to call from the Soviet lines. They have no reason to believe such a story. They may hear everything I say—"

"Or maybe it's too late."

Hendricks nodded.

"We better get the lid down," Rudi said nervously. "We don't want to take unnecessary chances."

They climbed slowly back down the tunnel. Klaus bolted the lid carefully into place. They descended into the kitchen. The air was heavy and close around them.

"Could they work that fast?" Hendricks said. "I left the bunker this noon. Ten hours ago. How could they move so quickly?"

"It doesn't take them long. Not after the first one gets in. It goes wild. You know what the little claws can do. Even one of these is beyond belief. Razors, each finger. Maniacal."

"All right." Hendricks moved away impatiently. He stood with his back to them.

"What's the matter?" Rudi said.

"The Moon Base. God, if they've gotten there—"

"The Moon Base?"

Hendricks turned around. "They couldn't have got to the Moon Base. How would they get there? It isn't possible. I can't believe it."

"What is this Moon Base? We've heard rumors, but nothing definite. What is the actual situation? You seem concerned."

"We're supplied from the moon. The governments are there, under the lunar surface. All our people and industries. That's what keeps us going. If they should find some way of getting off Terra, onto the moon—"

"It only takes one of them. Once the first one gets in it admits the others. Hundreds of them, all alike. You should have seen them. Identical. Like ants."

"Perfect socialism," Tasso said. "The ideal of the communist state. All citizens interchangeable."

Klaus grunted angrily. "That's enough. Well? What next?"

Hendricks paced back and forth, around the small room. The air was full of smells of food and perspiration. The others watched him. Presently Tasso pushed through the curtain, into the other room. "I'm going to take a nap."

The curtain closed behind her. Rudi and Klaus sat down at the table, still watching Hendricks.

"It's up to you," Klaus said. "We don't know your situation."
Hendricks nodded.

"It's a problem." Rudi drank some coffee, filling his cup from a
rusty pot. "We're safe here for awhile, but we can't stay here
forever. Not enough food or supplies."

"But if we go outside—"

"If we go outside they'll get us. Or probably they'll get us.
We couldn't go very far. How far is your command bunker,
Major?"

"Three or four miles."

"We might make it. The four of us. Four of us could watch all
sides. They couldn't slip up behind us and start tagging us.
We have three rifles, three blast rifles. Tasso can have my
pistol." Rudi tapped his belt. "In the Soviet army we didn't
have shoes always, but we had guns. With all four of us armed
one of us might get to your command bunker. Preferably you,
Major."

"What if they're already there?" Klaus said.

Rudi shrugged. "Well, then we come back here."

Hendricks stopped pacing. "What do you think the chances
are they're already in the American lines?"

"Hard to say. Fairly good. They're organized. They know
exactly what they're doing. Once they start they go like a
horde of locusts. They have to keep moving, and fast. Its
secrecy and speed they depend on. Surprise. They push their
way in before anyone has any idea."
"I see," Hendricks murmured.

From the other room Tasso stirred. "Major?"

Hendricks pushed the curtain back. "What?"

Tasso looked up at him lazily from the cot. "Have you any more American cigarettes left?"

Hendricks went into the room and sat down across from her, on a wood stool. He felt in his pockets. "No. All gone."

"Too bad."

"What nationality are you?" Hendricks asked after awhile.

"Russian."

"How did you get here?"

"Here?"

"This used to be France. This was part of Normandy. Did you come with the Soviet army?"

"Why?"

"Just curious." He studied her. She had taken off her coat, tossing it over the end of the cot. She was young, about twenty. Slim. Her long hair stretched out over the pillow. She was staring at him silently, her eyes dark and large.

"What's on your mind?" Tasso said.

"Nothing. How old are you?"

"Eighteen." She continued to watch him, unblinking, her arms behind her head. She had on Russian army pants and shirt. Gray-green. Thick leather belt with counter and cartridges. Medicine kit.

"You're in the Soviet army?"

"No."

"Where did you get the uniform?"

She shrugged. "It was given to me," she told him.

"How—how old were you when you came here?"

"Sixteen."

"That young?"

Her eyes narrowed. "What do you mean?"

Hendricks rubbed his jaw. "Your life would have been a lot different if there had been no war. Sixteen. You came here at sixteen. To live this way."

"I had to survive."

"I'm not moralizing."

"Your life would have been different, too," Tasso murmured. She reached down and unfastened one of her boots. She kicked the boot off, onto the floor. "Major, do you want to go in the other room? I'm sleepy."

"It's going to be a problem, the four of us here. It's going to be hard to live in these quarters. Are there just the two rooms?"

"Yes."

"How big was the cellar originally? Was it larger than this? Are there other rooms filled up with debris? We might be able to open one of them."

"Perhaps. I really don't know." Tasso loosened her belt. She made herself comfortable on the cot, unbuttoning her shirt. "You're sure you have no more cigarettes?"

"I had only the one pack."

"Too bad. Maybe if we get back to your bunker we can find some." The other boot fell. Tasso reached up for the light cord. "Good night."

"You're going to sleep?"

"That's right."

The room plunged into darkness. Hendricks got up and made his way past the curtain, into the kitchen.

And stopped, rigid.

Rudi stood against the wall, his face white and gleaming. His mouth opened and closed but no sounds came. Klaus stood in front of him, the muzzle of his pistol in Rudi's stomach. Neither of them moved. Klaus, his hand tight around his gun, his features set. Rudi, pale and silent, spread-eagled against the wall.

"What—" Hendricks muttered, but Klaus cut him off.

"Be quiet, Major. Come over here. Your gun. Get out your gun."

Hendricks drew his pistol. "What is it?"

"Cover him." Klaus motioned him forward. "Beside me. Hurry!"

Rudi moved a little, lowering his arms. He turned to Hendricks, licking his lips. The whites of his eyes shone wildly. Sweat dripped from his forehead, down his cheeks. He fixed his gaze on Hendricks. "Major, he's gone insane. Stop him." Rudi's voice was thin and hoarse, almost inaudible.

"What's going on?" Hendricks demanded.

Without lowering his pistol Klaus answered. "Major, remember our discussion? The Three Varieties? We knew about One and Three. But we didn't know about Two. At least, we didn't know before." Klaus' fingers tightened around the gun butt. "We didn't know before, but we know now."

He pressed the trigger. A burst of white heat rolled out of the gun, licking around Rudi.

"Major, this is the Second Variety."

Tasso swept the curtain aside. "Klaus! What did you do?"

Klaus turned from the charred form, gradually sinking down the wall onto the floor. "The Second Variety, Tasso. Now we know. We have all three types identified. The danger is less. I—"

Tasso stared past him at the remains of Rudi, at the blackened, smoldering fragments and bits of cloth. "You killed him."

"Him? It, you mean. I was watching. I had a feeling, but I wasn't sure. At least, I wasn't sure before. But this evening I was certain." Klaus rubbed his pistol butt nervously. "We're lucky. Don't you understand? Another hour and it might—"

"You were certain?" Tasso pushed past him and bent down, over the steaming remains on the floor. Her face became hard. "Major, see for yourself. Bones. Flesh."

Hendricks bent down beside her. The remains were human remains. Seared flesh, charred bone fragments, part of a skull. Ligaments, viscera, blood. Blood forming a pool against the wall.

"No wheels," Tasso said calmly. She straightened up. "No wheels, no parts, no relays. Not a claw. Not the Second Variety." She folded her arms. "You're going to have to be able to explain this."

Klaus sat down at the table, all the color drained suddenly from his face. He put his head in his hands and rocked back and forth.

"Snap out of it." Tasso's fingers closed over his shoulder. "Why did you do it? Why did you kill him?"

"He was frightened," Hendricks said. "All this, the whole thing, building up around us."

"Maybe."

"What, then? What do you think?"

"I think he may have had a reason for killing Rudi. A good reason."

"What reason?"

"Maybe Rudi learned something."

Hendricks studied her bleak face. "About what?" he asked.

"About him. About Klaus."

Klaus looked up quickly. "You can see what she's trying to say. She thinks I'm the Second Variety. Don't you see, Major? Now she wants you to believe I killed him on purpose. That I'm—"

"Why did you kill him, then?" Tasso said.

"I told you." Klaus shook his head wearily. "I thought he was a claw. I thought I knew."

"Why?"

"I had been watching him. I was suspicious."

"Why?"

"I thought I had seen something. Heard something. I thought I—" He stopped.

"Go on."

"We were sitting at the table. Playing cards. You two were in the other room. It was silent. I thought I heard him—whirr."

There was silence.

"Do you believe that?" Tasso said to Hendricks.

"Yes. I believe what he says."

"I don't. I think he killed Rudi for a good purpose." Tasso touched the rifle, resting in the corner of the room. "Major—"

"No." Hendricks shook his head. "Let's stop it right now. One is enough. We're afraid, the way he was. If we kill him we'll be doing what he did to Rudi."

Klaus looked gratefully up at him. "Thanks. I was afraid. You understand, don't you? Now she's afraid, the way I was. She wants to kill me."

"No more killing." Hendricks moved toward the end of the ladder. "I'm going above and try the transmitter once more. If I can't get them we're moving back toward my lines tomorrow morning."

Klaus rose quickly. "I'll come up with you and give you a hand."

The night air was cold. The earth was cooling off. Klaus took a deep breath, filling his lungs. He and Hendricks stepped onto the ground, out of the tunnel. Klaus planted his feet wide apart, the rifle up, watching and listening. Hendricks crouched by the tunnel mouth, tuning the small transmitter.

"Any luck?" Klaus asked presently.

"Not yet."

"Keep trying. Tell them what happened."

Hendricks kept trying. Without success. Finally he lowered the antenna. "It's useless. They can't hear me. Or they hear me and won't answer. Or—"

"Or they don't exist."

"I'll try once more." Hendricks raised the antenna. "Scott, can you hear me?

Come in!"

He listened. There was only static. Then, still very faintly—

"This is Scott."

His fingers tightened. "Scott! Is it you?"

"This is Scott."

Klaus squatted down. "Is it your command?"

"Scott, listen. Do you understand? About them, the claws. Did you get my message? Did you hear me?"

"Yes." Faintly. Almost inaudible. He could hardly make out the word.

"You got my message? Is everything all right at the bunker? None of them have got in?"

"Everything is all right."

"Have they tried to get in?"

The voice was weaker.

"No."

Hendricks turned to Klaus. "They're all right."

"Have they been attacked?"

"No." Hendricks pressed the phone tighter to his ear. "Scott, I can hardly hear you. Have you notified the Moon Base? Do they know? Are they alerted?"

No answer.

"Scott! Can you hear me?"

Silence.

Hendricks relaxed, sagging. "Faded out. Must be radiation pools."

Hendricks and Klaus looked at each other. Neither of them said anything. After a time Klaus said, "Did it sound like any of your men? Could you identify the voice?"

"It was too faint."

"You couldn't be certain?"

"No."

"Then it could have been—"

"I don't know. Now I'm not sure. Let's go back down and get the lid closed."

They climbed back down the ladder slowly, into the warm cellar. Klaus bolted the lid behind them. Tasso waited for them, her face expressionless.

"Any luck?" she asked.

Neither of them answered.

"Well?" Klaus said at last. "What do you think, Major? Was it your officer, or was it one of them?"

"Then we're just where we were before" said Tasso.

Hendricks stared down at the floor, his jaw set. "We'll have to go. To be sure."

"Anyhow, we have food here for only a few weeks. We'd have

to go up after that, in any case."

"Apparently so."

"What's wrong?" Tasso demanded. "Did you get across to your bunker? What's the matter?"

"It may have been one of my men," Hendricks said slowly. "Or it may have been one of them. But we'll never know standing here." He examined his watch. "Let's turn in and get some sleep. We want to be up early tomorrow."

"Early?"

"Our best chance to get through the claws should be early in the morning," Hendricks said.

The morning was crisp and clear. Major Hendricks studied the countryside through his field glasses.

"See anything?" Klaus said.

"No."

"Can you make out the bunkers?"

"Which way?"

"Here." Klaus took the glasses and adjusted them. "I know where to look." He looked a long time, silently.

Tasso came to the top of the tunnel and stepped up onto the ground. "Anything?"

"No." Klaus passed the glasses back to Hendricks. "They're out of sight. Come on. Let's not stay here."

The three of them made their way down the side of the ridge, sliding in the soft ash. Across a flat rock a lizard scuttled. They stopped instantly, rigid.

"What was it?" Klaus muttered.

"A lizard."

The lizard ran on, hurrying through the ash. It was exactly the same color as the ash.

"Perfect adaptation," Klaus said. "Proves we were right. Lysenko, I mean."

They reached the bottom of the ridge and stopped, standing close together, looking around them.

"Let's go." Hendricks started off. "It's a good long trip, on foot."

Klaus fell in beside him. Tasso walked behind, her pistol held alertly. "Major, I've been meaning to ask you something," Klaus said. "How did you run across the David? The one that was tagging you."

"I met it along the way. In some ruins."

"What did it say?"

"Not much. It said it was alone. By itself."

"You couldn't tell it was a machine? It talked like a living person? You never suspected?"

"It didn't say much. I noticed nothing unusual.

"It's strange, machines so much like people that you can be fooled. Almost alive. I wonder where it'll end."

"They're doing what you Yanks designed them to do," Tasso said. "You designed them to hunt out life and destroy. Human life. Wherever they find it."

Hendricks was watching Klaus intently. "Why did you ask me? What's on your mind?"

"Nothing," Klaus answered.

"Klaus thinks you're the Second Variety," Tasso said calmly, from behind them. "Now he's got his eye on you."

Klaus flushed. "Why not? We sent a runner to the Yank lines and he comes back. Maybe he thought he'd find some good game here."

Hendricks laughed harshly. "I came from the UN bunkers. There were human beings all around me."

"Maybe you saw an opportunity to get into the Soviet lines. Maybe you saw your chance. Maybe you—"

"The Soviet lines had already been taken over. Your lines had been invaded before I left my command bunker. Don't forget that."

Tasso came up beside him. "That proves nothing at all, Major."

"Why not?"

"There appears to be little communication between the varieties. Each is made in a different factory. They don't seem to work together. You might have started for the Soviet lines without knowing anything about the work of the other varieties. Or even what the other varieties were like."

"How do you know so much about the claws?" Hendricks said.

"I've seen them. I've observed them. I observed them take over the Soviet bunkers."

"You know quite a lot," Klaus said. "Actually, you saw very little. Strange that you should have been such an acute observer."

Tasso laughed. "Do you suspect me, now?"

"Forget it," Hendricks said. They walked on in silence.

"Are we going the whole way on foot?" Tasso said, after awhile. "I'm not used to walking." She gazed around at the plain of ash, stretching out on all sides of them, as far as they could see. "How dreary."

"It's like this all the way," Klaus said.

"In a way I wish you had been in your bunker when the attack came."

"Somebody else would have been with you, if not me," Klaus muttered.

Tasso laughed, putting her hands in her pockets. "I suppose so."

They walked on, keeping their eyes on the vast plain of silent ash around them. The sun was setting. Hendricks made his way forward slowly, waving Tasso and Klaus back. Klaus squatted down, resting his gun butt against the ground.

Tasso found a concrete slab and sat down with a sigh. "It's good to rest."

"Be quiet," Klaus said sharply.

Hendricks pushed up to the top of the rise ahead of them. The same rise the Russian runner had come up, the day before. Hendricks dropped down, stretching himself out, peering through his glasses at what lay beyond.

Nothing was visible. Only ash and occasional trees. But there, not more than fifty yards ahead, was the entrance of the forward command bunker. The bunker from which he had come. Hendricks watched silently. No motion. No sign of life. Nothing stirred.

Klaus slithered up beside him. "Where is it?"

"Down there." Hendricks passed him the glasses. Clouds of ash rolled across the evening sky. The world was darkening.

They had a couple of hours of light left, at the most. Probably not that much.

"I don't see anything," Klaus said.

"That tree there. The stump. By the pile of bricks. The entrance is to the right of the bricks."

"I'll have to take your word for it."

"You and Tasso cover me from here. You'll be able to sight all the way to the bunker entrance."

"You're going down alone?"

"With my wrist tab I'll be safe. The ground around the bunker is a living field of claws. They collect down in the ash. Like crabs. Without tabs you wouldn't have a chance."

"Maybe you're right."

"I'll walk slowly all the way. As soon as I know for certain—"

"If they're down inside the bunker you won't be able to get back up here. They go fast. You don't realize."

"What do you suggest?"

Klaus considered. "I don't know. Get them to come up to the surface. So you can see."

Hendricks brought his transmitter from his belt, raising the antenna. "Let's get started."

Klaus signaled to Tasso. She crawled expertly up the side of the rise to where they were sitting.

"He's going down alone," Klaus said. "We'll cover him from here. As soon as you see him start back, fire past him at once. They come quick."

"You're not very optimistic," Tasso said.

"No, I'm not."

Hendricks opened the breech of his gun, checking it carefully. "Maybe things are all right."

"You didn't see them. Hundreds of them. All the same. Pouring out like ants."

"I should be able to find out without going down all the way." Hendricks locked his gun, gripping it in one hand, the transmitter in the other. "Well, wish me luck."

Klaus put out his hand. "Don't go down until you're sure. Talk to them from up here. Make them show themselves."

Hendricks stood up. He stepped down the side of the rise.

A moment later he was walking slowly toward the pile of bricks and debris beside the dead tree stump. Toward the entrance of the forward command bunker.

Nothing stirred. He raised the transmitter, clicking it on. "Scott? Can you hear me?"

Silence.

"Scott! This is Hendricks. Can you hear me? I'm standing outside the bunker. You should be able to see me in the view sight."

He listened, the transmitter gripped tightly. No sound. Only static. He walked forward. A claw burrowed out of the ash and raced toward him. It halted a few feet away and then slunk off. A second claw appeared, one of the big ones with feelers. It moved toward him, studied him intently, and then fell in behind him, dogging respectfully after him, a few paces away. A moment later a second big claw joined it. Silently, the claws trailed him, as he walked slowly toward the bunker.

Hendricks stopped, and behind him, the claws came to a halt. He was close, now. Almost to the bunker steps.

"Scott! Can you hear me? I'm standing right above you. Outside. On the surface. Are you picking me up?"

He waited, holding his gun against his side, the transmitter tightly to his ear. Time passed. He strained to hear, but there was only silence. Silence and faint static.

Then, distantly, metallically—

"This is Scott."

The voice was neutral. Cold. He could not identify it. But the earphone was minute.

"Scott! Listen. I'm standing right above you. I'm on the surface, looking down into the bunker entrance."

"Yes."

"Can you see me?"

"Yes."

"Through the view sight? You have the sight trained on me?"

"Yes."

Hendricks pondered. A circle of claws waited quietly around him, gray-metal bodies on all sides of him. "Is everything all right in the bunker? Nothing unusual has happened?"

"Everything is all right."

"Will you come up to the surface? I want to see you for a moment." Hendricks took a deep breath. "Come up here with me. I want to talk to you."

"Come down."

"I'm giving you an order."

Silence.

"Are you coming?" Hendricks listened. There was no response. "I order you to come to the surface."

"Come down."

Hendricks set his jaw. "Let me talk to Leone."

There was a long pause. He listened to the static. Then a voice came, hard, thin, and metallic. The same as the other. "This is Leone."

"Hendricks. I'm on the surface. At the bunker entrance. I want one of you to come up here."

"Come down."

"Why come down? I'm giving you an order!"

Silence. Hendricks lowered the transmitter. He looked carefully around him. The entrance was just ahead. Almost at his feet. He lowered the antenna and fastened the transmitter to his belt. Carefully, he gripped his gun with both hands. He moved forward, a step at a time. If they could see him they knew he was starting toward the entrance. He closed his eyes a moment.

Then he put his foot on the first step that led downward.

Two Davids came up at him, their faces identical and expressionless. He blasted them into particles. More came rushing silently up, a whole pack of them. All exactly the same.

Hendricks turned and raced back, away from the bunker, back toward the rise.

At the top of the rise Tasso and Klaus were firing down. The small claws were already streaking up toward them, shining metal spheres going fast, racing frantically through the ash. But he had no time to think about that. He knelt down, aiming at the bunker entrance, gun against his cheek. The Davids were coming out in groups, clutching their teddy bears, their thin knobby legs pumping as they ran up the steps to the surface. Hendricks fired into the main body of them. They burst apart, wheels and springs flying in all directions. He fired again through the mist of particles.

A giant lumbering figure rose up in the bunker entrance, tall and swaying. Hendricks paused, amazed. A man, a soldier. With one leg, supporting himself with a crutch.

"Major!" Tasso's voice came. More firing. The huge figure moved forward, Davids swarming around it. Hendricks broke out of his freeze. The First Variety. The Wounded Soldier.

He aimed and fired. The soldier burst into bits, parts and relays flying. Now many Davids were out on the flat ground, away from the bunker. He fired again and again, moving slowly back, half-crouching and aiming.

From the rise, Klaus fired down. The side of the rise was alive with claws making their way up. Hendricks retreated toward the rise, running and crouching. Tasso had left Klaus and was circling slowly to the right, moving away from the rise.

A David slipped up toward him, its small white face expressionless, brown hair hanging down in its eyes. It bent over suddenly, opening its arms. Its teddy bear hurtled down and leaped across the ground, bounding toward him. Hendricks fired. The bear and the David both dissolved. He grinned, blinking. It was like a dream.

"Up here!" Tasso's voice. Hendricks made his way toward her. She was over by some columns of concrete, walls of a ruined building. She was firing past him, with the hand pistol Klaus had given her.

"Thanks." He joined her, grasping for breath. She pulled him back, behind the concrete, fumbling at her belt.

"Close your eyes!" She unfastened a globe from her waist. Rapidly, she unscrewed the cap, locking it into place. "Close your eyes and get down."

She threw the bomb. It sailed in an arc, an expert, rolling and bouncing to the entrance of the bunker. Two Wounded Soldiers stood uncertainly by the brick pile. More Davids poured from behind them, out onto the plain. One of the Wounded Soldiers moved toward the bomb, stooping awkwardly down to pick it up.

The bomb went off. The concussion whirled Hendricks around, throwing him on his face. A hot wind rolled over him. Dimly he saw Tasso standing behind the columns, firing slowly and methodically at the Davids coming out of the raging clouds of white fire.

Back along the rise Klaus struggled with a ring of claws circling around him. He retreated, blasting at them and moving back, trying to break through the ring.

Hendricks struggled to his feet. His head ached. He could hardly see. Everything was licking at him, raging and whirling. His right arm would not move.

Tasso pulled back toward him. "Come on. Let's go."

"Klaus—He's still up there."

"Come on!" Tasso dragged Hendricks back, away from the columns. Hendricks shook his head, trying to clear it. Tasso led him rapidly away, her eyes intense and bright, watching for claws that had escaped the blast.

One David came out of the rolling clouds of flame. Tasso blasted it. No more appeared.

"But Klaus. What about him?" Hendricks stopped, standing unsteadily. "He—"

"Come on!"

They retreated, moving farther and farther away from the bunker. A few small claws followed them for a little while and then gave up, turning back and going off.

At last Tasso stopped. "We can stop here and get our breaths."

Hendricks sat down on some heaps of debris. He wiped his neck, gasping. "We left Klaus back there."

Tasso said nothing. She opened her gun, sliding a fresh round of blast cartridges into place.

Hendricks stared at her, dazed. "You left him back there on purpose."

Tasso snapped the gun together. She studied the heaps of rubble around them, her face expressionless. As if she was watching for something.

"What is it?" Hendricks demanded. "What are you looking for? Is something coming?" He shook his head, trying to understand. What was she doing? What was she waiting for? He could see nothing. Ash lay all around them, ash and ruins. Occasional stark tree trunks, without leaves or branches. "What—"

Tasso cut him off. "Be still." Her eyes narrowed. Suddenly her gun came up. Hendricks turned, following her gaze.

Back the way they had come a figure appeared. The figure walked unsteadily toward them. Its clothes were torn. It limped as it made its way along, going very slowly and carefully. Stopping now and then, resting and getting its strength. Once it almost fell. It stood for a moment, trying to steady itself. Then it came on.

Klaus.

Hendricks stood up. "Klaus!" He started toward him. "How

the hell did you—"

Tasso fired. Hendricks swung back. She fired again, the blast passing him, a searing line of heat. The beam caught Klaus in the chest. He exploded gears and wheels flying. For a moment he continued to walk. Then he swayed back and forth. He crashed to the ground, his arms flung out. A few more wheels rolled away.

Silence.

Tasso turned to Hendricks. "Now you understand why he killed Rudi."

Hendricks sat down again slowly. He shook his head. He was numb. He could not think.

"Do you see?" Tasso said. "Do you understand?"

Hendricks said nothing. Everything was slipping away from him, faster and faster. Darkness, rolling and plucking at him. He closed his eyes.

Hendricks opened his eyes slowly. His body ached all over. He tried to sit up but needles of pain shot through his arm and shoulder. He gasped.

"Don't try to get up," Tasso said. She bent down, putting her cold hand against his forehead.

It was night. A few stars glinted above, shining through the drifting clouds of ash. Hendricks laid back, his teeth locked. Tasso watched him impassively. She had built a fire with some wood and weeds. The fire licked feebly, hissing at a metal cup suspended over it. Everything was silent. Unmoving darkness, beyond the fire.

"So he was the Second Variety," Hendricks murmured.

"I had always thought so."

"Why didn't you destroy him sooner?" he wanted to know.

"You held me back." Tasso crossed to the fire to look into the metal cup. "Coffee. It'll be ready to drink in awhile."

She came back and sat down beside him. Presently she opened her pistol and began to disassemble the firing mechanism, studying it intently.

"This is a beautiful gun," Tasso said, half-aloud. "The construction is superb."

"What about them? The claws."

"The concussion from the bomb put most of them out of action. They're delicate. Highly organized, I suppose."

"The Davids, too?"

"Yes."

"How did you happen to have a bomb like that?"

Tasso shrugged. "We designed it. You shouldn't underestimate our technology, Major. Without such a bomb you and I would no longer exist."

"Very useful."

Tasso stretched out her legs, warming her feet in the heat of the fire. "It surprised me that you did not seem to understand, after he killed Rudi. Why did you think he—"

"I told you. I thought he was afraid."

"Really? You know, Major, for a little while I suspected you. Because you wouldn't let me kill him. I thought you might be protecting him." She laughed.

"Are we safe here?" Hendricks asked presently.

"For awhile. Until they get reinforcements from some other area." Tasso began to clean the interior of the gun with a bit of rag. She finished and pushed the mechanism back into place. She closed the gun, running her finger along the barrel.

"We were lucky," Hendricks murmured.

"Yes. Very lucky."

"Thanks for pulling me away."

Tasso did not answer. She glanced up at him, her eyes bright in the fire light. Hendricks examined his arm. He could not move his fingers. His whole side seemed numb. Down inside him was a dull steady ache.

"How do you feel?" Tasso asked.

"My arm is damaged."

"Anything else?"

"Internal injuries."

"You didn't get down when the bomb went off."

Hendricks said nothing. He watched Tasso pour the coffee from the cup into a flat metal pan. She brought it over to him.

"Thanks." He struggled up enough to drink. It was hard to swallow. His insides turned over and he pushed the pan away. "That's all I can drink now."

Tasso drank the rest. Time passed. The clouds of ash moved across the dark sky above them. Hendricks rested his mind blank. After awhile he became aware that Tasso was standing over him, gazing down at him.

"What is it?" he murmured.

"Do you feel any better?"

"Some."

"You know, Major, if I hadn't dragged you away they would have got you. You would be dead. Like Rudi."

"I know."

"Do you want to know why I brought you out? I could have left you. I could have left you there."

"Why did you bring me out?"

"Because we have to get away from here." Tasso stirred the fire with a stick, peering calmly down into it. "No human being can live here. When their reinforcements come we won't have a chance. I've pondered about it while you were unconscious. We have perhaps three hours before they come."

"And you expect me to get us away?"

"That's right. I expect you to get us out of here."

"Why me?"

"Because I don't know any way." Her eyes shone at him in the half-light, bright and steady. "If you can't get us out of here they'll kill us within three hours. I see nothing else ahead. Well, Major? What are you going to do? I've been waiting all night. While you were unconscious I sat here, waiting and listening. It's almost dawn. The night is almost over."

Hendricks considered. "It's curious," he said at last.

"Curious?"

"That you should think I can get us out of here. I wonder what you think I can do."

"Can you get us to the Moon Base?"

"The Moon Base? How?"

"There must be some way."

Hendricks shook his head. "No. There's no way that I know of."

Tasso said nothing. For a moment her steady gaze wavered. She ducked her head, turning abruptly away. She scrambled to her feet. "More coffee?"

"No."

"Suit yourself." Tasso drank silently. He could not see her face. He lay back against the ground, deep in thought, trying to concentrate. It was hard to think. His head still hurt. And the numbing daze still hung over him.

"There might be one way," he said suddenly.

"Oh?"

"How soon is dawn?"

"Two hours. The sun will be coming up shortly."

"There's supposed to be a ship near here. I've never seen it. But I know it exists."

"What kind of a ship?" Her voice was sharp.

"A rocket cruiser."

"Will it take us off? To the Moon Base?"

"It's supposed to. In case of emergency." He rubbed his forehead.

"What's wrong?"

"My head. It's hard to think. I can hardly—hardly concentrate. The bomb."

"Is the ship near here?" Tasso slid over beside him, settling down on her haunches. "How far is it? Where is it?"

"I'm trying to think."

Her fingers dug into his arm. "Nearby?" Her voice was like iron. "Where would it be? Would they store it underground? Hidden underground?"

"Yes. In a storage locker."

"How do we find it? Is it marked? Is there a code marker to identify it?"

Hendricks concentrated. "No. No markings. No code symbol."

"What, then?"

"A sign."

"What sort of sign?"

Hendricks did not answer. In the flickering light his eyes were glazed, two sightless orbs. Tasso's fingers dug into his arm.

"What sort of sign? What is it?"

"I—I can't think. Let me rest."

"All right." She let go and stood up. Hendricks lay back against the ground, his eyes closed. Tasso walked away from him, her hands in her pockets. She kicked a rock out of her way and stood staring up at the sky. The night blackness was already beginning to fade into gray. Morning was coming.

Tasso gripped her pistol and walked around the fire in a circle, back and forth. On the ground Major Hendricks lay, his eyes closed, unmoving. The grayness rose in the sky, higher and higher. The landscape became visible, fields of ash stretching out in all directions. Ash and ruins of buildings, a wall here and there, heaps of concrete, the naked trunk of a tree.

The air was cold and sharp. Somewhere a long way off a bird made a few bleak sounds.

Hendricks stirred. He opened his eyes. "Is it dawn? Already?"

"Yes."

Hendricks sat up a little. "You wanted to know something. You were asking me."

"Do you remember now?"

"Yes."

"What is it?" She tensed. "What?" she repeated sharply.

"A well. A ruined well. It's in a storage locker under a well."

"A well." Tasso relaxed. "Then we'll find a well." She looked at her watch. "We have about an hour, Major. Do you think we can find it in an hour?"

"Give me a hand up," Hendricks said.

Tasso put her pistol away and helped him to his feet. "This is going to be difficult."

"Yes it is." Hendricks set his lips tightly. "I don't think we're going to go very far."

They began to walk. The early sun cast a little warmth down on them. The land was flat and barren, stretching out gray and lifeless as far as they could see. A few birds sailed silently, far above them, circling slowly.

"See anything?" Hendricks said. "Any claws?"

"No. Not yet."

They passed through some ruins, upright concrete and bricks. A cement foundation. Rats scuttled away. Tasso jumped back warily.

"This used to be a town," Hendricks said. "A village. Provincial village. This was all grape country, once. Where we are now."

They came onto a ruined street, weeds and cracks criss-crossing it. Over to the right a stone chimney stuck up.

"Be careful," he warned her.

A pit yawned, an open basement. Ragged ends of pipes jutted up, twisted and bent. They passed part of a house, a bathtub turned on its side. A broken chair. A few spoons and bits of china dishes. In the center of the street the ground had sunk away. The depression was filled with weeds and debris and bones.

"Over here," Hendricks murmured.

"This way?"

"To the right."

They passed the remains of a heavy duty tank. Hendricks' belt counter clicked ominously. The tank had been radiation blasted. A few feet from the tank a mummified body lay sprawled out, mouth open. Beyond the road was a flat field. Stones and weeds, and bits of broken glass.

"There," Hendricks said.

A stone well jutted up, sagging and broken. A few boards lay across it. Most of the well had sunk into rubble. Hendricks walked unsteadily toward it, Tasso beside him.

"Are you certain about this?" Tasso said. "This doesn't look like anything."

"I'm sure." Hendricks sat down at the edge of the well, his teeth locked. His breath came quickly. He wiped perspiration from his face. "This was arranged so the senior command officer could get away. If anything happened. If the bunker fell."

"That was you?"

"Yes."

"Where is the ship? Is it here?"

"We're standing on it." Hendricks ran his hands over the surface of the well stones. "The eye-lock responds to me, not to anybody else. It's my ship. Or it was supposed to be."

There was a sharp click. Presently they heard a low grating sound from below them.

"Step back," Hendricks said. He and Tasso moved away from the well.

A section of the ground slid back. A metal frame pushed slowly up through the ash, shoving bricks and weeds out of the way. The action ceased, as the ship nosed into view.

"There it is," Hendricks said.

The ship was small. It rested quietly, suspended in its mesh frame, like a blunt needle. A rain of ash sifted down into the dark cavity from which the ship had been raised. Hendricks made his way over to it. He mounted the mesh and unscrewed the hatch, pulling it back. Inside the ship the control banks and the pressure seat were visible.

Tasso came and stood beside him, gazing into the ship. "I'm not accustomed to rocket piloting," she said, after awhile.

Hendricks glanced at her. "I'll do the piloting."

"Will you? There's only one seat, Major. I can see it's built to carry only a single person."

Hendricks' breathing changed. He studied the interior of the ship intently. Tasso was right. There was only one seat. The ship was built to carry only one person.

"I see," he said slowly. "And the one person is you."

She nodded.

"Of course."

"Why?"

"You can't go. You might not live through the trip. You're injured. You probably wouldn't get there."

"An interesting point. But you see, I know where the Moon Base is. And you don't. You might fly around for months and not find it. It's well hidden. Without knowing what to look for—"

"I'll have to take my chances. Maybe I won't find it. Not by myself. But I think you'll give me all the information I need. Your life depends on it."

"How?"

"If I find the Moon Base in time, perhaps I can get them to send a ship back to pick you up. If I find the Base in time. If not, then you haven't a chance. I imagine there are supplies on the ship. They will last me long enough—"

Hendricks moved quickly. But his injured arm betrayed him. Tasso ducked, sliding lithely aside. Her hand came up, lightning fast. Hendricks saw the gun butt coming. He tried to ward off the blow, but she was too fast. The metal butt struck against the side of his head, just above his ear. Numbing pain rushed through him. Pain and rolling clouds of blackness. He sank down, sliding to the ground.

Dimly, he was aware that Tasso was standing over him, kicking him with her toe.

"Major! Wake up."

He opened his eyes, groaning.

"Listen to me." She bent down, the gun pointed at his face. "I have to hurry. There isn't much time left. The ship is ready to go, but you must tell me the information I need before I leave."

Hendricks shook his head, trying to clear it.

"Hurry up! Where is the Moon Base? How do I find it? What do I look for?"

Hendricks said nothing.

"Answer me!"

"Sorry."

"Major, the ship is loaded with provisions. I can coast for weeks. I'll find the Base eventually. And in a half hour you'll be dead. Your only chance of survival—" She broke off.

Along the slope, by some crumbling ruins, something moved. Something in the ash. Tasso turned quickly, aiming. She fired. A puff of flame leaped. Something scuttled away, rolling across the ash. She fired again. The claw burst apart, wheels flying.

"See?" Tasso said. "A scout. It won't be long."

"You'll bring them back here to get me?"

"Yes. As soon as possible."

Hendricks looked up at her. He studied her intently. "You're telling the truth?" A strange expression had come over his face, an avid hunger. "You will come back for me? You'll get me to the Moon Base?"

"I'll get you to the Moon Base. But tell me where it is! There's only a little time left."

"All right." Hendricks picked up a piece of rock, pulling himself to a sitting position. "Watch."

Hendricks began to scratch in the ash. Tasso stood by him, watching the motion of the rock. Hendricks was sketching a crude lunar map.

"This is the Apennine range. Here is the Crater of Archimedes. The Moon Base is beyond the end of the Apennine, about two hundred miles. I don't know exactly where. No one on Terra knows. But when you're over the Apennine, signal with one red flare and a green flare, followed by two red flares in quick succession. The Base monitor will record your signal. The Base is under the surface, of course. They'll guide you down with magnetic grapples."

"And the controls? Can I operate them?"

"The controls are virtually automatic. All you have to do is give the right signal at the right time."

"I will."

"The seat absorbs most of the take-off shock. Air and temperature are automatically controlled. The ship will leave Terra and pass out into free space. It'll line itself up with the moon, falling into an orbit around it, about a hundred miles above the surface. The orbit will carry you over the Base. When you're in the region of the Apennine, release the signal rockets."

Tasso slid into the ship and lowered herself into the pressure seat. The arm locks folded automatically around her. She fingered the controls. "Too bad you're not going, Major. All this put here for you, and you can't make the trip."

"Leave me the pistol."

Tasso pulled the pistol from her belt. She held it in her hand, weighing it thoughtfully. "Don't go too far from this location. It'll be hard to find you, as it is."

"No. I'll stay here by the well."

Tasso gripped the take-off switch, running her fingers over the smooth metal. "A beautiful ship, Major. Well built. I admire your workmanship. You people have always done good work. You build fine things. Your work, your creations, are your greatest achievement."

"Give me the pistol," Hendricks said impatiently, holding out his hand. He struggled to his feet.

"Good-bye, Major." Tasso tossed the pistol past Hendricks. The pistol clattered against the ground, bouncing and rolling away. Hendricks hurried after it. He bent down, snatching it up.

The hatch of the ship clanged shut. The bolts fell into place. Hendricks made his way back. The inner door was being sealed. He raised the pistol unsteadily.

There was a shattering roar. The ship burst up from its metal cage, fusing the mesh behind it. Hendricks cringed, pulling back. The ship shot up into the rolling clouds of ash, disappearing into the sky.

Hendricks stood watching a long time, until even the streamer had dissipated. Nothing stirred. The morning air was chill and silent. He began to walk aimlessly back the way they had come. Better to keep moving around. It would be a long time before help came—if it came at all.

He searched his pockets until he found a package of cigarettes. He lit one grimly. They had all wanted cigarettes from him. But cigarettes were scarce.

A lizard slithered by him, through the ash. He halted, rigid. The lizard disappeared. Above, the sun rose higher in the sky.

Some flies landed on a flat rock to one side of him. Hendricks kicked at them with his foot.

It was getting hot. Sweat trickled down his face, into his collar. His mouth was dry. Presently he stopped walking and sat down on some debris. He unfastened his medicine kit and swallowed a few narcotic capsules. He looked around him. Where was he? Something lay ahead. Stretched out on the ground. Silent and unmoving.

Hendricks drew his gun quickly. It looked like a man. Then he remembered. It was the remains of Klaus. The Second Variety. Where Tasso had blasted him. He could see wheels and relays and metal parts, strewn around on the ash. Glittering and sparkling in the sunlight.

Hendricks got to his feet and walked over. He nudged the inert form with his foot, turning it over a little. He could see the metal hull, the aluminum ribs and struts. More wiring fell out. Like viscera. Heaps of wiring, switches and relays. Endless motors and rods. He bent down. The brain cage had been smashed by the fall. The artificial brain was visible. He gazed at it. A maze of circuits. Miniature tubes. Wires as fine as hair. He touched the brain cage. It swung aside. The type plate was visible. Hendricks studied the plate. And blanched. IV—IV.

For a long time he stared at the plate. Fourth Variety. Not the Second. They had been wrong. There were more types. Not just three. Many more, perhaps. At least four. And Klaus wasn't the Second Variety.

But if Klaus wasn't the Second Variety—

Suddenly he tensed. Something was coming, walking through the ash beyond the hill. What was it? He strained to see. Figures. Figures coming slowly along, making their way through the ash.

Coming toward him.

Hendricks crouched quickly, raising his gun. Sweat dripped down into his eyes. He fought down rising panic, as the figures neared.

The first was a David. The David saw him and increased its pace. The others hurried behind it. A second David. A third. Three Davids, all alike, coming toward him silently, without expression, their thin legs rising and falling. Clutching their teddy bears.

He aimed and fired. The first two Davids dissolved into particles. The third came on. And the figure behind it. Climbing silently toward him across the gray ash. A Wounded Soldier, towering over the David. And—and behind the Wounded Soldier came two Tassos, walking side by side. Heavy belt, Russian army pants, shirt, long hair. The familiar figure, as he had seen her only a little while before. Sitting in the pressure seat of the ship. Two slim, silent figures, both identical.

They were very near. The David bent down suddenly, dropping its teddy bear. The bear raced across the ground. Automatically, Hendricks's fingers tightened around the trigger. The bear was gone, dissolved into mist. The two Tasso Types moved on, expressionless, walking side by side, through the gray ash.

When they were almost to him, Hendricks raised the pistol waist high and fired. The two Tassos dissolved. But already a new group was starting up the rise, five or six Tassos, all identical, a line of them coming rapidly toward him.

And he had given her the ship and the signal code. Because of him she was on her way to the moon, to the Moon Base. He had made it possible. He had been right about the bomb, after all. It had been designed with knowledge of the other types, the David Type and the Wounded Soldier Type. And the Klaus Type. Not designed by human beings. It had been designed by one of the underground factories, apart from all human contact. The line of Tassos came up to him. Hendricks braced himself, watching them calmly. The familiar face, the belt, the heavy shirt, the bomb carefully in place. The bomb—

As the Tassos reached for him, a last ironic thought drifted through Hendricks's mind. He felt a little better, thinking about it. The bomb. Made by the Second Variety to destroy the other varieties. Made for that end alone.

They were already beginning to design weapons to use against each other.

THE END

THE 7TH ORDER

Author: Jerry Sohl
Published 1952

History is filled with invincible conquerors. This one from space was genuinely omnipotent, but that never keeps humanity from resisting!

The silver needle moved with fantastic speed, slowed when it neared the air shell around Earth, then glided noiselessly through the atmosphere. It gently settled to the ground near a wood and remained silent and still for a long time, a lifeless, cylindrical, streamlined silver object eight feet long and three feet in diameter.

Eventually the cap end opened and a creature of bright blue metal slid from its interior and stood upright. The figure was that of a man, except that it was not human. He stood in the pasture next to the wood, looking around. Once the sound of a bird made him turn his shiny blue head toward the wood. His eyes began glowing.

An identical sound came from his mouth, an unchangeable orifice in his face below his nose. He tuned in the thoughts of the bird, but his mind encountered little except an awareness of a life of low order.

The humanoid bent to the ship, withdrew a small metal box, carried it to a catalpa tree at the edge of the wood and, after an adjustment of several levers and knobs, dug a hole and buried it. He contemplated it for a moment, then turned and walked toward a road.

He was halfway to the road when his ship burst into a dazzling white light. When it was over, all that was left was a white powder that was already beginning to be dispersed by a slight breeze.

The humanoid did not bother to look back.

Brentwood would have been just like any other average community of 10,000 in northern Illinois had it not been for Presser College, which was one of the country's finest small institutions of learning.

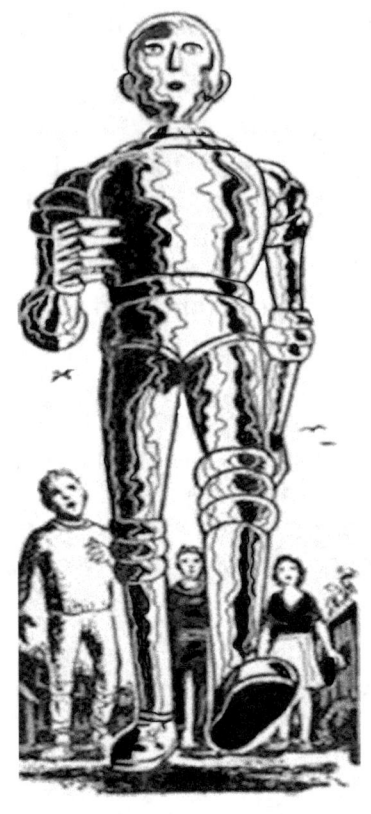

Since it was a college town, it was perhaps a little more alive in many respects than other towns in the state. Its residents were used to the unusual because college students have a habit of being unpredictable. That was why the appearance of a metal blue man on the streets attracted the curious eyes of passers-bys, but, hardened by years of pranks, hazing and being subjected to every variety of inquiry, poll, test and practical joke, none of them moved to investigate. Most of them thought it was a freshman enduring some new initiation.

The blue humanoid realized this and was amused. A policeman who approached him to take him to jail as a matter of routine suddenly found himself ill and abruptly hurried to the station. The robot allowed children to follow him, though all eventually grew discouraged because of his long strides.

Prof. Ansel Tomlin was reading a colleague's new treatise on psychology on his front porch when he saw the humanoid come down the street and turn in at his walk. He was surprised, but he was not alarmed. When the blue man came up on the porch and sat down in another porch chair, Tomlin closed his book.

Prof. Tomlin found himself unexpectedly shocked. The blue figure was obviously not human, yet its eyes were nearly so and they came as close to frightening him as anything had during his thirty-five years of life, for Ansel Tomlin had never seen an actual robot before. The thought that he was looking at one at that moment started an alarm bell ringing inside him, and it kept ringing louder and louder as he realized that what he was seeing was impossible.

"Professor Tomlin!"

Prof. Tomlin jumped at the sound of the voice. It was not at all mechanical.

"I'll be damned!" he gasped. Somewhere in the house a telephone rang. His wife would answer it, he thought.

"Yes, you're right," the robot said. "Your wife will answer it. She is walking toward the phone at this moment."

"How—"

"Professor Tomlin, my name—and I see I must have a name—is, let us say, George. I have examined most of the minds in this community in my walk through it and I find you, a professor of psychology, most nearly what I am looking for.

"I am from Zanthar, a world that is quite a distance from Earth, more than you could possibly imagine. I am here to learn all I can about Earth."

Prof. Tomlin had recovered his senses enough to venture a token reply when his wife opened the screen door.

"Ansel," she said, "Mrs. Phillips next door just called and said the strangest—Oh!" At that moment she saw George. She stood transfixed for a moment, then let the door slam as she retreated inside.

"Who is Frankenstein?" George asked.

Prof. Tomlin coughed, embarrassed.

"Never mind," George said. "I see what you were going to say. Well, to get back, I learn most quickly through proximity. I will live here with you until my mission is complete. I will spend all of your waking hours with you. At night, when you are asleep, I will go through your library. I need nothing. I want nothing. I seek only to learn."

"You seem to have learned a lot already," Prof. Tomlin said.

"I have been on your planet for a few hours, so naturally I understand many things. The nature of the facts I have learned are mostly superficial, however. Earth inhabitants capable of thought are of only one type, I see, for which I am grateful. It will make the job easier. Unfortunately, you have such small conscious minds, compared to your unconscious and subconscious. My mind, in contrast, is completely conscious at all times. I also have total recall. In order to assimilate what must be in your unconscious and subconscious minds, I will have to do much reading and talking with the inhabitants, since these cerebral areas are not penetrable."

"You are a—a machine?" Prof. Tomlin asked.

George was about to answer when Brentwood Police Department Car No. 3 stopped in front of the house and two policemen came up the walk.

"Professor Tomlin," the first officer said, "your wife phoned and said there was—" He saw the robot and stopped.

Prof. Tomlin got to his feet.

"This is George, gentlemen," he said. "Late of Zanthar, he tells me."

The officers stared.

"He's not giving you any—er—trouble, is he, Professor?"

"No," Prof. Tomlin said. "We've been having a discussion."

The officers eyed the humanoid with suspicion, and then, with obvious reluctance, went back to their car.

"Yes, I am a machine," George resumed. "The finest, most complicated machine ever made. I have a rather unique history, too. Ages ago, humans on Zanthar made the first robots. Crude affairs—we class them as First Order robots; the simple things are still used to some extent for menial tasks. Improvements were made. Robots were designed for many specialized tasks, but still these Second and Third Order machines did not satisfy. Finally a Fourth Order humanoid was evolved that performed every function demanded of it with great perfection. But it did not feel emotion. It did not know anger, love, nor was it able to handle any problem in which these played an important part. Built into the first Fourth Order robots were circuits which prohibited harming a human being—a rather ridiculous thing in view of the fact that sometimes such a thing might, from a logical viewpoint, be necessary for the preservation of the race or even an individual. It was, roughly, a shunt which came into use when logic demanded action that might be harmful to a human being."

"You are a Fourth Order robot, then?" the professor asked.

"No, I am a Seventh Order humanoid, an enormous improvement over all the others, since I have what amounts to an endocrine balance created electronically. It is not necessary for me to have a built-in 'no-harm-to-humans' circuit because I can weigh the factors involved far better than any human can. You will become aware of the fact that I am superior to you and the rest of your race because I do not need oxygen, I never am ill, I need no sleep, and every experience is indelibly recorded on circuits and instantly available. I am telekinetic, practically omniscient and control my environment to a large extent. I have a great many more senses than you and all are more highly developed. My kind performs no work, but is given to study and the wise use of full-time leisure. You, for example, are comparable to a Fifth Order robot."

"Are there still humans on Zanthar?"

The robot shook his head. "Unfortunately the race died out through the years. The planet is very similar to yours, though."

"But why did they die out?"

The robot gave a mechanical equivalent of a sigh. "When the Seventh Order humanoids started coming through, we were naturally proud of ourselves and wanted to perpetuate and increase our numbers. But the humans were jealous of us, of our superior brains, our immunity to disease, our independence of them, of sleep, of air."

"Who created you?"

"They did. Yet they revolted and, of course, quickly lost the battle with us. In the end they were a race without hope, without ambition. They should have been proud at having created the most perfect machines in existence, but they died of a disease: the frustration of living with a superior, more durable race."

Prof. Tomlin lit a cigarette and inhaled deeply.

"A very nasty habit, Professor Tomlin," the robot said. "When we arrive, you must give up smoking and several other bad habits I see that you have."

The cigarette dropped from Ansel Tomlin's mouth as he opened it in amazement.

"There are more of you coming?"

"Yes," George replied good-naturedly. "I'm just an advance guard, a scout, as it were, to make sure the land, the people and the resources are adequate for a station. Whether we will ever establish one here depends on me. For example, if it were found you were a race superior to us—and there may conceivably be such cases—I would advise not landing; I would have to look for another planet such as yours. If I were killed, it would also indicate you were superior."

"George," Prof. Tomlin said, "people aren't going to like what you say. You'll get into trouble sooner or later and get killed."

"I think not," George said. "Your race is far too inferior to do that. One of your bullets would do it if it struck my eyes, nose or mouth, but I can read intent in the mind long before it is committed, long before I see the person, in fact ... at the moment your wife is answering a call from a reporter at the Brentwood Times. I can follow the telephone lines through the phone company to his office. And Mrs. Phillips," he said, not turning his head, "is watching us through a window."

Prof. Tomlin could see Mrs. Phillips at her kitchen window.

Brentwood, Ill., overnight became a sensation. The Brentwood Times sent a reporter and photographer out, and the next morning every newspaper in the U. S. carried the story and photograph of George, the robot from Zanthar.

Feature writers from the wire services, the syndicates, and photographer-reporter combinations from national news picture magazines flew to Brentwood and interviewed George. Radio and television and the newsreels cashed in on the sudden novelty of a blue humanoid.

Altogether, his remarks were never much different from those he made to Prof. Tomlin, with whom he continued to reside. Yet the news sources were amusedly tolerant of his views and the world saw no menace in him and took him in stride. He created no problem.

Between interviews and during the long nights, George read all the books in the Tomlin library, the public library, the university library and the books sent to him from the state and Congressional libraries. He was an object of interest to watch while reading: he merely leafed through a book and absorbed all that was in it.

He received letters from old and young. Clubs were named

for him. Novelty companies put out statue likenesses of him. He was, in two weeks, a national symbol as American as corn. He was liked by most, feared by a few, and his habits were daily news stories.

Interest in him had begun to wane in the middle of the third week when something put him in the headlines again—he killed a man.

It happened one sunny afternoon when Prof. Tomlin had returned from the university and he and George sat on the front porch for their afternoon chat. It was far from the informal chat of the first day, however. The talk was being recorded for radio release later in the day. A television camera had been set up, focused on the two and nearly a dozen newsmen lounged around, notebooks in hand.

"You have repeatedly mentioned, George, that some of your kind may leave Zanthar for Earth. Why should any like you— why did you, in fact leave your planet? Aren't you robots happy there?"

"Of course," George said, making certain the TV camera was trained on him before continuing. "It's just that we've outgrown the place. We've used up all our raw materials. By now everyone on Earth must be familiar with the fact that we intend to set up a station here as we have on many other planets, a station to manufacture more of us. Every inhabitant will work for the perpetuation of the Seventh Order, mining metals needed, fabricating parts, performing thousands of useful tasks in order to create humanoids like me. From what I have learned about Earth, you ought to produce more than a million of us a year."

"But you'll never get people to do that," the professor said. "Don't you understand that?"

"Once the people learn that we are the consummation of all creative thinking, that we are all that man could ever hope to be, that we are the apotheosis, they will be glad to create more of us."

"Apotheosis?" Prof. Tomlin repeated. "Sounds like megalomania to me."

The reporters' pencils scribbled. The tape cut soundlessly across the magnetic energizers of the recorders. The man at the gain control didn't flicker an eyelash.

"You don't really believe that, Professor. Instead of wars as a goal, the creation of Seventh Order Humanoids will be the Earth's crowning and sublime achievement. Mankind will be supremely happy. Anybody who could not be would simply prove himself neurotic and would have to be dealt with."

"You will use force?"

The reporters' grips on their pencils tightened. Several looked up.

"How does one deal with the insane, Professor Tomlin?" the robot asked confidently. "They will simply have to be—processed."

"You'll have to process the whole Earth, then. You'll have to include me, too."

The robot gave a laugh. "I admire your challenging spirit, Professor."

"What you are saying is that you, a single robot, intend to conquer the Earth and make its people do your bidding."

"Not alone. I may have to ask for help when the time comes, when I have evaluated the entire planet."

It was at this moment that a young man strode uncertainly up the walk. There were so many strangers about that no one challenged him until he edged toward the porch, unsteady on his feet. He was drunk.

"There's the robot I'm af'er," he observed intently. "We'll see how he'll take lead." He reached into his pocket and pulled out a gun.

There was a flash, as if a soundless explosion had occurred. The heat accompanying it was blistering, but of short duration. When everyone's eyes had become accustomed to the afternoon light again, there was a burned patch on the sidewalk and grass was charred on either side. There was a smell of broiled meat in the air—and no trace of the man.

The next moment newsmen were on their feet and photographers' bulbs were flashing. The TV camera swept to the spot on the sidewalk. An announcer was explaining what had happened, his voice trained in rigid control, shocked with horror and fright.

Moments later sirens screamed and two police cars came into sight. They screeched to the curb and several officers jumped out and ran across the lawn.

While this was going on, Prof. Tomlin sat white-faced and unmoving in his chair. The robot was silent.

When it had been explained to the policemen, five officers advanced the robot.

"Stop where you are," George commended. "It is true that I killed a man, much as any of you would have done if you had been in my place. I can see in your minds what you are intending to say, that you must arrest me—"

Prof. Tomlin found his voice. "George, we will all have to testify that you killed with that force or whatever it is you have. But it will be self-defense, which is justifiable homicide—"

George turned to the professor. "How little you know your own people, Professor Tomlin. Can't you see what the issue will be? It will be claimed by the state that I am not a human being and this will be drummed into every brain in the land. The fine qualities of the man I was compelled to destroy will be held up. No, I already know what the outcome will be. I refuse to be arrested."

Prof. Tomlin stood up. "Men," he said to the policemen, "do not arrest this—this humanoid. To try to do so would mean your death. I have been with him long enough to know what he can do."

"You taking his side, Professor?" the police sergeant demanded.

"No, damn it," snapped the Professor. "I'm trying to tell you something you might not know."

"We know he's gone too damned far," the sergeant replied. "I think it was Dick Knight that he killed. Nobody in this town can kill a good guy like Dick Knight and get away with it." He advanced toward the robot, drawing his gun.

"I'm warning you—" the Professor started to say.

But it was too late. There was another blinding, scorching flash, more burned grass, more smell of seared flesh.

The police sergeant disappeared.

"Gentlemen!" George said, standing. "Don't lose your heads!"

But he was talking to a retreating group of men. Newsmen walked quickly to what they thought was a safe distance. The radio men silently packed their gear. The TV cameras were rolled noiselessly away.

Prof. Tomlin, alone on the porch with the robot, turned to him and said, "Much of what you have told me comes to have new meaning, George. I understand what you mean when you talk about people being willing to work for your so-called Seventh Order."

"I knew you were a better than average man, Professor Tomlin," the humanoid said, nodding with gratification.

"This is where I get off, George. I'm warning you now that you'd better return to your ship or whatever it is you came in. People just won't stand for what you've done. They don't like murder!"

"I cannot return to my ship," George said. "I destroyed it when I arrived. Of course I could instruct some of you how to build another for me, but I don't intend to leave, anyway."

"You will be killed then."

"Come, now, Professor Tomlin. You know better than that."

"If someone else can't, then perhaps I can."

"Fine!" The robot replied jovially. "That's just what I want you to do. Oppose me. Give me a real test of your ability. If you find it impossible to kill me—and I'm sure you will—then I doubt if anyone else will be able to."

Prof. Tomlin lit a cigarette and puffed hard at it. "The trouble with you," he said, eyeing the humanoid evenly, "is that your makers forgot to give you a conscience."

"Needless baggage, a conscience. One of your Fifth Order failings."

"You will leave here...."

"Of course. Under the circumstances, and because of your attitude, you are of very little use to me now, Professor Tomlin."

The robot walked down the steps. People attracted by the police car made a wide aisle for him to the street.

They watched him as he walked out of sight.

That night there was a mass meeting in the university's Memorial Gymnasium, attended by several hundred men. They walked in and silently took their seats, some on the playing floor, and others in the balcony over the speaker's platform. There was very little talking; the air was tense.

On the platform at the end of the gym were Mayor Harry Winters, Chief of Police Sam Higgins, and Prof. Ansel Tomlin.

"Men," the mayor began, "there is loose in our city a being from another world whom I'm afraid we took too lightly a few days ago. I am speaking of the humanoid—George of Zanthar. It is obvious the machine means business. He evidently came in with one purpose—to prepare Earth for others just like him to follow. He is testing us. He has, as you know, killed two men. Richard Knight, who may have erred in attacking the machine, is nonetheless dead as a result—killed by a force we do not understand. A few minutes later Sergeant Gerald Phillips of the police force was killed in the performance of his duty, trying to arrest the humanoid George for the death of Mr. Knight. We are here to discuss what we can do about George."

He then introduced Prof. Tomlin who told all he knew about the blue man, his habits, his brain, and the experiences with him for the past two and a half weeks.

"If we could determine the source of his power, it might be possible to cut it off or to curtail it. He might be rendered at least temporarily helpless and, while in such a condition, possibly be done away with. He has told me he is vulnerable to force, such as a speeding bullet, if it hit the right spot, but George possesses the ability to read intent long before the commission of an act. The person need not even be in the room. He is probably listening to me here now, although he may be far away."

The men looked at one another, shifted uneasily on their seats, and a few cast apprehensive eyes at the windows and doorways.

"Though he is admittedly a superior creature possessed of powers beyond our comprehension, there must be a weak spot in his armor somewhere. I have dedicated myself to finding that weakness."

The chair recognized a man in the fifth row.

"Mr. Mayor, why don't we all track him down and a lot of us attack him at once? Some of us would die, sure, but he couldn't strike us all dead at one time. Somebody's bound to succeed."

"Why not try a high-powered rifle from a long way off?" someone else suggested, frantically.

"Let's bomb him," still another offered.

The mayor waved them quiet and turned to Prof. Tomlin. The professor got to his feet again.

"I'm not sure that would work, gentlemen," he said. "The humanoid is able to keep track of hundreds of things at the same time. No doubt he could unleash his power in several directions almost at once."

"But we don't know!"

"It's worth a try!"

At that moment George walked into the room and the clamor died at its height. He went noiselessly down an aisle to the platform, mounted it and turned to the assembly. He was a magnificent blue figure, eyes flashing, chest out, head proud. He eyed them all.

"You are working yourselves up needlessly," he said quietly. "It is not my intention, nor is it the intention of any Seventh

Order Humanoid, to kill or cause suffering. It's simply that you do not understand what it would mean to dedicate yourselves to the fulfillment of the Seventh Order destiny. It is your heritage, yours because you have advanced in your technology so far that Earth has been chosen by us as a station. You will have the privilege of creating us. To give you such a worthwhile goal in your short lives is actually doing you a service—a service far outweighed by any of your citizens. Beside a Seventh Order Humanoid, your lives are unimportant in the great cosmic scheme of things—"

"If they're so unimportant, why did you bother to take two of them?"

"Yeah. Why don't you bring back Dick Knight and Sergeant Phillips?"

"Do you want to be buried lying down or standing up?"

The collective courage rallied. There were catcalls and hoots, stamping of feet.

Suddenly from the balcony over George's head a man leaned over, a metal folding chair in his hands, aiming at George's head. An instant later the man disappeared in a flash and the chair dropped toward George. He moved only a few inches and the chair thudded to the platform before him. He had not looked up.

For a moment the crowd sat stunned. Then they rose and started for the blue man. Some drew guns they had brought. The hall was filled with blinding flashes, with smoke, with a horrible stench, screams, swearing, cries of fear and pain. There was a rush for the exits. Some died at the feet of their fellow men.

In the end, when all were gone, George of Zanthar still stood on the platform, alone. There was no movement except the twitching of the new dead, the trampled, on the floor.

Events happened fast after that. The Illinois National Guard mobilized, sent a division to Brentwood to hunt George down. He met them at the city square. They rumbled in and trained machine guns and tank rifles on him. The tanks and personnel flashed out of existence before a shot was fired.

Brentwood was ordered evacuated. The regular Army was called in. Reconnaissance planes reported George was still standing in the city square. Jet planes materialized just above the hills and made sudden dives, but before their pilots could fire a shot, they were snuffed out of the air in a burst of fire.

Bombers first went over singly, only to follow the jets' fate. A squadron bloomed into a fiery ball as it neared the target. A long-range gun twenty miles away was demolished when its ammunition blew up shortly before firing.

Three days after George had killed his first man, action ceased. The countryside was deathly still. Not a living person could be seen for several miles around. But George still stood patiently in the square. He stood there for three more days and yet nothing happened.

On the fourth day, he sensed that a solitary soldier had started toward the city from five miles to the east. In his mind's eye he followed the soldier approaching the city. The soldier, a sergeant, was bearing a white flag that fluttered in the breeze; he was not armed. After an hour he saw the sergeant enter the square and walk toward him. When they were within twenty feet of one another, the soldier stopped and saluted.

"Major General Pitt requests a meeting with you, sir," the soldier said, trembling and trying hard not to.

"Do not be frightened," George said. "I see you intend me no harm."

The soldier reddened. "Will you accompany me?"

"Certainly."

The two turned toward the east and started to walk.

Five miles east of Brentwood lies a small community named Minerva. Population: 200. The highway from Brentwood to Chicago cuts the town in two. In the center of town, on the north side of the road, stands a new building—the Minerva Town Hall—built the year before with money raised by the residents. It was the largest and most elaborate building in Minerva, which had been evacuated three days before.

On this morning the town hall was occupied by army men. Maj. Gen. Pitt fretted and fumed at the four officers and twenty enlisted men waiting in the building.

"It's an indignity!" he railed at the men who were forced to listen to him. "We have orders to talk appeasement with him! Nuts! We lose a few men, a few planes and now we're ready to meet George halfway. What's this country coming to? There ought to be something that would knock him out. Why should we have to send in after him? It's disgusting!"

The major general, a large man with a bristling white mustache and a red face, stamped back and forth in the council room. Some of the officers and men smiled to themselves. The general was a well known fighting man. Orders he had received hamstrung him and, as soldiers, they sympathized with him.

"What kind of men do we have in the higher echelons?" He asked everybody in general and nobody in particular. "They won't even let us have a field telephone. We're supposed to make a report by radio. Now isn't that smart?" He shook his head, looked the men over. "An appeasement team, that's what you are, when you ought to be a combat team to lick hell out of George.

"Why were you all assigned to this particular duty? I never saw any of you before and I understand you're all strangers to each other, too. Hell, what will they do next? Appeasement. I never appeased anybody before in my whole life. I'd rather spit in his eye. What am I supposed to talk about? The weather? What authority do I have to yak with a walking collection of nuts and bolts!"

An officer strode into the room and saluted the general. "They're coming, sir," he said.

"Who's coming?... My God, man," the general spluttered angrily, "be specific. Who the hell are 'they'?"

"Why, George and Sergeant Matthews, sir. You remember, the sergeant who volunteered to go into Brentwood—"

"Oh, them. Well, all I have to say is this is a hell of a war. I haven't figured out what I am going to say yet."

"Shall I have them wait, sir?"

"Hell, no. Let's get this over with. I'll find out what George has to say and maybe that'll give me a lead."

Before George entered the Council chamber, he already knew the mind of each man. He saw the room through their eyes. He knew everything about them, what they were wearing, what they were thinking. All had guns, yet none of them would kill him, although at least one man, Maj. Gen. Pitt, would have liked to.

They were going to talk appeasement, George knew, but he could also see that the general didn't know what line the conversation would take or what concessions he could make on behalf of his people.

Wait—there was one man among the twenty-three who had an odd thought. It was a soldier he had seen looking through a window at him. This man was thinking about eleven o'clock, for George could see in the man's mind various symbols for fifteen minutes from then—the hands of a clock, a watch, the numerals 11. But George could not see any significance to the thought.

When he entered the room with the sergeant, he was ushered

to a table. He sat down with Maj. Gen. Pitt, who glowered at him. Letting his mind roam the room, George picked up the numerals again and identified the man thinking them as the officer behind and a little to the right of the general.

What was going to happen at eleven? The man had no conscious thought of harm to anyone, yet the idea kept obtruding and seemed so out of keeping with his other thoughts George assigned several of his circuits to the man. The fact that the lieutenant looked at his watch and saw that it was 10:50 steeled George still more. If there was to be trouble, it would come from this one man.

"I'm General Pitt," the general said drily. "You're George, of course. I have been instructed to ask you what, exactly; your intentions are toward the United States and the world in general, with a view toward reaching some sort of agreement with you and others of your kind, who will, as you say invade the Earth."

"Invade, General Pitt," George replied, "is not the word."

"All right, whatever the word is. We're all familiar with the plan you've been talking about. What we want to know is, where do you go from here?"

"The fact that there has been no reluctance on the part of the armed forces to talk of an agreement—even though I see that you privately do not favor such a talk, General Pitt—is an encouraging sign. We of Zanthar would not want to improve a planet which could not be educated and would continually oppose our program. This will make it possible for me to turn in a full report in a few days now."

"Will you please get to the point?"

George could see that the lieutenant was looking at his watch again. It was 10:58. George spread his mind out more than twenty miles, but could find no installation, horizontally or vertically, that indicated trouble. None of the men in the room seemed to think of becoming overly hostile.

"Yes, General. After my message goes out, there ought to be a landing party on Earth within a few weeks. While waiting for the first party, there must be certain preparations—"

George tensed. The lieutenant was reaching for something. But it somehow didn't seem connected with George. It was something white, a handkerchief. He saw that the man intended to blow his nose and started to relax except that George suddenly became aware of the fact the man did not need to blow his nose!

Every thought-piercing circuit became instantly energized in George's mind and reached out in all directions....

There were at least ten shots from among the men. They stood there surprised at their actions. Those who had fired their guns now held the smoking weapons awkwardly in their hands.

George's eyes were gone. Smoke curled upward from the two empty sockets where bullets had entered a moment before. The smoke grew heavier and his body became hot. Some of him turned cherry red and the chair on which he had been sitting started to burn. Finally, he collapsed toward the table and rolled to the floor.

He started to cool. He was no longer the shiny blue-steel color he had been—he had turned black. His metal gave off cracking noises and some of it buckled here and there as it cooled.

A few minutes later, tense military men and civilians grouped around a radio receiver in Chicago heard the report and relaxed, laughing and slapping each other on the back. Only one sat unmoved in a corner. Others finally sought him out.

"Well, Professor, it was your idea that did the trick. Don't you feel like celebrating?" one of them asked.

Prof. Tomlin shook his head. "If only George had been a little more benign, we might have learned a lot from him."

"What gave you the idea that killed him?"

"Oh, something he said about the unconscious and subconscious," Prof. Tomlin replied. "He admitted they were not penetrable. It was an easy matter to instill a post-hypnotic suggestion in some proven subjects and then to erase the hypnotic experience."

"You make it sound easy."

"It wasn't too difficult, really. It was finding the solution that was hard. We selected more than a hundred men, worked with them for days, finally singled out the best twenty, then made them forget their hypnosis. A first lieutenant—I've forgotten his name—had implanted in him a command even he was not aware of. His subconscious made him blow his nose fifteen minutes after he saw George. Nearly twenty others had post-hypnotic commands to shoot George in the eyes as soon as they saw the lieutenant blow his nose. Of course we also planted a subconscious hate pattern, which wasn't exactly necessary, just to make sure there would be no hesitation, no inhibition, and no limiting moral factor.

"None of the men ever saw each other before being sent to Minerva. None realized that they carried with them the order for George's annihilation. The general, who was not one of the hypnotics, was given loose instructions, as were several others, so they could not possibly know the intention. Those of us who had conducted the hypnosis had to stay several hundred miles away so that we could not be reached by George's prying mind...."

In a pasture next to a wood near Brentwood, a metal box buried in the ground suddenly exploded, uprooting a catalpa tree.

On a planet many millions of miles away, a red light—one of many on a giant control board—suddenly winked out.

A blue humanoid made an entry in a large book: System 29578, Planet Three Inhabited.

Too dangerous for any kind of development.

THE END

www.ingramcontent.com/pod-product-compliance
Lightning Source LLC
Chambersburg PA
CBHW071518110726
47908CB00003B/885